PERSUASION, CAPTAIN WENTWORTH AND CRACKLIN' CORNBREAD

Center Point
Large Print

Also by Mary Jane Hathaway and available from Center Point Large Print:

Pride, Prejudice and Cheese Grits
Emma, Mr. Knightley and Chili-Slaw Dogs

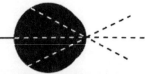

**This Large Print Book carries the
Seal of Approval of N.A.V.H.**

PERSUASION, CAPTAIN WENTWORTH AND CRACKLIN' CORNBREAD

JANE AUSTEN TAKES THE SOUTH
BOOK #3

MARY JANE HATHAWAY

CENTER POINT LARGE PRINT
THORNDIKE, MAINE

This Center Point Large Print edition
is published in the year 2015 by arrangement with
Howard Books, a division of Simon & Schuster, Inc.

The text of this Large Print edition is unabridged.
In other aspects, this book may vary
from the original edition.
Printed in the United States of America on permanent paper.
Set in 16-point Times New Roman type.

ISBN: 978-1-62899-440-7

Library of Congress Cataloging-in-Publication Data

Hathaway, Mary Jane.
 Persuasion, Captain Wentworth and cracklin' cornbread : Jane Austen
takes the south / Mary Jane Hathaway. — Center Point large print
edition.
 pages cm
 Summary: "A lively Southern retelling of Jane Austen's *Persuasion*,
featuring Lucy Crawford, who is thrown back into the path of her first
love while on a quest to save her beloved family home"
 —Provided by publisher.
 ISBN 978-1-62899-440-7 (library binding : alk. paper)
 1. Austen, Jane, 1775–1817—Parodies, imitations, etc.
  2. Large type books. I. Austen, Jane, 1775–1817. Persuasion.
  II. Title.
 PS3608.A8644P47 2015
 813′.6—dc23
                                                      2014041787

To my husband, Crusberto. You are my Jem. We are like night and day, like the sun and the moon, and just possibly from completely different planets. I couldn't live without fiction, and you don't read anything that doesn't have schematics inside. You never stop singing and I'm always wishing for a little bit of quiet. My Spanish is atrocious and your English isn't much better. But in the ways that matter, we are alike. You believe the martyrs had it right, that babies are a little bit of heaven and that we are called to live in this world, but not of it.

PS. You're a really good cook and I like the way you smell. Oh, and thanks for passing on your good teeth, dark skin that tans/never burns and excellent eyesight to our six kids. Well done!

To my children, always. Without you, I would be all work and no play, and a very dull girl indeed.

No: the years which had destroyed
her youth and bloom had only given
him a more glowing, manly, open look,
in no respect lessening his personal
advantages. She had seen the same
Frederick Wentworth.
—ANNE ELLIOT

CHAPTER ONE

"This is an effort to collect a debt. Any information obtained will be used for that purpose."

Lucy Crawford leaned her forehead against the wall and closed her eyes. The mechanical voice droned on, rattling through an 800 number and requesting a call back. The time stamp was an hour ago.

There was a brief pause and the next message began: "This call is for William Crawford. I am a debt collector and this is an effort to collect a debt. Any information—"

Lucy reached out and punched the skip button. The message machine flashed three more calls in the queue. She didn't know if she could listen to them all at one time. It was too depressing, like watching the recap, over and over, of the Bulldogs falling to Alabama by thirty points. Except that there was always next year for her favorite football team, and there wasn't any end in sight to her daddy's financial issues.

Skip. Skip. Skip. Maybe all the calls were from the same creditor, but probably not. Lucy heaved herself upright and trudged into the foyer. She might as well get the mail now while she was already feeling low. The black-and-white tile expanse of the entrance area gleamed dully in the summer light shining through the leaded panes of the double doors. In all of her twenty-eight years she had never seen them so scuffed. Old Zeke polished the floors of every room in the house once a week and always spent extra time on the entrance. He was proud of his job and being part of keeping up the historic Crawford House. Or at least he had been, until Lucy had fired him.

She paused in front of the side table, where a five-inch stack of bills waited neatly. The conversation with Zeke flashed through her mind and she felt the unfamiliar burn of tears. She wasn't a crier. When she'd sat Zeke down, she had done well, speaking clearly and confidently until he had bowed his head. The defeat in his posture was like a stab of hot iron in her heart. Zeke had always seemed larger than his five-foot-five frame, probably because Lucy remembered being very little, pulling on his pant leg and looking far, far up at the Crawford House handyman. He was like family, and she was telling him he wasn't going to be part of their daily lives any longer.

Then he had glanced up, black eyes still bright despite his seventy-five years. "Miss Lucy, I know'd this time be coming. I's not as strong as I once was."

She had wanted to drop to her knees, wrap her arms around his fragile shoulders and cry like a little girl. She'd wanted to cry like the time she'd lost her dolly down the irrigation pipe in the back pasture, before Zeke had retrieved it for her. Like the time she'd broken her heart into tiny pieces and he sat beside her, patting her shoulder and whispering, "There, there," until she fell asleep, soggy and exhausted.

But she hadn't. Lucy had explained, again, about the debts and the home equity loan and the repairs they couldn't afford. No matter what she'd said about bills and bankruptcy and foreclosure, old Zeke hadn't quite seemed convinced. The memory of it was so strong she felt chilled, even standing in the stifling air of the foyer. Lucy reached out and grabbed up the pile of envelopes, not even bothering to glance at the addresses. They wouldn't be able to pay them, or any new ones that would have come in.

"Honey, is that you?" Her daddy's rich baritone echoed through the large entrance hall. Seconds later he appeared around the corner, dressed in a perfectly pressed pair of yellow-and-green-plaid golf pants, Ralph Lauren polo shirt casually unbuttoned at the neck. Willy Crawford's close-cropped hair was still black, except for a bit of gray at each temple, and for a man of sixty, he was still lean and fit. "I'm headed to the club for a quick round with Theon James."

Lucy winced inside. Theon James excelled in three things: golf, business and goading her daddy into spending money to keep up his reputation as the richest man in town. She suspected Theon was playing a game, enjoying how easy it was to convince Willy Crawford that it was time to get a newer car or take a monthlong vacation to St. Simons Island.

"Will you be home for lunch? I have a casserole in the oven I think you'd really like, Daddy."

He cocked an eyebrow. "Does it have any meat in it?"

She was tempted to lie. Really, he acted as if vegetarian cooking were poison. "No, but the eggplant tastes just like—"

"Nah." He pulled on a matching green-and-yellow-plaid golfer's cap and shouldered his bag. "You know I don't like that sort of thing. Put some ham in it next time. And don't say I always need my meat, because I eat some of that vegetarian food, too. Your mama was a great cook. Her beignets were so light and fluffy, fried just right, a good bit of powdered sugar on top. . . ." He paused, a small smile on his face. Lucy knew just what he felt. Sweet memories were all they had left of her mama.

"Before you go," she started to say, holding out the mail.

He cut her off. "No time now, sugar. Theon's already there." Her daddy leaned in and gave her a quick kiss on the head, leaving a whiff of Old Spice and cigars.

"It's just I thought you were fixin' to sort through some of these on Sunday after church, but you went out to lunch. We need to see if there are a few we could pay off right away. It would save a lot on interest in the long run and . . ."

He wasn't listening to her. Bending over his golf bag, he rummaged inside. "When I get back, I'll take care of it. And there's no *we* about payin' these bills. I've got the money, just need to cash out a few old savings accounts and I'll be settled up with those people."

Lucy almost sighed out loud. *Those people.* Her daddy always drew a thick black line between their family and the rest of the world. If she tried to suggest that they were close to bankruptcy, he would point out how the Crawfords had owned the finest home in Brice's Crossroads, Mississippi, since right after the Civil War had ended, or how his great-granddaddy had founded the area's first African-American business league, or how the Crawfords had attended Harvard before the Roosevelts. The Crawfords were good stock. They were on the boards of hospitals, joined exclusive clubs, were admired by everyone. They didn't have financial issues, and they certainly didn't worry out loud if they did.

"Some of these are probably Paulette's," Lucy said. "You've got to get those credit cards from her. She's got closets full of designer clothes and she just buys more."

"Your sister is a fine-lookin' woman in search of a husband. I won't be interfering with that." He winked at her.

"But Janessa managed to get a husband without spending sprees in Atlanta." Lucy crossed her arms over her chest. Her middle sister had many faults, but being a fashionista wasn't one of them.

"You leave Paulette be. She's not like you. She's still young and hasn't given up on men. I don't mind her spending a bit to make herself look presentable. It's part of keeping up appearances. She certainly doesn't want to live in her daddy's house the rest of her days." His voice was light, but there was a warning in his eyes.

Did he think she'd given up on men? She swallowed past the hurt of his words and said, "Alrighty, as soon as you get back, let's go over these bills together. Mama's not here. You need to keep track of these things."

"Don't be disrespectful." His face was stiff with anger. "I didn't raise you like that."

Lucy dropped her gaze to the floor. When she

was little, her daddy had heard her mouth off to her mama. He hadn't used the switch on her, the way she'd thought he would. He'd sat her on his knee and explained he could forgive a lot of sins, but he could never love a stubborn, strong-willed girl. She'd apologized to her mama and tried her very best to be a good girl ever since. She was a grown woman now, but Lucy still couldn't seem to balance on that fence between gentle coaxing and shrewish nagging.

"I didn't mean to offend, Daddy."

The door was already closing on the end of her sentence, and Lucy listened to him cross the wide, wooden porch. His footsteps faded with each step toward his shiny red Miata. She sagged against the side table and resisted the urge to throw the whole stack of letters against the door. He wouldn't listen. She had done everything possible to keep the bank from foreclosing on the house, but it was only a matter of time before they lost everything. Her mama had been so good at managing the household finances. Maybe too good. Her daddy had been happy to turn it all over to her and focus on his golf game. He was the face of Crawford Investments, but her mama had been the brains. When she passed, he'd just pretended that nothing had changed, creating chaos at home and disaster for the business.

Just the thought of her mama gave Lucy a sharp pain, even though it had been close to nine years now she'd been gone. One early morning she'd collapsed in the kitchen and Lucy's life had changed forever.

Lucy breathed a prayer of thanksgiving for the time they'd had together, all the way through her teens. She used to love sitting in the bright-blue kitchen and watching her mama cook. Their housekeeper, Mrs. Hardy, made perfectly fine meals, but her mama wasn't happy if she didn't mix up a batch of gumbo or hush puppies once in a while. Straight from Cane River, she spoke with the lyrical accent of a native Creole speaker and had eyes the color of Kentucky bluegrass. She liked to sing, all the time, and it was like having a radio you could never turn off. Gospel hymns, blues, low-country ballads. The house was so quiet without her. Lucy had the dark eyes and skin of her daddy, but her curves and throaty laugh were all her mama's doing.

She still had the curves, but it had been months since she'd heard herself laugh.

A rap at the door sounded like a gunshot in the quiet foyer. Lucy hesitated, wondering if bill collectors ever came to the door in their "attempts to collect a debt." Peeking through the beveled glass, she let out a breath. When trouble comes, family arrives close behind, for better or for worse.

"Auntie," she said, swinging the door wide.

Aunt Olympia held out both hands and stuck out

14

her lower lip. "Oh, honey, come here." She gripped Lucy's hands and hauled herself over the threshold like a shipwreck victim grabbing hold of a life raft.

"You got my message," Lucy said into her aunt's elaborately braided updo. Lucy was being squeezed and rocked from side to side, and her words sounded as if she were running.

"Yes, bless your heart. And I've been busy solving your problems," Aunt Olympia said. Letting go of Lucy, she shut the door behind her and started toward the kitchen. "Come let me tell you all about it over a little sweet tea."

Lucy knew better than to laugh. There was no way Aunt Olympia could have solved anything in the hours since Lucy had called, giving the dire news of the impending foreclosure. Instead, Lucy trailed along behind her, wondering how such a tiny woman could exude such force. Where Olympia went, everyone followed.

"Aren't you supposed to be at the museum today?" her aunt called over one shoulder. Of course she would have noticed Lucy's jeans-and-T-shirt ensemble right away. Her aunt didn't believe in casual clothes. Her neon-green track suit said JUICY on the rear, and her earrings bounced with every movement. She was all flash, all the time.

"They're closed for maintenance, and it's an interpretive center, not a museum." Lucy didn't want to talk about her job. Aunt Olympia would say Lucy should have a better position, maybe something with a fancy title and a yearly bonus.

"Which means what? Cleaning?" Aunt Olympia moved around the cheery kitchen, reaching into the fridge for the pitcher of tea.

Lucy dropped into a chair. "Yes. Cleaning." Maintenance made it sound as if the center might get a new roof or any of the other desperately needed repairs. But upgrading access to a Civil War battlefield site wasn't high on the list of popular causes in Tupelo.

"I don't know why you work over there. You probably are only gettin' the people who wander through from the Elvis museum."

Lucy said nothing. The sad fact was, if Elvis had been born in Brice's Crossroads, they'd have an event center with a full kitchen, green rooms and a theater—not to mention a chapel and a gift shop with its own apparel line. As it was, they had to make do with folding chairs, a microwave and a yearly budget that wouldn't cover Graceland's electric bill.

"Hun, you need to find yourself a better job. Iola is working on the top floor of a smoked-glass high-rise in Atlanta. She wears the prettiest outfits and has a whole closet for her shoes. She says—"

"I know," Lucy interrupted, unable to stand hearing one more time about her cousin's happiness at being a secretary for a group of slick

16

lawyers in pin-striped suits. "I know," she said more slowly. "But working at the center is perfect for me, Auntie. I love this area, these people. If I could have majored in the history of Tupelo, Mississippi, I would have. Being a curator doesn't come with fame or glory, but it makes me happy."

Aunt Olympia's frown softened into a sigh. "You deserve a little happiness, that's for sure."

Lucy wondered for a moment if she meant because of the way her mama had passed away so suddenly, or if Olympia was talking about another time, long before. An image of a laughing, blond-haired boy flashed through her mind and she shoved it away. Her present was bad enough without wallowing in the past.

Her aunt glanced in the oven. "Is that lasagna? You know your daddy doesn't like ethnic dishes."

"It's baked ziti, and he's already taken a pass."

"Oh, honey, you need to learn how to cook. You're never going to catch a man with that kind of food." Aunt Olympia shook her head, as if knowing the perfect fried chicken recipe would solve Lucy's single status.

She didn't want the conversation to veer off into marriage talk. "What sort of plan did you come up with for the house?"

"I've got a surefire idea to get you all out of this mess," Aunt Olympia said, taking a sip of tea. A bright smear of orange lipstick decorated the rim of her glass.

Surefire. That couldn't be good. Aunt Olympia had flair, beauty, style and one of the finest Southern mansions in the state, but she had about the same amount of business sense as Lucy's daddy. She knew how to spend money, not make it.

She leaned forward, resting her hand on Lucy's. Her long nails were sunset orange with tiny black palm trees. "I called my friend Pearly Mae and she—"

Letting out a groan, Lucy slumped in the chair. "Oh, boy."

Aunt Olympia paused, lips a thin line. "You can make all the fun you want, but Pearly Mae knows everything about everyone."

"Now she knows everything about us, too."

"Yes, well, that's part of the bargain, isn't it? You tell her what you need and she tries to help out."

"While calling every friend of hers on the way." Lucy had just enough pride left to be horrified at the idea of her family troubles being spread around town.

Ignoring that last comment, Aunt Olympia went on, "She heard that the Free Clinic of Tupelo needed a new space. They got a big grant from the state to upgrade all their equipment, but the place over on Yancey Avenue is too little for all their clientele. Crawford House has thirteen large bedrooms upstairs and—"

Lucy held up a hand, eyes closed. "Wait, now. Wait just a minute here."

"I know you think they'll destroy the place," her aunt said. "But they won't make any significant changes and you all can still live here, too."

Lucy cracked an eye and stared at her. "Live here. With the Free Clinic of Tupelo." She wasn't sure which was worse: the idea of Crawford House being rented out as a medical facility or living in what would amount to a waiting room for sick people.

"You wouldn't have to interact with them at all, of course. You and Willy keep the front part of the house with the library, sitting room, kitchen and your bedrooms. The back part could be turned into a reception area and consultation rooms."

Something about her aunt's wording rang a warning bell. "You've already been talking to someone about this? Someone other than Pearly Mae?"

"Lucy, it happened so fast, it must be God's will." Aunt Olympia sat forward beaming. "And Dr. Stroud says he knows you. Last Christmas he was here with his wife at Crawford House's annual party, and you two stood by the punch bowl half the night, chatting about battlefield amputations."

Lucy remembered Dr. Stroud. Bushy white mustache, bow tie, seersucker suit. She'd figured he was retired and no longer practicing medicine because he seemed to spend all his time on

Civil War collections and reenactments. He'd said that he was surprised the African-American community wasn't more involved with Brice's Crossroads, since half of the Union dead were part of Bouton's Brigade of United States Colored Troops, and then he'd tried to recruit her for the next battle. She'd wavered under his charm. The idea of battling mosquitoes in five layers of Civil War dress made it easy to say no.

She chewed the inside of her lip. If Aunt Olympia had named any other person in the area, she would never think of agreeing, but Dr. Stroud understood the history of a place like Crawford House. He wouldn't be setting his coffee cup on the hundred-year-old white-oak fireplace mantel from Philadelphia, or hanging his coat from the cast-iron wall sconces.

"How much will they pay? And what are the terms of the lease?"

"See, I knew you would agree," Aunt Olympia said. "It's enough that you can pay off that home equity in a few years. They'll be over in about fifteen minutes. I told him to give me a little time to get you comfy with the idea."

"I'm not agreeing to anything. Daddy's not even here to make a decision." Lucy stood up, glancing around the kitchen. Mrs. Hardy only came on Tuesdays and Thursdays now. There were dishes in the sink, crumbs on the counters and her daddy's coffee mugs dotted the drainboard.

As if following Lucy's train of thought, Aunt Olympia wandered to the sink and stood in front of it, blocking the view of the mess. "Honey, I can convince Willy to do what's right. I'm more worried about getting you on board. This is the best thing that could have happened. You won't have to move, Willy can get out of debt and the house will be used for something other than gathering dust. Plus, I know Paulette is counting on having a big, fancy wedding as soon as she finds her man."

Lucy leaned around her aunt and held a dishrag under the faucet, saying nothing. She wasn't agreeing to this so that Paulette could have the wedding of the year when she finally chose between all her boyfriends.

"There is one small detail I should mention." The tone of forced cheerfulness in her aunt's voice made Lucy pause.

She turned, wet rag in one hand. "What? Will they put a sign on the front of the house? Install bars on the windows?"

"I'm not sure about any of that." Aunt Olympia's cheeks turned darker and the sight filled her with dread. Her aunt was never embarrassed. It was practically impossible to shame the woman. She firmly believed she was in the right at all times.

When Lucy didn't respond, her aunt hurried on, "They're bringing in a new doctor. He's part of the Rural Physicians Scholarship Program, and now that he's graduated, he's coming back to practice in a rural community so he can erase his school debt."

Lucy reached out for the back of the kitchen chair. She could hardly feel the smooth wooden top rail under her hand. *Please, Lord. Not him.* The kitchen had turned small, her aunt's voice fading away. A flash of a crooked smile, blond hair tousled from the wind, a gentle voice, the warmth of large hands against her back.

"Honestly, it's not a big deal." Aunt Olympia let out a sigh as if her niece were being difficult.

"Who is it?" Even as she asked the question, Lucy knew the answer. Her aunt wouldn't have saved this point for last if it wasn't important.

"Jeremiah Chevy." Her aunt reached out to pat Lucy's hand, changing her mind when she saw the wet rag clenched in one of Lucy's fists. "You'll be fine. It's been a long time. Ten years almost. It was the right thing to do and you know it. First of all, that name. Did you really want to be Mrs. Chevy?"

Lucy slid into a chair. *Mrs. Chevy.* She'd actually practiced that name on the inside cover of her school notebooks, over and over in her best handwriting. *Mrs. Lucy Crawford Chevy.*

Her aunt waved a hand, as if the concept had let off a terrible smell. "Can you imagine? It was insanity, being attached at eighteen to a boy like that."

"Like what, Auntie?" Lucy could hear the trembling in her voice. She didn't know if it was from shock or fury or both. "White? Poor? Or was it that Jem has a teen dropout for a mama?"

"Well, sure, all of those things." Aunt Olympia wasn't embarrassed now. "It never would have worked. He didn't even know if he could get into college. I don't know how he got through medical school, and he must have mountains of debt. Probably in the hundreds of thousands."

Lucy stared at her aunt, wondering if the woman honestly believed medical-school debt was any worse than what her daddy had accrued with bad investments and lavish vacations.

"He had nothing but his daddy's name, which he couldn't trade for beans. And if you thought your mama would have been happy with you marrying a white boy, you're wrong."

Lucy felt her throat close up. Had her mama been a racist? She hadn't said much at the time, not about his color. "Mama had green eyes. Someone somewhere didn't care about color," she whispered.

"Oh, don't start with that. You know better." Her aunt's face was stony. "There's no chance those pretty eyes came from a mixed couple in love a hundred years ago. Somebody knew the story but didn't want to pass it down, and that tells us enough right there."

Lucy dropped her chin to her chest. The news

had sucked every logical thought from her head. Oh, the irony was laughable. She'd been persuaded to break it off with him because she was wealthy, Black and guaranteed a good job after being accepted to Harvard. Only one of those things was still true.

The doorbell sounded dimly in the distance.

"Oh, there they are," her aunt said, jumping to her feet.

Lucy's stomach turned to ice. "They?"

"Dr. Stroud and Jem. I can show them around if you want. I know you didn't get a chance to put on anything nice." Aunt Olympia paused, cocking her head. "And you haven't been to the hairdresser's in too long. You need one of those coconut-oil treatments under the hair dryer and maybe some extensions. You're hardly fit to entertain guests. You just stay in the kitchen, hear?"

She sat frozen to the spot as Aunt Olympia sashayed out of the doorway. She would have given anything in the world to rewind the last ten minutes and keep this from happening. She would have called them, told them it wouldn't work, made some excuse, any excuse.

Deep voices carried faintly to her and she wanted to clap her hands over her ears. She hadn't heard anything from Jem in ten years. Not an e-mail, not a text. Completely understandable, really. Once they had been the best of friends, finishing each other's sentences and talking for hours into the night. And love, there had always been love. She never let herself think of it, but now, in a flash, she remembered clearly the overwhelming need to be near him, to touch him. He was like air to her then, and she couldn't live without him.

And yet, she had. When her aunt had convinced her it would never work out, Lucy had stood on his rickety front porch and told him she had decided it was better if they saw other people. It was such a stupid thing to say, something she copied from a TV show about teenagers who swapped boyfriends like shoes. There were no other people to see, was no one else she wanted, then or after. The memory of the shock and hurt on Jem's face haunted her dreams, stole her appetite and gnawed away at her peace of mind. By the time she reached her breaking point months later, he was gone. There was nothing for her to do but sleep in the proverbial bed she had made.

The kitchen was silent except for the sound of her own breathing. Time seemed suspended, as if the world were waiting on her next move.

Lucy ran a hand over her hair, feeling the slight frizz at her hairline, the dryness at the ends. She wasn't wearing much makeup, had only a pair of simple pearl studs in her ears. She glanced down, taking in her battered running shoes, straight-leg jeans and last year's marathon T-shirt, which had a tiny hole at the hem. When she'd known Jem, she'd put in about the same amount of time on her appearance as any wealthy teenage girl. But after he'd gone, there wasn't any reason to get her nails done or a facial at her favorite spa. She'd thrown herself into her studies and done her best to keep her mind off her heartache. This was who she was now. Putting off this meeting until she made it to the hairdresser's implied that something could be changed. She heaved herself to her feet. There was no choice except to walk in there like the grown woman she was and welcome them into her home. "Please give me strength," she whispered. And it would be nice if she didn't trip, stutter, or blush.

It seemed to take hours to walk down the hallway, but finally she reached the end, emerging into the foyer. Her gaze landed on Dr. Stroud first, as he swept an arm out toward the seating in the entryway. He was saying something about the Civil War–era sewing bench and square nails.

Lucy tried to focus on Dr. Stroud, but her attention was pulled, against her will, to Jem. He was half-turned away, looking out the large windows onto the rose garden. At first glance, it was surreal to see him standing there in her house, as if ten years hadn't passed. But a closer look showed the years between. Wearing a charcoal-gray suit that fit him well, his hands were at his sides. He was taller than she remembered. Bulkier around the shoulders, more heft and muscle. As a teen he had always managed to get his feet tied up in chair legs or trip over wrinkles in the carpet or bump his head on a low doorframe. He had changed, but was still the same, so much the same that she could have recognized him from the back. The muscles under his jacket tensed, and she knew that he would turn and see her. The moment before their eyes met, Lucy felt as if she were dangling off the side of a cliff, holding on to one slim branch as it bent toward the ground. If he let on, in any way, with a smirk or a glint of laughter, what a humorous reversal of fortune this was, she didn't think she would survive.

He met her gaze steadily, emotionless. It was as if they didn't know each other at all. His blond hair still stick-straight, brows two shades darker, the long nose he inherited from his mom's side, the blue eyes from his dad's Irish grandparents. She looked at him, not able to think of a word to say. She wanted to catalog his features, to spend hours noting every tiny difference from ten years ago, but he wasn't hers and hadn't been for a long time.

"Oh, here you are. Miss Lucy Crawford, let me introduce my colleague, Dr. Jeremiah Chevy. He's just completed his residency at Boston Children's Hospital." Dr. Stroud beckoned her forward, bushy mustache twitching with excitement. "He's also quite a fan of our local history. You might have crossed paths, with being the curator over at Brice's Crossroads."

"We've met before," Jem said casually. "Nice to see you again."

She nodded. "And you."

He'd already looked away, gazing up at the high ceiling and the brass chandelier, probably noticing how shabby the ornate ceiling medallion looked, small bits of paint flaking off at the curves of the motif.

"Excellent. Then we're all introduced and we can talk about the future of the Free Clinic." Dr. Stroud clapped his hands together. "Miss Lucy, will you lead the way?"

She tried to look as if her pulse weren't pounding in her ears. "My aunt said you'd like to look at the back of the house, near the former servants' quarters?"

"Let's start there. If the rooms are big enough, we can make them examination rooms." Dr. Stroud glanced around. "What a magnificent old place. Your family must be incredibly proud."

Proud. She cringed at the word. If they had been proud, her daddy would have made sure that their home was safe, instead of adding equity loan after equity loan on the old place. No bank in the state would forgive that kind of debt just because it was a Civil War–era home. They didn't care that her great-granddaddy Whittaker had brought that pie safe all the way from Philadelp... or that her grandmama Honor had handpicked the wallpaper. Family history didn't matter to a big bank, and if her daddy had been truly proud, then he would have been more careful.

"Follow me back, then." She turned and crossed the foyer, knowing she would do whatever it took to save her home, but wishing with all her heart that this day had never come.

ow they were as strangers; nay worse
than strangers, for they could never
become acquainted.
—ANNE ELLIOT

CHAPTER TWO

He hadn't expected Lucy to be home. Jem smoothed his tie and checked his shirt for stains, evidence of his lunch of catfish nachos. Not that it mattered. She wouldn't notice. He was old news to her, and he could tell by the straight line of her mouth that there wouldn't be any friendly chatter between them.

She hadn't smiled and he was thankful for that. He'd loved her smile. And her deep, rich laugh. He'd loved everything about her, once. Although she had always been shy, now she seemed withdrawn. He would have said it was impossible, but she was more beautiful now. Her cheeks had lost their adolescent roundness, and the heart shape of her face was more pronounced.

She had glanced at him, dark eyes somber, and it was as if he were reliving every humiliating episode of their romance all at once. From the time he'd brought cracklin' cornbread to her catered garden party, to the moment she stood on the little built-on porch of his mama's mobile home and told him she was going to see other people. He shouldn't have been shocked, not with everything else, but somehow he had believed that their love was enough. Maybe she had never loved him. That was always a possibility.

He needed to focus on his future, not on the bad history here. The air in the old house felt sluggish in his lungs. He concentrated on breathing slow and deep. It took an enormous amount of hard work to get into the Rural Physicians program and he wasn't going to jeopardize it by letting himself be pulled into old drama.

The hallway was filled with the delicious scent of cooking. He took a few sniffs, trying to narrow the possibilities. Definitely Italian.

Their little group filed into the back parlor. The view out the floor-to-ceiling windows was just as he remembered, and the green hills of the property glowed lushly in the sunshine. The hardwood parquet flooring was scuffed and battered, wallpaper peeled at the corners of the room. He fought to stay in the present, but his mind flashed back to the first time he'd stepped into this room.

Brought together by a mutual love of history and friends in common, Lucy sought him out at every gathering. He thought maybe, just maybe, she liked him, but he wasn't sure until the day she offered to show him Crawford House. The Greek Revival architecture, with its massive white columns and sweeping front steps, was nothing compared to the inside. Family antiques dating back centuries were everywhere, on mantels and tables and hung on the walls. He'd been amazed at how much she'd known about it all, from the glazed stoneware to the quilts to the grain scoop in the kitchen flour cabinet.

Now the furniture was sparse, as if someone had been clearing the space for some other project, or maybe the Crawfords had resorted to selling off antiques to keep up their lifestyle. If they had, the funds certainly weren't being passed to Lucy. He shot a look at her, noting her simple clothing and jewelry. She never was much into fashion. Turning her head at that moment, she caught his eye and he looked away. He walked toward the windows, letting Dr. Stroud carry the conversation.

"I'm not sure how many seats we could put in here. Our daily patient load runs anywhere from ten to forty." Dr. Stroud frowned at the space.

"One row of seats would be just fine, surely. The others can stand." Olympia shrugged.

Jem felt the muscles in his shoulders contract. This woman irked him, always had. She enjoyed running roughshod over every situation. He'd never liked her, even before she'd convinced Lucy to dump him. Now, even with all the years he'd spent fighting his bitterness, the woman still made his hackles rise. "We'll need a small area for children to play. Just a corner, but that space will cut down on seating. And don't forget the intake area," he said.

"Play area? It's not Disneyland," Olympia said.

"Jem is right," Dr. Stroud said. "When the kids are occupied, the wait is easier on everyone." He paced the area, moving his lips, counting off steps.

"You could set it up in this little room." Lucy walked past Stroud, opening a narrow door to the right. It revealed a space cluttered with household materials, old paint cans and boxes of cleaning supplies. "Zeke used this for storage, but we won't need it now."

The sadness in her voice rang an alarm and Jem spoke before thinking. "Zeke passed away?"

"No," she said without meeting his eyes. "I had to let him go."

There was no good way to respond to that news. Zeke had been part of Crawford House from before Lucy was born. The old man loved her like his own child, and Lucy loved him back.

Dr. Stroud peeked over Lucy's shoulder. "That could work, for sure. We'd have to remove the door. Paint the walls and put in some small shelves and kid-sized furniture. But before we make too many plans, we'd better check out those servants' quarters and see if they can be turned into exam rooms."

"This way," Olympia called out, her voice echoing around the small foyer. Dr. Stroud followed, and there was an awkward moment where Jem wasn't sure if Lucy would stay. He knew exactly why she hesitated and his face went hot. Finally, she seemed to realize he was waiting for her, and she quickly followed the others.

Walking down the back hallway was a painful sort of déjà vu. He'd had this tour before, many years ago. Lucy had led him to the servants' quarters, little rooms along a narrow hallway at the back of the house. He'd mentioned his mama's battered, old trunk and Lucy was looking to show him a similar one that was tucked into a corner somewhere. What he'd done then was so impulsive and foolish; he gritted his teeth just to think of it. Lucy had been midsentence, maybe even midword, when he'd backed her up against the wall and kissed her.

As a grown man he'd learned some manners, but as a kid, heady with the smell of her perfume and the sound of that husky laugh, he'd taken a chance. His instincts hadn't been wrong. She'd kissed him back, wrapping her arms around his neck.

"We might have to install a few more lights along this passage, but I really think this could be the perfect answer to our problem of space," Dr. Stroud said. He excitedly opened and closed each of the six little doors, wandering up and down the long hallway. "It will be a much smoother operation, having the nurses do some of the preliminary intake while we examine patients." He beamed at Jem. "Thanks to this fine young man, the Free Clinic of Tupelo will be serving more of the neediest families in the area. I can't thank him enough for coming back to his hometown. I know he wasn't eager to make the move, but we're sure glad to have him."

"Well, your family is still here, aren't they?" Olympia asked.

"My mother has moved to Birmingham." Jem had moved her away from Tupelo as soon as he'd been able. She loved it in Birmingham, working part-time as a reading tutor in a grade school. His mama had always wanted to be a teacher, and he was hoping to convince her to return to school. She said she was too old for that sort of thing, but she always smiled when she said it, as if she liked the thought.

"Well, it's always easier to come home than to make your way in a big city. Right, Lucy?" Olympia had a hand on one neon hip, her orange lips turned up in a bright smile. "She's had plenty of opportunities to move, especially right after she graduated from UGA."

Jem frowned. "University of Georgia? I thought you went to Harvard."

Raising her eyes from her shoes, Lucy said, "I did. One year. But I had to . . . I transferred to be closer to home."

Jem was starting to see that the Crawfords' financial issues had started a lot further back than a few years. It explained a lot about Lucy's willingness to rent out the house. He pretended to examine the inside of one of the rooms, forcing himself to keep quiet. He wanted to say how sorry he was, how he'd known how much Harvard had meant to her, how hard she'd worked to get there. Mostly he wanted to tell her that he knew how it felt to be poor, to be choosing the lesser of two evils, and how she would survive it all just fine. But he didn't. It was something a friend would say, and they weren't friends.

"What do you think, Jem?" Stroud asked. "Do we tell the board we've found the perfect spot?"

"It's definitely a step up from that little building on Yancey. This is a good location, too. Right on the bus line because of that new cross street." Jem paused. "It might be a longer ride for most of our patients, though."

"True, true." Dr. Stroud stroked his mustache. "But they'll be more comfortable here. Miss Olympia, you're sure that Mr. Crawford will agree?"

"Oh, yes." She laughed. "I can persuade him, never fear. I'm very good at that."

Jem clenched his jaw. The woman was bragging about her ability to bend her family to her will. He looked up at that moment and met Lucy's gaze. Her expression was stark. Pain, regret and

36

embarrassment flickered across her features. It gave him a little bit of satisfaction that she felt anything so many years after she'd broken his heart.

"I say we move the clinic, Dr. Stroud," Jem said.

"Excellent." He clapped his hands together and smiled at each of them. "I'll get the paperwork drawn up as soon as possible. Now, if you'll excuse me, I should probably get back to work. Dr. Harris is covering my appointments, and we've still got to get Jem settled in to the routine."

"Follow me," Olympia said. "Jem, I admire your commitment to serving the community that raised you. So many young people leave Tupelo and never return, even after receiving so much support from the people here."

"I was placed here by the Rural Physicians Program." Jem wanted to add that he didn't feel a whit of gratitude toward the community that barely tolerated his trailer-trash family.

As they paused in the foyer, Lucy walked past them to the front door. She smiled at Stroud, but didn't look Jem in the face.

"We'll see you at the center, Miss Lucy? I wouldn't miss that presentation on battlefield medical care on the thirtieth." Dr. Stroud was already headed out.

"I'll see you there. And come again soon," she said, but it was clearly just a polite saying. She looked as if she would rather do anything other than head up another Crawford House tour.

Jem said his good-byes and followed Stroud down the steps. He heard the door close behind him and imagined Lucy on the other side, letting out a sigh of relief. They had trooped into her home, scoped out the area, and planned on bringing hordes of poor folk around. Times must be desperate for her to entertain that as a solution to her family's debts.

Stroud clapped him on the shoulder as they walked down the flagstone path toward the parking area. "Now there's a fine family for you, Jem. Their history stretches back to before the Civil War. If I remember correctly, they're related to the Medal of Honor winner Aaron Anderson. Of course, poor man, they spelled his name wrong on it, but that's how things happened in those days. Even the most honored African Americans weren't treated with much respect."

Pausing near the rose-garden entrance, Stroud looked around at the slightly overgrown hedges. "They've fallen on hard times, but as long as they hold on to their family history, they'll be just fine. Everything else can be replaced, but you can't buy a good family name."

Jem stared up at the arbor, where red climbing roses sprung out in all directions like broken beads from a necklace. The old doctor was charming, educated and committed to helping the people of Tupelo. But he was blind to his own bias. A person who loved history would always admire the noble heritage of others, of course. That was natural. Stroud didn't realize how he sounded to someone who barely knew his grand-parents, or to someone who had never been invited to the best parties, the nicest houses, or the good ol' boys' clubs. Jem remembered the sharp pain of hunger that lasted from the moment he got up, to the free lunch at school. He remem-bered the sound of his mama crying at night when the electricity was going to be shut off, again. He remembered the look on her face when he asked about his daddy and if he would come back someday.

Jem fought to shrug off the old bitterness. He knew moving back to Tupelo would bring back a lot of bad memories. It was completely expected.

Stroud flashed him a smile, blue eyes twinkling behind his round glasses. "You certainly made a fine impression with the Crawfords. I'd be surprised if you weren't invited back for dinner."

He choked and covered it with a cough. He was absolutely certain that was not going to happen.

"And you'll be coming to the presentation at the interpretive center. You can ride over with me, if you like." Dr. Stroud turned back toward the parking area, patting his pockets for his keys. "Don't tell me you'll be busy. I've seen your collection of Civil War medical kits. You wouldn't miss it for the world."

But Jem would, if he could. He said nothing. He had planned to spend his evenings working on his Confederate costume and traveling to reenactments on the weekends, but now he wanted to stay as far from Brice's Crossroads as possible.

Stroud located his keys; his forties-era, red Ford pickup gleamed in the bright sunshine. He paused, shooting Jem a look, before saying softly, "I know you've got some history here, being a hometown boy. But good or bad, it is what it is, and there's no getting away from it."

Jem opened his mouth to deny he had any such issue, but Stroud was already sliding behind the wheel of his truck. With a roar of the old engine and a snappy salute, the doctor reversed out of the driveway and headed onto the main road.

Jem looked up at Crawford House, three stories of proud Southern heritage and hundreds of years of history. Jem admired a fine antebellum mansion as much as any other Southerner, but once upon a time this place had meant more to him than architecture or Civil War battles. There had been a girl with a dry sense of humor and beautiful black eyes living here and she had won his heart. Then she'd gone and broken it.

Jem let out a breath and fumbled at getting the key in the door of his Honda. He'd forgiven her for that long ago. They were miles and years away from that summer as teenagers. Hormones and wishful thinking had created a potent brew, leading to what he had thought would be the love of his life. But he wasn't even thirty and that love was long gone, a distant memory.

Settling behind the wheel, Jem didn't allow himself another look toward Crawford House. He would be there plenty in the coming weeks and months. Now that the first awkward meeting was over, they should be able to greet each other with distant smiles and murmured niceties. It would be almost easy, really, now that he'd faced the past.

There was so much more to do in Tupelo than to pine after Lucy Crawford. He was determined to keep his head down and put in his time, without drama or complications. Once his school debt was erased, his real life as a fully qualified medical doctor could begin . . . somewhere other than Tupelo, Mississippi.

"Well, isn't Jem just the tomcat's kitten? I don't remember him being so handsome," Aunt Olympia said. "I think that went real well. I'm going to call your daddy. I know he's out golfing, but if I can get him to answer his phone, I'll tell him what we're doing." Aunt Olympia didn't wait for a response and headed back to the kitchen.

Lucy leaned against the door and let out a long, slow breath. It was fine. Everything was fine. The sick feeling she had in the pit of her stomach was because Crawford House was now slated to host the Free Clinic of Tupelo. Nothing more.

She squeezed her eyes closed, unable to resist bringing up his image. His suit wasn't fancy, but it fit him well. The coal-gray vest was striking against the white, button-up shirt and had a timeless feel, as if he could have been from any era. He had always been handsome, in a lanky sort of way, but it was that quiet demeanor that made her mouth go dry. He wasn't like Dr. Stroud, grinning and slapping men on the back and showering the women with compliments. Jem was watchful, considerate, forming his impressions and tucking them away somewhere inside.

Lucy pushed away from the heavy oak door and smoothed back her hair. He had hardly looked at her, so who cared whether she'd had her hair straightened recently. Janessa always said Lucy was letting herself go, and Paulette made noises over Lucy's complete lack of style, but none of it mattered. It had been years since she'd worried how she looked, and even longer since she'd had the disposable income to spend on her appearance. All of her tiny curator's salary went into keeping Crawford House afloat.

For all that, there was a hot, little coal of regret lodged somewhere in her throat. He had looked much as he always had, so handsome, and she must have seemed an older, scruffier version of the girl he had once loved. She didn't always wear makeup, so she was naturally only wearing a bit of mascara, but lifting her hands to her cheeks, she wondered if her skin looked dry. It would have been nice if she'd been wearing something other than jeans and a T-shirt. Maybe that pretty shirt-dress she'd found at the thrift shop, with tiny red and yellow flowers and the pearl buttons down the front. She looked down at her ancient running shoes. A pair of leather flats, or even some flirty summer sandals, would have been better. Holding out a hand, she frowned at her nails. Short, plain, and a bit dry around the cuticles.

She wrapped her arms around her middle, as if to keep all her emotions from tumbling around inside like shoes in a dryer. This deep, dark hole of self-pity had no bottom. She refused to let herself be drawn into an endless recital of things she could have done differently when it didn't matter at all what he thought. The hardest part was now over. They would be able to greet each other with no awkward pauses on either side.

At least, that was what she prayed could happen. If all else failed, she would do her best to stay as far out of his way as possible.

"If there is anything disagreeable going on, men are always sure to get out of it."
—MARY MUSGROVE

CHAPTER THREE

Lucy looked up at the knock on the door. Alda Huggins stood in the crack, an irritated look on her face. Her coworker's long, blond hair was pulled back and tinted pink and blue. Her style could best be described as couldn't-care-less, and her attitude hovered between sassy and downright frightening. "The Dramavore called and she's fixin' to come see you."

Lucy sighed. She should probably correct Alda and have her use Janessa's actual name, but that definition of a person who fed off emotional conflict was pretty accurate. "Okay, thanks for letting me know. Are you headed to lunch?"

"Sure am, and you're comin' with me."

"I can't. The diary arrived today and I need to get this display sorted." Lucy gestured to the pile of papers on her desk. "You go on, I'll hold down the fort."

"It's not a fort. It's a battlefield," Alda said. "It's because I ate that big burger last time, isn't it?

It just looked so good, with all those grilled mushrooms and Swiss cheese. It probably smelled like a dead carcass to you, but it was delicious. Mmm, just thinkin' about it makes me want another one."

Lucy shook her head. "It's nothing to do with your carnivorous habits, my friend."

Alda dropped into the chair near the door. "Then what is it? You haven't gone to lunch with me for weeks. I hardly ever see you."

Lucy snorted. "You see me every single weekday." Alda was the only other full-time staff member. She handled tour appointments, sold tickets, fielded phone calls, and made sure Lucy came out of her cave every so often.

Alda frowned at her slacks, picking off a bit of lint. The interpretive center didn't have a dress code, but Alda always wore subdued clothing that mostly covered the mermaid tattoo on one bicep and the flowering dogwood on the other. She'd mentioned her piercings once, but Lucy couldn't see any and certainly didn't want to ask for the details. "Sure, I see you when I come deliver a message or tell you that someone is waiting, but it's not the same."

Lucy rubbed her forehead. She missed chatting with Alda, it was true. But everything that had happened at Crawford House had made her shrink inward, pulling herself tight into a ball. It was hard to chat and make lighthearted conversation over lunch when all she wanted to do was lie in bed with the covers over her head.

"Give me a few days and we can go anywhere you want."

"Promise?" Alda stood up, skeptical look on her face.

"Cross my heart and all that jazz." Lucy put on a bright smile.

"I'm holdin' you to it." Alda closed the door behind her and Lucy let out a soft sigh.

It had been a week since she had seen Jem standing in her foyer, and the promise of the arrival of this little book was the only thing that had kept her sane.

Lucy opened the archival museum box and ran a gloved finger over the small leather diary. Now part of the museum's collection, the diary of Hattie Winter was one of the few first-person accounts of a woman joining the battle for the South while disguised as a man. It was a bright spot in her nerdy curator's life, and she was going to shove all her anxiety aside to focus on the treasure. During the days, she had managed to keep busy with projects around the house or organizing displays at the museum, but her dreams had turned into emotional minefields. She hadn't slept more than a few hours at a time before she would wake in a cold sweat, heart pounding painfully in her chest, visions of Jem fading in the darkness.

Every day she came home to face more changes

at Crawford House. The receptionist's desk, examining tables, waiting-room chairs, and the smell of bleach all spoke of the impending arrival of the Free Clinic. And Dr. Jeremiah Chevy. She could only hope that seeing him on a daily basis might be less torturous than waiting for the moment they would meet next. As it was, every day she drove down the tree-lined drive, pulse thudding in her ears, fingers numb on the steering wheel, waiting to see if his car was in the parking spot. Every time it was empty, she wondered if he had come to Crawford House with someone else and might be waiting inside with his somber demeanor and quiet voice.

Gently spreading the brittle pages of the diary, Lucy inhaled deeply. Here, in her office, she felt at home. She hadn't been very happy at Crawford House, but it had been a place to disappear. Now only the interpretive center was left for her, and even that wasn't completely secure. In a few weeks, Jem and Dr. Stroud would come to listen to her talk on Civil War medical kits.

She dropped her head onto her palm. She couldn't avoid Jem, and it was impossible to try. The best she could hope for was never being in a small space with him or having to have an actual conversation. Meanwhile, she would do her job, just as she always had, forgetting her own trouble by falling into the story of someone who lived long ago.

Most curators had a special fondness for one area of their collection. For Lucy, it was the handwritten diaries and letters. The accounts of long-dead soldiers were a comfort to her, their words like a guide in the confusion of modern life. Some kept a diary during the war but some only poured out their thoughts and fears at the end of their lives, as if to purge themselves from the memories. Most wrote in a diary without ever considering that anyone would read their words. They made inside jokes, referred to loved ones with simple initials, and abbreviated everything to the point of near illegibility. Her favorite moments were discovering a treasured bit of verse, a chorus of a folk song, or even a silly limerick. The soldiers never knew their words would be read hundreds of years later, and she usually loved the idea of private musings becoming immortal. But not today. Today she only wanted to touch the pages and remember that all things pass with time.

Her eyes burned with unexpected tears. Usually the tragedy of the war didn't grieve her, but this morning was different. Probably the lack of sleep. Maybe because her birthday was next week and she didn't feel like celebrating. Even if she had many friends to invite, it would be awkward to have people over for dinner. Walking past the brand-new sign for the Tupelo Free Clinic wasn't something they could ignore.

When they asked, she'd have to explain, and explaining meant talking about her family's debts. She wasn't living in a fantasyland, but she didn't feel like having that conversation on her birthday either.

Shifting in her chair, she refocused on the little book. The diary's author had written this at the very end of her life, and since she had never married, it had been handed to a nephew, then on down through the family until it turned up at auction. Lucy wondered if Hattie Winter knew she would be famous in certain circles years after she had passed away. Surely not. She couldn't have revealed her secret while she was alive, and even now only a small group of historians cared about the women who fought in the War Between the States. But Lucy cared and she was willing to spend a quarter of the center's artifact-acquisition funding to have Hattie's diary in its collection.

"We'll make you a nice display, with a silk-covered stand. It will be temperature and humidity controlled so you won't get moldy," she murmured. She might be embarrassed if anyone heard her, but her office door was closed, and the rest of the center's bare-bones staff was off at lunch. The air conditioner hummed comfortingly in the background.

"But first we need to know why you pretended to be a man, Miss Hattie Winter." Sometimes the *why* came much later than the *how,* but Lucy couldn't help looking for a reason for the wildly brave acts these women committed.

The first few pages of the diary were filled with birth and death dates, then a few lines of Emily Dickinson's poetry: *They dropped like Flakes, they dropped like Stars, like Petals from a Rose.* Lucy stared at the spidery cursive, tracing the letters with her finger. So much loss, so many friends and comrades vanished from the earth.

The next page answered her question. *To Bismarck Johnson. The Lord says if we seek, we shall find. I looked for you at each battle, every roll call, in the rows of the injured and the dead. I never did find you, my love, but you will always remain in my heart. If God will hear my prayer, we shall see each other in heaven.*

Lucy closed her eyes, feeling hot tears slide from under her lids. *Oh, Hattie.* What kind of love made a woman risk everything to follow her man into war? She would have said she had known heartbreak, but she hadn't been strong enough to follow her man across the railroad tracks, let alone into battle. Drawing in a shaky breath, she wiped her cheeks. She was different now. If she got another chance at love, she wouldn't let anyone stand in her way.

It had been ten years and she had never wanted anyone else. She might die an old woman still living in the shadows of a lost love. She imagined a cold lump of sadness, lifeless and still, sat under her ribs where her heart should be. She laid the diary back in the folds of archival paper. She needed to take a break before she started sobbing at her desk. Maybe some sunlight would lift her mood. It had been days since she'd been for a run, and her mental state was fraying along with her nerves.

Standing up, she stretched her arms up as far as she could reach, holding her breath and letting it out as she swung her fingers down to her toes. Just as she reached the ground, there was a knock at her office door and it swung open. Lucy straightened up with a snap. Her first thought was of Jem, and her second was irritation at the idea. Jem wasn't going to be waltzing into her office on a Tuesday afternoon.

"Surprise," someone called out.

"Rebecca?" Lucy started to laugh. Her cousin taught at Midlands College, only a few hours away, but she didn't visit very often. Maybe only a few times a term, and then just for lunch and never unannounced. But there she was, bright-red silk shirt contrasting with her black ringlets, her slim form perfectly sheathed in narrow jeans, with red patent leather ballet flats on her feet.

"I thought you didn't recognize me for a moment," Rebecca said, holding out her arms.

Lucy squeezed her tight and then stood back. "You look amazing, and extra happy. Come sit down. Tell me there's a special reason for this visit."

Rebecca dropped into a chair and swept her hair off one shoulder in an attitude of extreme nonchalance. "I have no idea what you mean. Just because I don't travel to Tupelo to see my Southern cousins very often doesn't mean that there is any particular reason for me to be here."

Lucy grinned. They called each other cousin, but the exact nature of their connection was vague. They knew Rebecca's great-uncle Martin had married Lucy's third cousin Pearl, which made them related in a way they still hadn't figured out. Rebecca had contacted the Crawfords when she had moved to Spartainville, and Lucy's daddy had welcomed Rebecca with pride. A professor of literature was a relative to brag about, even if she was a Northerner.

"I was going to wait until later, but if you insist . . ." Rebecca pulled a small, white envelope from her pocket. "An invitation."

Lucy tried not to show her disappointment. Another party. She'd had enough parties to last a lifetime. She slid her finger under the flap and popped it open. As soon as she saw the delicate rosebud-patterned liner, her heart skipped a beat. She withdrew the card, eyes going wide at the elegant script on the front. Just two initials, intertwined.

She glanced up and almost laughed at Rebecca's

expression. She had both hands over her mouth, eyes brimming with happiness. Lucy slowly unfolded the card, reading the words once, twice. *Mr. and Mrs. Joseph Hughes request the honor of your presence at the marriage of their daughter, Rebecca Anne, to Thomas Paul Nelson, son of Mr. and Mrs. Ronald Nelson . . .*

They stared at each other for a moment and then Lucy hugged Rebecca so hard that the invitation was crushed between them. "I can't believe it. I mean, I can. I just, I'm so surprised. I'm not sure why, really. I always knew you would get married, and Tom is a wonderful guy. It's that I didn't even know you were engaged." Lucy's words tumbled out, hitching their way past the sudden lump in her throat.

"Everything happened so fast." Rebecca let her go, smiling hugely. "We got engaged a week ago and we'll be married at the end of next month. In September, I'm leaving for a sabbatical year in Bath, so we thought we should just get married. He works remotely most of the time, so he could come with me, although my mother was pitching a fit about the quick wedding. She's sure everyone will think it's a shotgun wedding since it's all such short notice and then I'm leaving the country."

Lucy laughed, shaking her head. "That's your mama."

"I'm surprised they're giving their blessing, really. She was set on picking out my husband."

Glancing at the invitation again, Lucy paused. "The wedding is in Oxford?"

"Since he's from Miami, and I'm from DC, we thought we'd meet in the middle."

Lucy felt her eyes go wide.

"No, I'm kidding. He lives in Miami right now, but his family still lives around here." Rebecca leaned closer. "Don't tell, but I've always wanted a big Southern magnolia wedding."

"No, you haven't."

"You're right, I haven't," she said. "Did you read the whole thing?"

Lucy bent her head and read the invitation more slowly . . . *at St. Mark's Catholic Church, Oxford, Mississippi, July 26th, 2014, at 1:00 p.m. The Regency-themed reception will be held at Rowan Oak, Old Taylor Road.*

"I didn't know the William Faulkner House did wedding receptions."

"One of the perks of being an English literature professor. Plus, we've promised not to let anyone deface the scribbles on the study wall."

Lucy blinked, searching her memory for anything about Faulkner and his walls.

"Don't tell me you've never been there," Rebecca said. "I'm going to rescind your Southerner's card."

"You can't. It's tattooed on at birth. But what about the scribbles?"

"He outlined his Pulitzer Prize–winning novel *A*

Fable on the study wall. They've preserved it as part of the tour." Rebecca sighed. "Actually, the entire reception will be held outside. There's no way they would agree to let a big wedding party run through that place. The good news is that Bailey's Woods will be the perfect setting for my Regency dance."

Lucy glanced back to the invitation. " 'Regency-themed'? Is everyone supposed to come in costume?"

"Only if they want, but you should see my dress." Rebecca searched for her phone, then held it out. "It's patterned after an original Regency wedding gown. There's a dressmaker in Oxford and she's working on it as we speak."

"It's beautiful," Lucy said, and meant it. She wasn't wild about 1800s fashion, but this dress was stunning. The bodice was gently gathered, and the neckline was decorated with tiny roses. A long, graceful column of white silk fell from the Empire waist, and embroidery circled the hem.

"I'm glad you like the style because the bridesmaids' dresses will be the same, just simpler and a pale color."

It took Lucy a moment to understand her words. "You mean . . ."

"Will you? Be a bridesmaid? I promise not to be a total bridezilla and make you drive me around so I don't ruin my manicure or anything like that."

"Of course," Lucy practically shouted. "Of

course I would love to be part of the wedding. And you can dress me in anything you want. I'll drive you around and rub your feet when you've been dancing all evening, and hold up the train of your dress when you have to go to the bathroom, and—"

"Whoa. Not so fast." Rebecca looked horrified. "I'll be handling my own potty breaks, thank you."

"Oh, well, Janessa needed a lot of help on her big day." Not that Lucy had enjoyed any of it. If her mama had been there, she would have told Janessa to act like she had some raisin', but she hadn't been. Janessa spent the day screaming, "Bride's day, bride's way," until everyone got the message and just stayed out of the area if they could help it.

Rebecca reached out and grabbed Lucy's hands. "I'm not Janessa. I want to celebrate my wedding, with friends and family, while having a really good time. If someone spills punch on my dress, I'm not going to cry about it."

Lucy raised an eyebrow.

"Okay, I may cry just a bit, but it's only because it's an Austen-era reproduction and anybody would feel the pain of destroying something so lovely."

"Does Tom love Jane Austen, too?" Lucy figured he must if he was willing to dress up in a cravat and tails.

Rebecca waved a hand. "He doesn't really care one way or the other. In fact, he's never read a single Austen novel."

"But . . . that's your whole life. That's all you study, all you teach." For a moment, Lucy felt a pang of fear for Rebecca. Maybe the marriage was doomed from the start. A literature professor from DC and a computer programmer from Miami might not be the best match after all.

"It's not my whole life." Rebecca had a dreamy look on her face. "And I like seeing it all new through his eyes. Almost everyone I know has read the books or at least seen a movie or two."

"I guess Tom and I will have a lot in common, then."

Lucy could have said she was joining the circus and Rebecca would have been less surprised. "You're kidding."

"Absolutely not. I think I read half of *Pride and Prejudice* when I was in high school."

"We're going to have to remedy that situation before the wedding. You can't wear a Regency gown without knowing how very special it is." Rebecca was smiling, but something in her tone promised that she would find a way to force-feed Lucy some Austen.

"And the bridezilla rears her head."

Rebecca snorted. "I wouldn't insist, but I'd love to have some people at the reception who could lead during the dances or felt comfortable in the costumes. I wish some of my JASNA friends could come, but the wedding is happening so fast that most are off on vacation or busy that weekend."

"JASNA?"

"Jane Austen Society of North America. I'm a member of the DC group and the Mississippi group, and if we spend any time in Miami, I'm going to join there."

"There are whole organizations of people like you?" Lucy wasn't sure whether she should be encouraged or worried that there were hundreds of other people so enamored of Austen.

"Strange, isn't it? People coming together to study and enjoy their passion. Just like all these Civil War buffs you hang around with," Rebecca said.

"Yes, but this is important history and that is . . ." Her words trailed off at the look on Rebecca's face. Lucy could tell she was treading on thin ice. "You're right. I do need to educate myself. And then maybe I can help out more during the reception."

Rebecca's expression softened and it seemed all was forgiven. "Anyway, even if I weren't having a wedding, it would be my solemn duty to make sure you were versed in all things Jane."

"You sound like my aunt Olympia. She feels it's her solemn duty to make me do a lot of things that every good Southern girl should do, like learn how to cook a turkey or fry up some chicken."

"Perfect activities for a vegetarian," Rebecca said, laughing. "I sort of miss your aunt. The way she bosses everyone around is kind of cute."

Lucy tried to smile, but her mouth didn't want to cooperate.

"Uh-oh."

"It's nothing, really." Lucy shuffled a few papers.

"What's her current project? Finding you a husband?"

Lucy wanted to cringe. Aunt Olympia had done the opposite of finding her a husband. "We've had some financial problems."

"I remember you mentioned that. Is it getting any better?" Rebecca leaned forward, concern on her face.

"No. Well, yes." Lucy rubbed her forehead, trying to straighten out her tangled thoughts. "Aunt Olympia found a way for Crawford House to make a bit of income. The Free Clinic of Tupelo is renting out the back rooms as their new space. It's enough to start paying off some of the home equity loans Daddy took out on the house."

"Well, that's a good thing, right?" Rebecca paused. "It must be really strange for you, though, to have people in your house."

Lucy stared at her hands, wishing she could tell Rebecca everything, but not knowing where to start. She would have to go back ten years, and even then it would be almost too complicated to explain. "It is. Really strange. But I'm glad we've got the chance to save the house."

"I'm sorry. I didn't know it was that bad."

Lucy nodded. "It was and it is. As long as we can keep the lease with the Free Clinic, we should be out from under some of the worst debt in about five years."

"So, this isn't a short-term project." Rebecca took a deep breath. "And how are the clinic people? Are they nice?"

"Sure, very nice." Lucy rubbed her nose.

Rebecca's eyes went wide. "They're not."

"What? They are. Very nice."

"You rub your nose when you lie. Did you know that?" Rebecca started to giggle.

"I do not," Lucy protested. She searched her memory but couldn't come up with any proof that Rebecca was wrong.

"Tom says that everyone has a 'tell,' something that betrays their subconscious when they're trying not to speak the truth. When we first met, he asked if I thought his job was cool, and I said I did, but I did this little shrug with one of my shoulders." Rebecca lifted one shoulder and dropped it. "He laughed and said most people think programmers are complete nerds, living like a Dilbert cartoon, in a cube farm. It was weird. I never knew I did that, but now I catch myself, especially when I'm talking to my mom about the wedding. Everything she suggests is awful, from the enormous centerpieces to the eighty-dollar-a-plate dinner."

Lucy smiled, imagining Rebecca shrugging her way through a lunch with her mother.

"So, spit it out. What's wrong with the clinic people? Are they loud or messy or rude?"

"No, nothing." Lucy lifted a hand and stopped it halfway to her nose. Rebecca crossed her arms and gave her best "gotcha" smirk.

Sliding out from behind her desk, Lucy went to the window and stared out. She'd wanted to talk about Jem, but now that she had the opportunity, she didn't know what to say. "One of the doctors is from this area."

Rebecca said nothing.

"We knew each other a long time ago."

"Uh-oh."

Lucy turned. "It's not a big deal. We're fine. We've talked to each other and everything."

"How long ago was this?"

"Senior year of high school. We met at a spoken-poetry group." Lucy shrugged. "I don't know why we started hanging out. We both loved words, I guess."

"Hmm." Rebecca stared at the ceiling for a moment. "Something tells me that you shared more than poetry. You wouldn't be upset about him moving back here if you'd been just friends."

"Of course we were more than friends." Lucy's face went hot. She couldn't admit it without flashing back on the memory of that one glorious summer, full of passion and yearning. "But we had nothing in common. We were from completely different economic groups, our families would never have gotten along, and he didn't even know if he was going to college."

"So, you guys broke up when you left for Harvard?"

The memory was still painfully clear in Lucy's mind. "A few weeks before that, right after a garden party at my house. I wanted to introduce him to my parents, but Daddy refused to shake his hand. My aunt persuaded me to break it off, to set things straight about our lack of a future, or he would be expecting us to get married. And that would never happen."

Rebecca cocked her head. "Your aunt Olympia?"

"Right." Lucy sat down again and moved a paper to the left, then back to its original spot. She spoke slowly, voicing thoughts she'd been mulling. "I think, I mean, I'm not sure, but maybe we would have been happy together. I know it looked like we had nothing in common, but we were so similar in the ways that really mattered."

"What was wrong with him? She must have had a reason other than money."

Lucy spread her hands on the desk. Rebecca might not understand, coming from DC, but race was important here, more important than almost anywhere else in the country. "I know your family doesn't object to Tom, but my family is very traditional. A Crawford girl couldn't just marry a redheaded programmer from Miami and get away with it."

"Are you saying he's white?" Rebecca's eyes were wide. "Now, I can see how that would be a problem. Your daddy didn't strike me as being particularly open-minded."

"Even worse, Jem was really poor in high school. His mom was a high school dropout and he never knew his dad. He lived in a terrible little trailer park off Lincoln Street. Umm, and he's Catholic."

Rebecca started to laugh.

After a few seconds, Lucy couldn't help smiling, then chuckling. Finally, she wiped tears from under her eyes. "I suppose it is a little funny when I say it all at once. We were like Romeo and Juliet."

"No"—Rebecca let out a final laugh—"you're just like Anne Elliot and Frederick Wentworth." At Lucy's confused expression, Rebecca went on, "You've really got to read some Austen. In *Persuasion*, the heroine breaks off an engagement with a poor sailor because he has no wealth or rank. Eight years later he returns, a ship captain, and all the girls want to marry him. Meanwhile, Anne is an old maid and her family is in debt and—"

"We weren't engaged." Lucy shook her head.

"And I object to that part about the old maid."

"I didn't mean it that way. But it's really odd how your story sounds just like *Persuasion*."

"Maybe some parts of it. I haven't read it, but I can tell you that our ending won't be a happy one, and I'm assuming Austen's is. We're just trying to keep out of each other's way."

"You never know. I'll pray that you two can—"

"No, don't do that." Lucy said, cutting into Rebecca's sentence. She paused. "I'm sorry. Of course you can pray. But I don't want to hope for what can never happen. The best we can pray for is that he can forgive me."

Rebecca's brown eyes were soft, her smile gone. "Then I'll pray for you both to forgive what happened in the past and feel free to be friends." She stood up, shouldering her tote bag. "I'll let you get back to work, but call me this weekend. I'll drive down and we can have lunch."

Lucy shot her a look. "Does this involve an Austen movie?"

"No, no ulterior motives. I just feel like it's been too long since we've really caught up with each other."

"All right, but no meddling. We're not literary characters and we're not going to be reenacting a romantic scene for you."

"Got it. No meddling." Rebecca leaned over the desk and gave her one last hug. "Don't work too hard, and I'll see you this weekend. You can help me pick out the bouquets."

Lucy felt her heart lift at the idea. "Deal."

Seconds later, Rebecca was gone, the door closing softly behind her. Lucy let out a breath. She loved weddings. It was incredible to witness the union of two people, pledging to honor and respect each other, before their family and friends. But there was a tiny pinch of jealousy somewhere near her heart. She didn't want to envy Rebecca. The woman deserved all the happiness in the world. She was kind, loving, faithful and strong. She'd found true love with Tom and it was going to be a beautiful ceremony, although it might be a little odd to have everyone dressed in Regency clothes.

Lucy felt the jealousy bloom, becoming an overwhelming tide for just a moment, before she pushed it deep down inside. Dropping her head into her hands, she felt the muscles in her back as tight as bowstrings. She'd made her bed, and now she had to sleep in it. Her chance at happiness was long gone.

Hot tears leaked out from under her lids and she brushed them away. Jem's coming back into town at the same time she was going to help plan a big wedding was a bit of bad timing. Horrible, ironically bad timing. But there wasn't anything to do about it but be happy for Rebecca and keep going. Just as she had been for the last ten years.

Lucy was going to have to live with the choice she'd made. It couldn't get any worse than it already had.

She said the words over and over, but in her gut she knew that it was a lie.

There could have been no two
hearts so open, no tastes so similar,
no feelings so in unison.
—ANNE ELLIOT

CHAPTER FOUR

Jem measured the baby's head and turned to scribble down the numbers, but by the time he put his pen to the paper, he'd forgotten them. Frustrated, he slipped the paper circle over the wiggling infant one more time. He had been like this all week. Disorganized, forgetful, spacey. Moving the Free Clinic to Crawford House wasn't too complicated, but he felt drained and grumpy by the end of every shift. Today was the clinic's last day in the tiny house on Yancey Avenue, and most of the staff were thrilled to be moving to the historic home. If only he could say the same.

"Kaniesha, your baby is looking much better." Jem glanced over the notes from their last visit. "When you brought her in last time, she hadn't gained any weight in three months."

"That new formula you told me to use doesn't make her spit up so much. My Tina takes after me. I got a real sensitive stomach." The young mom shook a pair of plastic keys in front of the baby's face.

"She probably had a form of milk allergy." Jem glanced across at Kaniesha's rounded tummy. "How far along are you now?"

"Huh?" She looked confused, her tired face wrinkling into a frown. "Oh, the new baby. I'm due in September."

"Have you thought about breast-feeding? Breast-fed babies don't struggle with milk allergies and they're all-around healthier." He held out a finger to Tina, smiling as she ignored the toys and grabbed for his hand.

"How do I do that when I'm workin'? My grammy lives with us and she watches her during my shift." Kaniesha heaved a sigh. "It's not that I don't want to, Dr. Chevy."

"Any amount of time breast-feeding can have a positive lifelong impact. Maybe you could breast-feed the first three months while you're on maternity leave."

Kaniesha laughed, a short bark of sound that echoed in the small examining room. "What are you talkin' about? Maternity leave?"

"By federal law you're allowed twelve weeks of maternity leave. Your employer is required to keep your position open until you return." He reached for a small pamphlet on the Family and Medical Leave Act.

"And I get paid for that?"

Jem's hand stilled on the stack of papers. "Well, no. It's an unpaid leave."

"Nobody got time to sit around in the house while the bills are comin' in. I went back to work two weeks after she was born." Glancing down, Kaniesha slid her hand over the soft skin of Tina's little leg. "She was so tiny." Her voice was barely a whisper.

"Working moms can also pump milk for their babies. You'll have to have a designated area in the freezer and teach your grammy how to gently warm it in hot water because it shouldn't be defrosted in the microwave, but it can be a huge benefit to your baby's health." He pulled open a file cabinet to the side of his desk and flipped through the tabs until he found what he needed.

Kaniesha took the paper and read through it silently. "How do I get the machine?"

Jem blinked. He hadn't thought about that. He knew a hospital-grade pump could run hundreds of dollars, but cheaper hand models were available. "Let me look into it."

She sighed. "I would love to stay home with them for a few months. My husband tries real hard, but he ain't makin' much more than I am. We're hardly keeping up with our two jobs. I wish they would give me a full-time position, but they keep 'em for folks who graduated."

"Have you ever thought of going back to get your GED? There are night classes here in town. I think they're on Tuesdays and Thursday at—" He looked up and left off the rest of his sentence. Kaniesha was staring at the floor, her expression filled with frustration.

He realized how he sounded, how everything he'd said was a request to improve, to change. He knew exactly how she felt. Growing up in this town, he'd heard a lot of advice, too. His high school counselor gave him job applications to the local hardware store. His friends jeered when he studied instead of going out. His aunt had yelled at him when his mama worked two shifts to help pay for his college tuition. A lot of people had thought they'd known better than he did, and no one cared that it was his life. Except Lucy and his mama. He pushed the thought of Lucy out of his mind. In the end, she had been like everyone else. But his mama had focused on what he was doing right, made him believe in himself. A different memory flooded through him: his mama at their tiny table, wiping tears away with a kitchen rag, refusing to tell him what was wrong. Had she sat in an office, just like this one, listening to an educated professional give her suggestions to better her life?

"But all of that can come later, if you want," Jem said. "You're doing a great job with Tina. She's healthy and happy. You've made a loving home for her and the new baby."

Kaniesha's lips tilted up. "Yeah, I have. We got

lots of love in our house. Not a lot of money, but lots of love."

"I was raised in a house just like that." Jem swallowed hard. He thought he'd know how to talk to the poorest patients at the clinic, but he'd fallen into the same old narrative that he'd heard his whole life. Not good enough, never good enough. And once a person believed that, life only went downhill.

"And look how you turned out. A doctor." Kaniesha smiled at her baby. "Maybe she'll be a doctor someday, too."

"Dr. Tina. It has a nice ring to it." Jem grinned. "A sight nicer than Dr. Chevy."

Kaniesha snorted. "Sorry. I don't mean to be pokin' fun at your name."

"It's fine. I'm used to it." He checked the sheet again. "Let's have you come back here in a month, just to make sure Tina's back on track with her growth. We're moving the clinic to Crawford House. Do you know where that is?"

She shifted, her eyes narrowing. "That big ol' place with the pillars? Did they move out?"

"No, the family is still living there, but we're renting the back portion of the house. There's a bus stop right on the corner of Dogwood." He could see she wasn't happy with the change. "Is it much farther for you?"

"Naw. It's just . . . I don't like them folks. They think they're so much better than everybody else."

Jem looked down at his hands. He couldn't argue. Once upon a time, Olympia had made it clear that he and his family were less than nothing. There was a brief moment he would have said one person in that family didn't care about his poverty, but he'd been wrong. "It's a better space for us. More rooms, a bigger reception area."

Kaniesha shrugged. "As long as I don't have to talk to them, maybe it'd be okay."

The Crawfords probably felt the same way. "I'll see you on the twelfth, then. Stop on the way out and let Leticia get you into the schedule."

She hoisted Tina onto one hip. "Okay, see ya, Dr. Chevy." She left the door open behind her.

Jem swiveled on his stool and jotted down his final notes. He felt scattered, distracted. The sun filtering in through the small examining-room window reminded him he hadn't exercised in days. Assisting in the moving to Crawford House didn't really count. He needed to plug in some music, go for a run and just clear his mind. The idea was a bright spark in the fog. Then it was extinguished in the next moment. It would have to wait until tomorrow because tonight was a party at the Strouds' place. He would just decline except that it was a fund-raiser, and heaven knew that the Free Clinic could use the donations.

And he could use more exercise. More sunlight. Less worry and stress. He blew out a long breath.

If only it were all that simple. His life was becoming impossibly complicated, and a long run on a sunny day wasn't going to fix it.

"I'm so glad you're here. I just had the worst experience." Janessa breezed into Lucy's office, her perfectly made-up face a picture of suffering. Tears shone at the corners of her eyes and her bright-red lips quivered. She plopped herself into Lucy's desk chair and pulled out a tiny pill-box. "They let anybody have a driver's license nowadays."

"Hi, Janessa." Lucy wasn't sure her sister even heard her, but she might as well be polite. It was definitely the day for unexpected visitors. "Our cousin Rebecca was just here. She's engaged."

"My doctor said these would help calm my nerves, but I don't think they're working." She didn't respond to Lucy's news. "He said one a day, but this is my fourth and I can't cope any better than before. Everything is a mess." She took out a pill and put it under her tongue, the rest of her complaint sounding muffled and awkward. "You know, if people would just realize that I need some space, and a little bit of consideration, I would be fine. But everyone is rushing around, honking at me to move over when I'm going the speed limit."

Lucy nodded. Janessa didn't really want her to respond. She usually kept going until she got tired, and nothing Lucy said would change her trajectory.

"I asked Isaiah if he would bring me down here but he was too busy. I mean, he's at the office every single day. He can't take one afternoon off? I'm with the kids all day and he gets to go to work and be by himself. I'm not asking for much, really, just a few hours." Janessa leaned back, closing her eyes, stretching her designer-jean-clad legs out in front of her, the picture of absolute exhaustion.

Lucy sighed. Her nieces were in third and fifth grade and therefore at school all day. Janessa had a housekeeper and no job, spending most of her time shopping or on the couch with a headache. Maybe that was the problem, actually. If Janessa had something to do other than wander through the mall in search of a deal, she might not imagine herself on the verge of a mental breakdown so often. Lucy liked her brother-in-law, but Isaiah had long ago given up trying to coax Janessa out of her hypochondria.

"I'm glad you made it. That road can be tricky with only the two lanes."

"Exactly." Janessa sat up straight, eyes wide. "They need to put in a barrier or something. My life was flashing before my very eyes. I'll be down with a migraine from all the stress."

She paused, wondering if Janessa would ever get to the reason she'd made the fifteen-minute trek out to Tupelo. Her sister didn't take hints or preferred to ignore them, so it was better to wait.

"Anyway, I'm here and that's all that matters." Janessa seemed to notice Lucy's red-rimmed eyes for the first time. "What? What are you crying about now?"

"I wasn't crying." Janessa acted as if she'd found Lucy crying at her desk before. Or anywhere, for that matter. Janessa glanced around, spying the little book in the archive box. "More sad poetry? You need to stop that. You like to wallow in all those death poems."

" 'Death poems'?" Lucy knew her sister was probably referring to anything that wasn't a Hallmark card.

"You know, like that one you had on your wall in your room? About the dead kid?"

Searching her memory, Lucy finally grasped a dim flash of a poem cut from a magazine. " 'Night Funeral in Harlem.' Langston Hughes. I guess it is sort of a death poem, but that's not what he meant, really. It was more about the friends who—"

"Okay, got it." Janessa rolled her eyes. "You should watch some TV once in a while. You get all depressed when you read that stuff. I was watching this new reality show the other night. It was so funny, all about the reasons people end up in the emergency room. They'd interview them while they were being stitched up, and guess what?" She leaned forward, arm wrapped around her stomach, already laughing.

"What?"

"It was usually something that happened in the bedroom. Know what I mean?" Janessa let out a cackle of laughter.

Sometimes Lucy wondered if they were actually related. It was beyond her how Janessa could dismiss Civil War diaries and Langston Hughes's poetry while smirking over ill-fated bedroom trysts. Lucy's head started to throb gently. "I was fixin' to go out and sit in the sun for a bit. Sometimes too much time in the office makes me feel down."

"In the sun? Girl, you are crazy. You're already darker than a coconut." Janessa smoothed her brow as if she could be sure her own skin hadn't darkened with the mere mention of sunlight. "I've been using this fade cream I bought off BNT. They had a great deal. I think I'm a few shades lighter already, and I'm not going outside to sit in the noonday sun."

Lucy searched for words. If the product worked, what sort of hideous chemicals did it take to fade a person's natural melatonin? Aunt Olympia had said her mama wouldn't have let her marry a white boy, but Janessa was bleaching her skin. Lucy thought of her daddy and tried to remember if he'd ever worried over his shade of brown. Or if he'd ever mentioned which of his daughters was lightest. And then she thought of another Langston Hughes poem that had something about being the darker brother, the one they send to the kitchen when company comes.

Janessa seemed to notice that Lucy hadn't responded. "Anyway, that's all off topic. I came to discuss this Free Clinic thing. It's got to be stopped. Our home is a historic landmark and there will be sick people all over it, *touching things,*" she emphasized, as if the germs they carried would infect the very structure of Crawford House.

Lucy's shoulders sagged. "It's not something I wanted, either."

"Then let's stop it now, before they starting bringing those people to our front door."

"It's not so simple. We need the money. The clinic will pay double the home equity payments so we'll be able to be out of debt in a few years. Daddy's latest investments didn't make anything near a profit, and he's drained all his accounts."

"Impossible. He has savings accounts set aside for times like this. He just needs to—"

"Right, transfer the money." Lucy chewed her lip. There was a fine line between setting her sister straight and causing a family rift. "He's told me that, too, but I'm not seeing it happen. We're going to lose the house. The bank will foreclose on it and we'll have to leave. Crawford House will no longer be owned by Crawfords."

Janessa's eyes went wide. "But banks always threaten that kind of thing."

"No, they don't. And there are more creditors than just the bank. " Lucy looked out the window, her throat tight. "Every day the message machine is full of calls from debt collectors. There are more bills than I can keep track of, and the minimum payments are too much for me, on this salary."

"Have you talked to Paulette? She should be responsible for some of that, right?"

Lucy wanted to laugh, but couldn't find the energy. "Paulette says that Daddy gave her permission to use those credits cards. She's not going to change her spending habits just because the bills are going unpaid. Plus, she says she's cut back a lot this year."

Janessa snorted. "She went to that bridal show in Atlanta and ordered samples of everything. By the time she actually gets engaged, she's going to have several apartments full of wedding material."

"That's another thing. If Paulette moved home, Daddy wouldn't have to pay for her apartment. She says she's an interior designer, but she never decorates anything but her own place."

Janessa flicked at an invisible speck on her white linen jacket. "You think anyone is going to be interested in a girl her age still living at home? She needs to be able to entertain in freedom."

Lucy grimaced. *Entertain* better not mean having

men sleep over. She wasn't a prude, but the Crawford women were better than that.

"I know what you're thinking. I can read it on your face." Janessa leaned forward, half-laughing, half-angry. "And let me tell you, I wish I'd dated around a bit more before I married Isaiah. Once you settle down and have kids, everything changes. There's no passion, no spark. When we have date nights, I just wish he would go out by himself and let me watch TV in bed."

"Maybe you should take a vacation together? Maybe you need more than one evening to get back into the groove." Lucy felt ridiculous giving her sister marriage advice, but she couldn't stand thinking of Isaiah being dismissed like a babysitter. He was a good man. Not particularly interesting, and he loved duck hunting a little too much, but he was solid. He was a good father, and that meant a lot when you had kids at home.

"Can I take that vacation with another man?" Janessa looked up and let out a belated laugh.

Lucy could tell her sister was well and truly done with her marriage, and it made Lucy's stomach twist to think of two adults living so unhappily together with the kids stuck in the middle of it.

"I'm just saying"—Janessa crossed one slim leg over another and adjusted her tailored shirt—"that Paulette should be able to sow her wild oats without any interference. That will be better for everybody."

Lucy nodded, gaze landing on the little leather diary. Hattie Winter had shorn off her hair, risked jail by impersonating a man and joined some of the nation's worst battles to find the man she loved. Lucy would wager Hattie hadn't sown any wild oats before she'd fallen in love with Bismarck.

"Anyway, Paulette won't want to live in Crawford House with all those people coming in and out. I was just there this morning and I ran into Jeremiah Chevy. You remember? The one you met at those spoken-poetry nights in East Tupelo? I knew who he was right away, and for a moment, I thought he was back to hanging around our house, waiting for you." Janessa let out a long laugh. "Remember that time he brought a big pan of cornbread to our garden party? Oh, my word, I can't think of that without laughing."

Lucy swallowed hard. That memory had become so nightmarish that just mentioning it made her break out in a sweat.

Janessa wiped tears of laughter from her eyes. "He just stood there in his nice jeans and plaid shirt, looking like a kitchen boy who got lost on the way to the serving tables. Except our caterers would never let the waiters wear anything like that. He looked like he'd crawled right out of the trailer park. And his little dish, with the foil wrapped all over the top . . ."

Lucy stared out the small window, letting

Janessa giggle her way into a hiccuping silence.

"Oh, now you're gonna be upset that I brought it up. It was a long time ago, and of course I didn't say anything to him now. I would never hold being poor against anybody. People can't help being born into a trashy family." Janessa paused, as if searching for a way to prove she'd been perfectly nice to Jem. "I asked him if he knew who I was, and he said he did. But he said he wouldn't have known you at all, you were so different looking."

Lucy froze. "He really said that?"

"Well, sure. And he was right sorry about Zeke being let go. He thought we would have kept him till the very end. But I told him it was your idea and you felt like it had to be done."

"Is there a reason you're here, Janessa? I mean, besides trying to talk me out of saving our home?" Lucy's words came out a bit more abrupt than she meant.

"Well, thank you, Billy Sunday." She stood up, shouldering her large designer tote bag. "I knew you wouldn't budge on that, but I drove myself all the way over here to see if you wanted to have a late lunch at Xander's. If you're going to be so negative, I might as well go back home and leave you to your little poetry books."

"It's a diary, not poetry." For just a moment, Lucy ached for someone to share Hattie's story with, to take turns reading aloud the pages and treasuring every word of a centuries-old love story. But instead, she had her status-obsessed older sister dropping by to harass her about going to the fanciest restaurant in Tupelo. Janessa had never invited Lucy to Xander's, ever. Either she had made up the idea on the spot, or she had been dumped by one of her friends and didn't want to cancel her reservation.

"Thank you for the offer, but everyone is gone to lunch. I'll have to pass."

Janessa sniffed, looking Lucy up and down. "Probably just as well. You're not really dressed for public. It wouldn't hurt you to wear heels once in a while. Just because you work in a museum doesn't mean you have to dress like you're from the fifties."

If Lucy dressed like a Southern woman in the fifties, she'd be wearing pearls, a shirtwaist dress and pantyhose with those heels, but she didn't bother to correct her sister. "There aren't very many people to impress here."

"That should tell you something." Janessa wagged a finger. "I guess I'll see you this evening. We're invited to the Strouds' for a party. It's sort of a fund-raiser for the Free Clinic, too, I guess."

"We're . . ." Lucy fought to catch up. "The Strouds'?"

Letting out a deep sigh of irritation, Janessa said, "Did you get my message? Last week?

Normally we wouldn't go, but since Dr. Stroud just won that award for service to the state of Mississippi, Daddy thinks we should accept."

Lucy vaguely remembered a message about a party, but she hadn't paid much attention to it. It had sounded like a reminder for every other party she'd been to that year.

"Daddy doesn't normally want anything to do with people like Dr. Stroud," Lucy said.

"He thinks it will look good for the business if he's known as a friend of that kind of person."

"What kind?" Lucy knew she shouldn't ask, but couldn't help herself.

"You know. The kind that spend all their time helping poor people. It looks good." With that, Janessa reached for the door. "And please wear something pretty."

Lucy nodded, not bothering to respond as her sister left the room. A fund-raiser for the Free Clinic, held at Dr. Stroud's house, would definitely be attended by Jem. She sank into her office chair. She knew it was impossible to stay out of his way completely, but the idea of socializing at one of those pretentious parties filled her with dread. Women dressed to the nines, men swaggered around in seersucker suits and everyone talked about new jewelry, cars, and vacations. She didn't like those parties at the best of times. She always found herself trapped in a circle of busybody women, fielding questions about her relationship status and professional trajectory. They must smell her shyness, like sharks tasting blood in the water. Now she would have to stand firm under the usual grilling, with Jem in the same room, maybe even close by to hear how her life had gone nowhere after she'd dumped him.

Lucy put her hands to her cheeks, feeling the heat against her cold fingers. He'd said she had changed so much he'd hardly recognized her. She walked her fingertips up her face, near her eyes. She gently swiped the area, noting the tiniest of grooves from her lids to her temples. Crow's-feet. She wasn't even thirty.

Pushing back from her desk, Lucy grabbed her keys. She didn't care if she turned as black as ebony and as wrinkled as a walnut. She needed some sun. And maybe after that she'd cook something without a bit of pork fat in it. If her love life was a lost cause, she might as well make herself happy the only way she knew how.

His cold politeness, his ceremonious
grace, were worse than anything.
—ANNE ELLIOT

CHAPTER FIVE

As soon as the Crawfords stepped over the threshold of the Strouds' home, Daddy hotfooted it over to a group of his golfing buddies. The large living room was packed with guests. At one side, double French doors were open to the evening air, and partyers dotted the large wooden deck outside and the lawn beyond. The sound of polite chitchat and politer laughter competed with that of the live band in the garden. Lucy took a moment to take in the high ceiling, the enormous brass chandelier, the deep-red wallpaper and velvet-cushioned antique settees. From the outside, the home had seemed charming, well kept. Inside the house, her historian's heart beat double time at the sight of so many well-preserved Civil War–era furnishings. It was almost as if she had walked into one of the exhibits at the interpretive center. It also made clear how much Crawford House had been updated in the name of current interior design.

"So glad you made it. Come on outside, Miss Lucy," Dr. Stroud said as he paused on his way past. He was wearing a three-piece, pale-blue seersucker suit and a matching bow tie, and his bushy white mustache seemed to have been groomed with extra care. He smelled of cigars and bourbon, and for some reason it made her smile. "We were just discussing the next reenactment at Brice's Crossroads." A group of older gentlemen waited by the doors for him, tumblers of amber liquid in hand and thumbs hooked into vest pockets.

"Wonderful, I'll be right there." She needed to track down Paulette and beg her not to drink too much. She hated to nag, but Paulette didn't worry about driving after a party like this. Lucy straightened her shoulders and navigated through the groups of partygoers. She might as well spend time with the Civil War buffs. She didn't know anyone else here except her father's golf friends, and her sisters were nowhere to be found. It was a much bigger party than she'd thought it would be. As she passed a tight-knit huddle, a slender woman in an low-cut dress scanned her up and down, then leaned back into the circle, whispering.

For once, Lucy was glad she'd followed Janessa's advice to dress up. She still wasn't approaching the level set by most of these women, in their designer dresses and diamond cuffs, but she was presentable. It had taken her hours, but she was happy with her thirties-inspired bob, the waves lying close to her cheeks. Her mother's perfectly preserved vintage dress swished softly against her skin as she moved. Pale pink wasn't her favorite color, but the bias-cut silk was a work of art. A pair of teardrop pearl earrings had been all she added for jewelry. No sequins, no dazzle. But she felt beautiful.

"Oh, my word," Paulette said, appearing out of nowhere. "What are you wearing? This isn't Halloween."

"Hi, dear sister, I'm fine. How are you?"

Paulette ignored Lucy's sarcasm and put a death grip on her elbow. "You couldn't find anything else? Were you raiding the attic? You shouldn't wear Mama's old clothes. Don't you think it hurts Daddy to see you in them?" Paulette's eyes were rimmed with bright-blue eyeliner, and her lashes sparkled with tiny gold flecks. The little black dress she wore plunged disconcertingly and Lucy averted her eyes. She wondered if anyone else felt uncomfortable knowing her sister wasn't wearing anything under her dress.

"Don't you think it might hurt him more to see you in yours? I hope you used some double-sided tape or you're going to have a wardrobe malfunction."

Paulette smirked. "Nothing wrong with a little side boob. I'd say you're the one with a wardrobe malfunction. What is this, anyway?" She swept a hand up and down Lucy's figure. "Pink is so far out of style you might as well be wearing plaid. The little handkerchief sleeves are kind of cute and the open back is pretty, but that high neckline and those ruffles? Really. You look like someone's old aunt in a nightie."

Lucy peered at the rows of tiny ruffles at the ankle-length hem. The gown was dramatic in a way that didn't mesh with this room of Tupelo's wealthiest in all black, and she didn't really care. "I *am* someone's old aunt, Paulette."

"Huh. Just don't tell anybody we're related. It'll ruin my reputation as the most fashion-forward girl in Tupelo."

Lucy wanted to tell her sister she was a woman, not a girl, but Paulette wouldn't see her point. Her attention was dragged to the brightly spangled item in her sister's hand. "What's that?"

"This?" Paulette's voice was carefully casual. She held up the little clutch, letting the crystals catch the light. "My new Judith Leiber minaudière. Rihanna has one just like it. I saw it in the pictures of her on the red carpet at the Grammy Awards."

Lucy shook her head. "Those cost thousands of dollars and this . . ." It was a bright-blue-topped cupcake as large as a grapefruit and impossible to miss. Her sister didn't understand that stars were loaned almost everything they wore. They used the items once and gave them back, while her sister was going to have this ridiculous purse forever.

"It's a conversation piece," Paulette sniffed, and hung the chain back over her shoulder. "If you can wear that something from the attic, I can carry this. It may have cost seven thousand dollars but it's *whimsical*." She said the word as if she'd never pronounced it before, carefully enunciating each syllable.

Lucy almost choked. "They told you that, didn't they? The people who sold you the shiny cupcake told you it was *whimsical*." She would have laughed if it hadn't been so awful. At least *her* ugly old thing was free. She didn't care what Paulette wore, but knew that little fashion gem carried a steep interest rate. Seven thousand dollars of new debt made Lucy's stomach clench. To be fair, it wasn't just the debt. If Harvard had let her pay her tuition with a credit card, she would gladly have stayed, ringing up semester after semester on her daddy's card. The idea of losing Crawford House because of something as stupid as a little cupcake purse carried by a pop singer made her want to grab her sister by the shoulders and shake her.

Lucy rubbed her forehead. "Never mind, Paulette. Forget I said anything. I'm trying to reach Dr. Stroud over there, so why don't I let you get back to hooking up with your man of the evening."

Paulette flipped her long, silky extensions over one shoulder and stalked off to a group of identical-looking young women, all in little black dresses and sky-high heels.

Lucy sighed. As she went to bed at night, she prayed for every member of her family. She asked God to bless them and keep them safe. And then she couldn't keep her temper for more than five minutes around her bratty little sister. All Lucy had were good intentions, and they were worth less than nothing when it came to showing love to the unlovable.

Dr. Stroud caught her eye again and motioned her to join them as they drifted onto the deck, and she lifted a hand. She was getting there, slowly but surely. Passing by the punch table, she couldn't help a bit of a smile at the crystal bowl of pink lemonade. Some things never changed, especially in the South. It wasn't a party without a bowl of pink lemonade. A crystal decanter off to the side caught her eye and she paused midstep. It was half-filled, with a slice of orange decorating the narrow mouth. The pale-pink liquid inside was topped with a thin layer of foam. She leaned closer, finally lifting the bottle to take a quick sniff before setting it back in its place. Another bowl was filled with a clear amber liquid that smelled definitely alcoholic, and the light of the room reflected around the edges of the silver rim. She was fairly certain what it was and smiled.

"Chatham Artillery Punch," said a woman's voice to her left.

Lucy glanced at her, taking in her simple but expensive-looking dark-blue dress, the cameo necklace, the gray curls brushing her shoulders. "Named after Georgia's oldest military unit. I would expect nothing less at Dr. Stroud's party."

"A full bar is the sign of a good party, and Johnny makes the finest drinks around, but I just have to have a punch table. As for this stuff, they say that when President Monroe stopped in Savannah in 1819, they mixed up a batch in a horse bucket."

Lucy peered into the bowl. "I hear it takes two days to make. I wonder what they used for a recipe."

"I can tell you, because I made it myself. A few ounces of green tea leaves in cold water for a day and a half, then add the lemon juice and half a pound of brown sugar. Add a quart of bourbon, dark rum and brandy each. Set to mingle for a day, then pour over a block of ice with three bottles of champagne. Now, you get a recipe like that and you know your party's bound to be a success."

Lucy couldn't help responding to the laughter in the woman's blue eyes. Her accent was the same as Lucy's mama's, straight from the low country of Louisiana. "You're Dr. Stroud's wife?" She held out her hand, introducing herself.

"Oh, goodness. I forgot my manners when I saw you examining my handiwork." Instead of shaking Lucy's hand, Mrs. Stroud reached out and gave her a quick squeeze. "I know who you are, of course. Jacob thinks a lot of all the work you've done at the interpretive center. He says it's one of the best preserved battle sites in the state."

She smiled, pleased at the compliment. Most residents of Tupelo didn't even know Brice's Crossroads existed. "You have a beautiful accent. My mama was from Cane River."

"Really? Well now, then we're almost related." Mrs. Stroud dropped her voice. "My husband has been tryin' to teach me to speak Mississippi for twenty years. It just won't stick."

"I'm glad." Lucy didn't realize how much she'd missed hearing those long, sweet vowels. The sudden ache of recognition took her by surprise and she searched for something else to say. She motioned to the crystal flask. "May I ask what this is?"

"Orgeat."

"I wasn't sure . . ." Lucy said. The orgeat recipe she knew was a simple clarified sugar syrup with almond flavoring that had no relation to the contents of the bottle in her hand.

"I told Jacob I was making some original orgeat, and he got excited." Leaning forward and whispering conspiratorially, she said, "He never asked which era I was using as inspiration. A lady needs to have a little bit of glamorous Regency in the middle of all this Civil War madness."

"Do you have a special interest in the Regency period, Mrs. Stroud?"

"Oh, call me Theresa. And no more than any warm-blooded woman." She shrugged, her deep-blue dress shimmering in the light. When Lucy didn't respond, she went on, "Jane Austen, of course," as if that cleared up any confusion.

"My cousin Rebecca teaches comparative English literature at Midlands College. She's always seeing Austen in the world around her."

"Exactly." Theresa beamed. "Life is easier to understand when you think of it in terms of *Pride and Prejudice*. And all the others."

"I didn't realize there were that many others." She thought for a moment. "Wait, I think I saw a bit of *Emma* on the BBC one year."

"Wasn't it amazing?" Theresa gripped her hand, blue eyes bright with excitement. "What was your favorite part? The dance? Or the proposal?"

Lucy searched her memory for any bit of the plot but came up empty. "I . . . I liked the hats," she said.

Theresa stared for a moment, then burst into laughter. Lucy felt her face warming as curious guests turned to watch. "You liked the hats. Oh, girl." She swiped a finger under her eyes and tried to stifle her giggles.

"I guess without knowing the story, the bit that I saw didn't make much of an impression."

"You're absolutely right. The story is what

makes an Austen romance so . . . romantic." Theresa tapped her chin with a forefinger. "My niece just sent me the new *Persuasion* movie for Christmas. You should come watch it with me."

"Thank you, but I couldn't intrude." Lucy felt her heart drop. She already knew the plot of *Persuasion*, and it wasn't anything she wanted to sit through.

"Intrude?" She swept a hand around the packed living room. "It will be just me and my lonesome."

"You don't have a group of Austen-loving friends?" Lucy didn't know much about period dramas, but she knew the televised events were popular. "Not even one?"

At this, Theresa's smile faded away. "I did. Just one, but she's gone now. My sister passed away last month." Her voice was soft, barely above a whisper.

"I'm so sorry." She saw the stark grief in Theresa's eyes.

"Thank you. There were three of us kids, all right together. I'm the oldest, she was the knee baby and my brother, Henry, came last. Funny, I miss her all the time, but I miss her most when I'm reading Austen. We'd been fans since we were in the seventh and eighth grade, two Creole girls gigglin' about marriage proposals gone bad. Our daddy teased us about reading each other passages during a Fourth of July crawfish boil, so he named the biggest one Mr. Darcy and threw him in the pot." Theresa looked up, a smile fighting the tears in her eyes. "We refused to eat him."

Lucy thought back to eighth grade and couldn't remember ever sharing a moment like that with her sisters. They'd always been so different. She was the oldest, so she'd watched out for them as best she could. It seemed as if her family role was more about making sure Daddy was happy than anything else.

Motioning to the orgeat on the table, Theresa said, "She taught me how to make that. Pound almonds into a paste, squeeze out the oil, let it rest for twenty-four hours. Then you mix with water, tartaric acid, then sugar and orange water." Her blue eyes glinted with tears. "Here, let me pour you some."

Lucy accepted a small glass and took a sip. It was a bit like amaretto, but creamier, leaving a sweet-bitter flavor in her mouth like a childhood memory. "It's very nice."

"Nicer with rum, some say." Theresa flashed a fragile smile. "I know you're a Civil War historian, but you should really acquaint yourself with Miss Jane."

"I would like that," Lucy answered on a whim. Her own relationship with her sisters was fraught with tension and aggravation, but she knew that losing them would throw her into a pit of grief. To have had a sister who was close enough to share a passion, such as Theresa and her sister had shared, must have been a real joy. Her heart ached for this older woman. "Let me know the day, and I'll come. I can be your Austen protégée."

"Well, I'll be. That orgeat must be real good to convince you that fast."

Lucy laughed. "My cousin Rebecca will be thrilled that I've been doing my homework before she gets married. She's having a Regency-themed wedding."

Theresa's eyes went wide. "I think I heard about this. My friend volunteers at the William Faulkner House. She said there was a wedding reception planned for the end of next month. They turned in details to get approval, and my friend noticed everything sounded like it was right out of an Austen book."

"That's Rebecca. I don't think her fiancé cares much about Jane Austen, but he loves her enough to not really care. She's leaving for an academic sabbatical in Bath, England."

"Bath! I've always wanted to visit that town. *Persuasion* is set there, partially. There's the Jane Austen Centre, and a festival in September that brings thousands of people from all over the world. You can stay in a Georgian-era apartment and take the Austen walking tour. I heard there was even a trip you could join that visited all the places they'd used for the BBC movies."

"Well, Rebecca is going to be in hog heaven because she'll be honeymooning, too."

Theresa shook her head. "I would be, too. And after you get a taste of an Austen romance, you'll understand."

"I hope so," Lucy said. She didn't usually read romance. Or ever, really, but she was willing to give it a try just to discover why millions of women were swooning over love stories written two hundred years ago. It was time that she filled the gap in her knowledge. A little less Civil War and a little more Austen couldn't be such a bad thing. "But shouldn't I read the book before I watch the movie?"

"Oh, *Persuasion* is a simple story. Love lost, love found, eight years between the two."

Lucy steeled herself to the idea. "As long as the love found part is there, I'm sure it will be good."

The sound of a throat being cleared drew Lucy's attention and she turned, looking up into Jem's eyes. He wasn't smiling, not even the sort of smile that was all show and no feeling. He quickly looked over her head, somewhere to the room beyond. "Dr. Stroud sent me to ask whether you needed rescuing. He's been waiting for you to come out for five minutes."

For a long moment, Lucy struggled to form some sort of response. All she could do was take in his dark suit, the white dress shirt that was casually unbuttoned at the neck, how he was freshly shaved. His dark blond hair always looked a bit disheveled. He adjusted his tie and she glimpsed the dark line of leather suspenders under his jacket. She got a whiff of soap and coffee, and wondered if he was going to stand around chatting in Stroud's group. She couldn't imagine him with a cigar clamped between his teeth, sipping on a Tennessee whiskey. But he'd been so much younger when they'd known each other.

"Oh, mercy. You tell Jacob to keep his bow tie on. We're coming right over. We were just talking about lost loves and second chances," Theresa said.

One dark eyebrow went up, and Jem's gaze snapped from the room at large to Theresa to Lucy. Lucy felt her face go hot and she stuttered out, "Jane Austen. You know, the movies."

Both brows were up now. And a corner of his mouth twitched. "I think she also wrote a few books."

Lucy let out a huff. "Yes, I know that." He looked as if he was trying not to laugh, and for just a moment it seemed as if they could almost be friends. Or at least, not such bitter enemies. "I was telling her that my cousin Rebecca is having a Regency-themed wedding before she moves to Bath, England. Theresa has volunteered to educate me on Austen."

"I'm no expert," Theresa said, laughing. "But a

historian like yourself should know at least a little about our Miss Jane." She turned to Jem. "Lucy's coming to my house to watch *Persuasion*. You should join us, Jem. It's such a wonderful story." She launched into a long description before either could respond. Lucy felt Theresa's rendition of the plot like stones dropping one by one into her stomach. It seemed as if she'd never be done, but finally, she reached the end. ". . . meanwhile her family has lost all their money, and their roles are reversed. It's the most romantic movie." Theresa opened her mouth to go on, but Jem was already shaking his head.

"I'm not a fan of romances, but that one sounds downright depressing." The almost-smile was gone from his lips. His eyes were cold. "How could a woman be convinced to break off an engagement? Either she didn't really love him, or she was hopelessly wishy-washy. You wouldn't be able to rely on a person like that. He should have run while he had the chance." Jem's jaw was tight, and his gaze fixed on Lucy's face.

"Nonsense. You're looking at it through the lens of modern sensibilities," Theresa said. "You're a reenactor, right? You're used to pretending. It doesn't take much to imagine how it was in the Regency time. Back then, the women had to find a spouse within narrow groups of approved men, usually only those with a title and money. We can't understand what it was like back then.

We're free to choose our mates, sometimes even to the utter dismay of our families."

This speech seemed to take hours, days. Lucy couldn't force her eyes from the hard lines of Jem's face, from the raw emotions that flashed behind those blue eyes.

"Yes, we are, aren't we?" Jem asked, his voice dropping an octave. "It's not illegal to marry someone without a title, or without money, or belonging to a different church, or even a different race. We have all the freedom in the world to follow our hearts, if we truly love someone."

Lucy focused on the lace cloth of the punch table. She understood him now, and whatever small hope she'd been hiding deep inside was extinguished. He could never forgive her. She had been weak when she had nothing to fear except her family's disapproval. She had been a free woman, able to make her own decisions, and she had turned her back on him. All those hot summer days they'd spent walking along the red-clay back roads by his trailer park, the humid nights at the spoken-poetry clubs around the city, threading their words with love and promise and passion . . . Gone.

The joy that grew from their friendship was spontaneous, a meeting of hearts and minds and souls, bringing them closer than any two people had a right to be. The loss was clear at that moment, clearer than she had ever seen it. As he stood inches from her, voice shadowed with anger, she knew she deserved every bit of his disdain. Everything that she had thrown away was outlined starkly in her mind, but one thing above all stood apart, and that was the way she'd felt with him. He had been hers, as surely as or more so than her own family, and loved her without condition. A chill went through her and she felt the blood drain from her face. She had once had what everyone dreams of, and she'd thrown it away.

He turned on his heel and left. The space where he'd been standing seemed to reverberate with his words.

"He sure got bowed up, didn't he? Must have a broken heart in his past." Theresa tutted under her breath.

Lucy's mama used to say that, too. Bowed up, like an angry snake, raising its head before it strikes. Jem had good reason to strike back at Lucy. She deserved whatever he had to say. She just wished it didn't hurt so much to hear it. Lucy bit the inside of her lip. Her mama used to say that if wishes were horses, then beggars would ride. The party had barely started and she was desperate to go home, so she had better stop wishing. There was nothing to do but to force herself through the next few hours and hope she made it to the safety of her own bed before she let the tears fall.

He had an affectionate heart. He must
love somebody.
—ANNE ELLIOT

CHAPTER SIX

Jem walked blindly back toward Stroud with
Theresa's words ringing in his ears. *Lost loves and
second chances.* It was all fine and good in the
movies, but reality was much harsher. Once a
person broke your heart, you didn't sign up for
another round. Although if anything would make
him give it a second thought, it might be that
dress. There wasn't another woman at this party,
probably not even another woman in the whole
state, more beautiful.

He frowned, searching for what had changed.
She was shy, that was still true. He could see
her choose her words carefully, weighing whether
to speak. But in high school Lucy had seemed
afraid to offend, nervous around any kind of
confrontation. Now she didn't seem to care what
anyone thought. That dress was a good example.

He ran a finger under his collar. Women thought
you needed to show cleavage or some thigh to get
a man's attention. Sometimes all a woman needed

was some nicely cut silk. Lucy looked like a movie star from the thirties, coolly elegant, perfectly poised. He'd seen most of the men give her a second look, and all of the women.

Jem stepped around a group of middle-aged men laughing loudly over their bourbons. He didn't want to admire her, but he couldn't help seeing how she outshone, without diamonds or jewels, every other woman here. Her beauty was classic, timeless. Just the line of her neck, the curve of her cheek, the way the dress draped her hips, was enough to stop the room. When she'd turned away to look at something on the table and he'd seen the back of the dress, he thought he might have to sit down. The smooth skin of her back looked impossibly soft, and he ached to reach out, just for a moment, and splay his hand against it.

Letting out a sigh, Jem wished he could give himself a good kick. Lucy was his weak spot. She always had been and she always would be. Whatever it was about her that had stolen his heart ten years ago was still there, right under the surface. All she needed was to recite some poetry and he'd be hanging around her porch again like a lost puppy.

It occurred to him he'd be hanging around her porch anyway, because of the clinic. *Lord, I just don't know what You're thinking most of the time.* Jem wasn't prone to spontaneous prayer, but seeing his future interwoven with Lucy filled him with panic. Coming back to Tupelo had been a very bad idea.

"We'd better get over there," Theresa said, slipping her arm through Lucy's and tugging her toward the open doors. Lucy nodded, saying nothing. Her feet felt leaden and she could imagine her heart beating sluggishly, barely strong enough to keep her upright. Was there anything worse than having Jem walk away from her without a good-bye? Yes, there was. She was going to follow in his footsteps all the way across the room, join his circle of friends and converse like a rational person while her whole being was begging to be released from this torture. If she had ever thought she'd moved on from their breakup, she'd been wrong. Nothing was farther than fine.

The band was louder out in the garden, but the scent of magnolias in the evening air was like a balm. Lucy inhaled deeply and felt the muscles in her shoulders relax a little. There were tiny lanterns strung on the trees around the wide expanse of thick lawn, and the band was playing a bluesy rendition of "Shady Grove." A few guests were dancing on the portable wooden dance floor at the edge of the garden. The sun was setting, and although the air was still humid, a bit of breeze had picked up and Lucy lifted her face to the clear sky. She wasn't a girl who enjoyed parties, but the tinkle of ice in tall glass and the murmur of quiet waiters sparked something deep in her Southern soul.

"Oh, honey, I see my friend Mr. Clark over there. You go ahead and I'll be over in a second." Theresa looked to an older gentleman seated in a white folding chair, his cane between his feet. He was tapping one black dress shoe to the music, his eyes closed and a smile on his lips.

"Of course," Lucy said, suddenly self-conscious, as if someone had taken away her clothes. It was easier to imagine standing across from Jem with Theresa at her side. She was irritated with herself for being weak. She was relying on a woman she'd only just met to give her confidence. Lucy lifted her chin and summoned a smile. It was time to put on her game face and make polite conversation. This was no time to brood and fret. Her mama had raised her to be cool and collected in moments such as these.

Jem looked away as she walked up. He didn't look angry. He didn't look as if he felt anything at all. If he weren't so intent on watching the rest of the party around the garden, Lucy might think he hadn't been furious just minutes before.

There were two older men on either side of Dr. Stroud, and a beautiful young woman next to Jem. Lucy recognized her as a friend of Paulette's. She had come by the house several times, usually on the way back from shopping in Birmingham. Her hair was the perfect shade of honey blond and her skin was milky pale, as if she never stepped into the sun. Her short black dress was simple, but obviously expensive, the halter neckline dotted with tiny crystals. She was slender, but not athletic. If it weren't for the gentle pink of her cheeks, she might look unhealthy, but she seemed simply genetically blessed.

As for the men, one was short, with a receding hairline and weak chin. He stared at Lucy, but his gaze never went above her chest. The other was vaguely familiar, but she couldn't quite place him. Something about his beard made her think of battlefield pictures of Confederate soldiers. Then he smiled wide and she remembered him as one of the reenactors who had volunteered at the center with the last school visit. He'd regaled the kids with tales of eating out of a billycan and having only one hobnail boot on a forty-mile hike.

"There you are, my dear." Dr. Stroud reached out a hand. "Lucy, let me introduce Regan Ross. She's Dr. Eugene Ross's daughter."

Lucy offered her hand and felt the quick, tight grip of a girl who didn't want to make friends. It occurred to her that Jem might have come to the party with a date. It shouldn't have been a surprise, but for just a moment it took her breath away.

"Nice to see you again, Regan," she said, but her sister's friend only nodded.

"And my friends, Albert Archer and John Gregory. You've probably seen John during the battles. He's made sacrifices no Southern man should be forced to make. This last time he had to wear a Union cavalry outfit and wrestle one of the twelve-pound cannons."

"A pleasure to meet you both. Mr. Gregory, how's your hearing?"

The group let out a collective chuckle. Lucy refused to take the bait of teasing him for dressing as a Union man and instead focused on the weapon. The howitzers were notoriously noisy artillery, and Lucy could hear the reenactors practicing from as far away as five miles.

"Excellent, thank you. What's good enough for Ulysses S. Grant is good enough for me. He hauled his up to a church belfry in Mexico City, so I don't complain about standing in the pasture with the sun at my back." John gave a slight shrug. "Some men prefer to run at the enemy with rifles raised, but I think it takes a real command of spirit to handle a howitzer. Right, Jem?"

Jem turned, as if just taking noticing of the conversation. "Sure does."

"I might be wrong, but I think Grant lugged an earlier brass version up that tower. What you all have out on the field is a redesigned bronze Napoleon 1857," Lucy said.

There was a short silence. Stroud beamed at her. "Men, this is what gives an old codger like me some hope. Between young Jem here coming back to work at the clinic instead of staying in Boston, and Lucy preserving our Southern history, I know that we can't go wrong."

Hearing their names in the same sentence was a peculiar kind of pain for Lucy. Coming directly from Boston, she wondered how dirty and backward the place must seem to him now.

"I would hope the future of the South is about more than relivin' old battles and knowing which cannon they used," Regan said. Her tone was light and she looked as if she might have been giving a compliment, but her words were a rebuke. "We're never going to get over our painful past if we don't stop focusing on what happened in the war."

Lucy hadn't really expected much from someone who spent so much time with Paulette, but if Regan thought that sort of comment would win points in a group of Civil War reenactors and the curator of a historical interpretive center, then she wasn't as smart as she looked.

"And wasn't Nathan Bedford Forrest the Confederate leader in that battle at Brice's Crossroads? I don't think we should be celebrating that man." Regan arched one lovely brow and waited for Lucy to respond.

An awkward silence hovered. Nobody liked to talk about Forrest. Most agree that he founded the KKK, then tried to disband it. That statue of him in Memphis was hotly contested, and most polite

Mississippians avoided discussing the man at all costs.

"Do you think we should pretend he wasn't there or just act as if the entire battle had never happened?" Lucy asked.

"As a Black girl, don't you feel it's wrong to glorify the man?" Regan asked. "Maybe it doesn't matter to you because your family is very prominent in the area, but most Blacks don't want anything to do with Forrest."

Lucy tried not to roll her eyes. Making sure history was accurate was hardly glorifying anybody. And to say that her race or family status kept her from understanding the horrors of lynching and oppression was downright offensive. "I'm a historian. I can't pick and choose who headed the Confederate army that day. Ignoring it all, for whatever reason, helps no one."

"So, you're saying we can learn from the past to make the world a better place?" Regan popped a hand to her hip.

Lucy watched Regan's face carefully, just to be certain that she wasn't kidding. Lucy almost wished the girl were putting on some sort of spacey act. The alternative was too awful. Lucy opened her mouth to answer, but Jem's voice derailed her thoughts.

"R. G. Collingwood said studying the past shows us what it is to be a man, what it is to be the kind of man you are and what it is to be the kind of man you are and nobody else." Jem looked over at Lucy. "And on a more practical note, if we simply forget the most painful episodes of the past, we might make the same mistakes over again."

Lucy felt as if someone had stolen the air from her lungs. She nodded meekly. "Yes, exactly," she managed. He wouldn't forget what had happened. And she never could.

"Honey, should we start the presentations?" Theresa asked, walking up to her husband and laying a hand on his arm. The question defused the tense moment. "I know you didn't want them to make a big fuss over you, but just smile and say thank you."

"Now, you deserve this award more than I do. When Mrs. Sussman presents it, feel free to stand up and set the record straight," Dr. Stroud said.

Theresa laughed, pink flooding her cheeks. "Oh, Jacob."

He stuck his thumbs in his vest pockets and pretended to be giving a speech. "Gentlemen and ladies, you think I'm a saint to dedicate so much of my time to the Free Clinic, but the true hero in this house is my wife. She works as hard as I do, or harder. She's been tireless in soliciting funds and directed the grant writing this year. We wouldn't be moving to Crawford House without her help."

Lucy watched the expressions pass between

them, and her throat grew tight. She swallowed hard. Not here, not now. She couldn't cry yet. This couple had something she might never have. And standing across from Jem while she faced that fact was almost too much.

"You inspire me," Theresa answered. "I want to make a difference when I see you offering yourself to this community." Her voice was soft, but sure. "I want to be by your side."

"Are you from around here, Mrs. Stroud?" Regan cut into the moment. "You don't sound like a native."

Theresa turned, her lips tilting up ever so slightly. "No, Regan. I'm from the low country of Louisiana."

"Don't you get lonely for your own folk?" Albert asked. "They say a woman is never happy away from her family."

Lucy blinked. One would think that decades of marriage would qualify them as a family, but they had no children, and some felt a couple without children wasn't on the same level as a couple with a brood of children and grandchildren. Albert either had a bone to pick with the Creole people or he was needling Stroud, knowing the best way to get to the man was through the woman he'd just expressed such admiration for.

"It's strange, really." Theresa didn't seem too upset by the question. "The only time I've ever been lonesome and feeling like the last pea at pea-time is when Jacob was working in Memphis. I stayed here by myself. He was interning at a hospital in a really rough part of the city, and we thought it would be better if I held down the fort."

"The hardest job I ever had," Dr. Stroud said. His white mustache turned down. "And not because of the gunshot wounds every weekend."

"Surely you wouldn't have wanted to be in the middle of a place like that," Regan said. "When Lucy's sister Paulette and I went to Birmingham last time, a man came up to our car while we were at a stoplight." Her eyes were wide, horror on her face at the memory.

"Did he have a weapon?" Jem asked.

"What?" Regan frowned at him. "No, he was washing our windshield with a nasty old rag and then wanted us to roll down the window and give him change. It was the scariest thing."

Lucy caught Jem's eye and almost laughed. Just the crook of his eyebrow said everything.

"Poverty can be quite frightening, I agree," Dr. Stroud said, his mustache twitching.

Regan slipped her arm through Jem's. "That's the last time we go alone. Our next shopping trip, I'm taking along a big, strong man like Jem."

All the laughter that had been building in Lucy faded away at the sight of Jem's tolerant smile. He bent his head and whispered, "I shall defend you from the scary window washers."

Wrapping both hands around his arm, Regan cooed, "I bet you will. Look at this muscle."

Lucy turned her head, scanning the garden party for Janessa, Paulette, anyone. She'd thought standing across from an angry Jem was as bad as it could get, but she was wrong. Watching a beautiful, brainless girl such as Regan touch Jem and to watch him flirt back was far, far worse.

"Really, Jacob, we should get started or the mayor will have had so much punch that the speech won't make any sense at all." Theresa nodded toward the drinks table, where a bald man in a wide, red tie served himself.

"Yes, m'dear." Jacob inclined his head to the group. "Excuse us."

Moments after their departure, Albert and John both decided to seek out more whiskey.

Lucy stepped to the side, hoping to ease away from their awkward trio, but Regan spoke first. "Paulette said you went to Harvard but had to drop out. Was it real hard? My cousin Shirley June is applying there."

Lucy blinked. "Are you asking if I flunked out?"

"I'm not trying to be nosy. I just want to know what to tell Shirley June."

"You can tell her it's a beautiful campus full of wonderful people." Lucy's voice had gone husky. The one year she'd spent there lived in her memory as a precious time, even as she dealt with her self-inflicted heartbreak.

"Well, don't feel bad about having to leave." Regan reached out and patted Lucy's arm. "I flunked a big test one time. It was on cellular biology. I mean, how do they expect us to memorize all that stuff? It should have been an open-book exam."

Lucy wanted to say she hadn't flunked out, but that her family had simply run out of money. She hated herself for being too proud to tell the truth, but she couldn't force the words out.

Looking up, she caught Jem searching her face. He seemed to be waiting for her to speak, and when she didn't, he glanced away.

"Excuse me, I need to find my sister before they start the speeches," Lucy said, her words tumbling over each other. She backed away, a smile fixed to her face. If she could just get away from Regan and her questions, away from the way she held on to Jem as if he were her property, then Lucy would be okay.

She turned her back and crossed the room blindly. She had to get control of her emotions. If he didn't have a girlfriend right now, he would very soon. Jem wouldn't stay single forever, especially surrounded by beautiful women who found him absolutely eligible now that he had a medical degree and a nice salary. They looked at him with admiration and respect. They looked at him the way she should have when he was only a poor white kid from the wrong side of the tracks who had nothing to offer her but his love.

Jem watched Lucy wend her way back through the small-knit groups of people. Regan was still chattering about how impossible it was to pass a science class, her words fading in and out of the strains of the music. Lucy hadn't corrected Regan about failing school, but it was unlikely—no, it was impossible—that she had failed. Lucy had one of the brightest minds he'd ever met. She loved all words, but poetry especially. She absorbed information in a way that made him simultaneously giddy and painfully jealous. He'd once said he admired Thoreau, and she'd read all his books by the time Jem had next seen her, reciting whole sections and debating with him whether a person could truly gain a more objective understanding of society through personal introspection.

"So that's why I decided to switch my major to psychology. Even though I've never found a job where I can use it, I knew I could really help all my friends with their problems. I could make a difference in the world," finished Regan.

Jem turned his head, blinking down at Regan. She'd uttered those last words with such conviction that he was pulled back to the conversation. "I admire you for wanting to help others."

She nodded, blue eyes impossibly wide.

"Exactly. Some people spend their whole lives focused on horrible things like wars from a long time ago, when people need help right now." She brushed back her hair. "My friends say I always solve their problems. Like, just yesterday someone called me and she was totally upset about this guy that had asked her out once, and then never again. So, I told her"—Regan glanced up to make sure Jem was ready to hear her wisdom—"call him. He's nervous. You're so pretty and smart that he doesn't know how to approach you."

"Didn't he already ask her out once?"

"Well, yes, but it was probably easier before he really knew her." Regan leaned back a bit, satisfied with her logic.

He wanted to laugh. Poor guy. One evening might have been enough for a lifetime. He liked Regan well enough, but his mama would have called her the type of person who didn't know whether to scratch her watch or wind her bottom. Pretty, but sort of clueless. Regan rambled on and he let her words float past him, adding a few affirmative sounds now and then.

Jem noticed Willy Crawford in the center of the large deck, pompously holding court over a group of similarly pompous-looking folks. Jem had always suspected Lucy's mother was the one with the business sense, and now he was sure. The picture came together for him with startling clarity. Lucy had left Harvard either because her mother had passed away or because they had run out of money. Lucy's family had suffered a true reversal of fortune, and so had he.

"Oh, I think they're starting," Regan said, and tugged him toward the front of the garden. The band rested their instruments on their knees, and Dr. Stroud tapped on a glass with a spoon, the clear tones echoing through the evening air.

"Before we start, I wanted to introduce our newest member of the Free Clinic staff. Jeremiah Chevy, fresh from his internship at Boston Children's Hospital, was born and reared in Tupelo, so don't worry when you address him. He speaks Southern real well," Dr. Stroud said.

Laughter greeted his words and Jem had to smile at the thought of all his fellow Mississippians working to make themselves understood to someone from up North. He'd had his share of conversational mishaps in Boston.

"Jem, would you care to come up and say a few words?" Stroud waved him forward. "I didn't warn him beforehand, nor did I monitor his consumption of the Chatham Artillery Punch, so brace yourselves."

The room rocked with laughter, and Jem felt a few hands pushing him forward, up to the front of the room. He didn't have a phobia of public speaking, but he would have liked to have prepared something.

"Go on, everybody's waiting," Regan said, pulling on his arm. As he reached Dr. Stroud, he realized she still had her arm through his, as if they were there to introduce themselves as a couple. He moved his hand, as if to ease away, but her grip was tight. There was no polite way to shake her off.

The guests waited for him to speak and he looked up, searching for something, anything, to say. "I'm glad to be back in my hometown, if only for a few years." And he realized he was, sort of. He'd missed the land, the accent of his community, the food and the music.

His gaze found Lucy, by herself off to the side, watching him. "There's a line of poetry that makes me think of this place, something about 'the quiet-colored end of evening smiles, miles and miles, on the solitary pastures.' Tupelo has grown a lot since I've been away, but the green grass and the landscape is the same, and the people are the same."

Lucy's eyes had narrowed, but not in anger. She looked as if someone had prodded an injury, her shoulders hunching a bit as if she wanted to curl in on herself. Her arms wrapped around her middle.

He gestured to Dr. Stroud. "It's an honor to work with you and I look forward to serving the community." So it wasn't the smoothest ending, but he needed to step away.

There was a polite wave of applause like a bag of popcorn reaching the end of its cycle in the microwave. He moved to the side, whispering, "I'll be right back." Regan's perfect mouth turned down in a pout, but she released her grip, and he scooted around the guests and headed for the porch. Stroud's voice followed Jem as he passed through the French doors and into the living room.

"The bathroom is on the left." A big man with a full beard pointed out a door as he passed. Jem nodded and went inside, closing the door behind him and locking it. He leaned his head against the wall and closed his eyes. Why had he recited those lines? Was he trying to cause Lucy—or himself—pain?

Only one other person in the room would recognize Robert Browning's poem "Love Among the Ruins." Lucy would, because he had learned it from her, one summer evening ten years ago.

They'd been arguing about whether the poem was about war or love. Of course it was about war, with the line *In one year they sent a million fighters forth North and South.* Sure, there was the girl with *eager eyes and yellow hair* waiting in the turret for the poet's return, but Jem insisted that was just a minor point.

Lucy had stepped forward, put her hands, so soft and warm, on either side of his face, and whispered the words of that poem as they stood on his run-down porch in the middle of a trailer park. The moths had fluttered around the naked lightbulb, bullfrogs had sung for a mate and she had seduced him with a dead man's words. The yearning in her voice was like an oath. *For whole centuries of folly, noise and sin! Shut them in with their triumphs and their glories and the rest! Love is best.*

And he'd believed her. Her hands on his cheeks, her words on her—and then his—lips, he had believed that the poem was more than a depressing reminder of the futility of war. He had believed for one perfect month that love could conquer all and that love would win out.

Jem turned to the sink, avoiding his own eyes in the mirror. Turning the brass fixtures, he splashed water on his face and wiped it with the spotless hand towel. Finally, he looked up. His dress shirt and suit were still perfectly pressed, but he felt ragged. There was a weariness in his eyes. If only the evening could be fast-forwarded and he could find himself alone, somewhere quiet. He was bone tired and it had nothing to do with sleep.

He had known coming back to Tupelo would be hard. He didn't need to make it any harder than it already was. No more poetry, no more dredging up old memories. He had work to do here, and as soon as his debt was paid, he would move. Maybe near his mama in Birmingham, maybe Boston, or even Los Angeles, where it would be always sunny and never humid.

Minutes later, he was back in the garden. It looked as if they'd already awarded Stroud his plaque or award, or whatever it had been. He hoped that meant the party was winding down and he'd be able to slip out soon without much notice. Lucy was gone from where she'd been at the edge of the garden. He glanced around the area, not wanting to seem obvious, hating himself for needing to know where she was, angry at not being able to stop looking.

Regan appeared at his side as if summoned. "You're not havin' a good time, are you? I can tell." She smiled up at him, tossing her hair over one bare shoulder. "I can read emotions really well and you're bored."

He nodded without listening. Bored wasn't the emotion he was feeling, but he didn't want to explain.

"I know!" She grabbed his hand. "Next weekend I'll throw a party and introduce you to all my friends. We totally know how to have a good time."

He looked down at their hands, intertwined, and wondered how it had happened. "Regan, I'm not sure . . ."

"It'll be fun. Come on, you can't spend all your time in that clinic. My daddy is a doctor and I know the type of man you are. Work, work, work. My mom has to drag him out on vacations or he'd work himself to death. I won't let you get all isolated and lonely." Regan seemed to become more and more animated as she considered how to save Jem from himself. She waved to a friend and called out. "Donna, listen to this. We're havin' a party for Jem next weekend."

In seconds he was surrounded by giggling girls, all shouting suggestions over each other. Jem had never felt less like a party, but there wasn't any good reason to refuse. It wouldn't hurt anyone. The evening couldn't be any worse than this one.

She hoped to be wise and reasonable in time; but alas! Alas! She must confess to herself that she was not wise yet.
—ANNE ELLIOT

CHAPTER SEVEN

Lucy was nearly to the stairs when she glanced up and froze. Jem was opening the patio doors, his gaze searching the groups of guests, probably looking for Regan. Lucy turned on her heel and walked as quickly as she could toward a row of crepe myrtle trees. If she could just blend in until he was distracted, then she might be able to slip back inside without having to come face-to-face.

Just the idea of meeting his eyes made her throat tighten. The remaining heat of the day, the crowd of bodies, the music, all pushed against her mind. Jem had only said a few words, but they were a message to her, reminding her of how she had treated him.

Regan appeared, grabbing on to Jem. He moved to the side, now only feet away from Lucy. He was still focused somewhere out in the garden and seemed to be barely listening to Regan's chatter.

Lucy edged farther into the low-hanging boughs

and swallowed hard, wishing she were some-where, anywhere, but here. She'd been so young then, but it wasn't an excuse. It was wrong to deliberately break someone's heart. It was the sort of wrong that stamped the rest of your life with a curse. She had asked God for forgiveness, but that didn't mean her life would be easy. A price had to be paid for that kind of action, and part of it must be standing here and watching Regan flirt with Jem. She couldn't help overhearing every word, every giggle. Lucy shot a glance to the left and thought, if she were very quiet, she might be able to move away without his noticing.

Just then, Regan waved a hand and a crowd of girls rushed over, surrounding the couple and effectively boxing Lucy into the tiny space left under the myrtle. And now they were planning a party. Well, at least she wouldn't be expected to go. She wrapped her arms around herself and resolved to wait until they had moved on, maybe to the dance floor or the bar.

Lucy glanced up, her gaze meeting Theresa's. Her blue eyes flashed surprise at seeing Lucy under the myrtle tree, clearly not part of the group. "Why are you hiding back there in the bushes?" Theresa called out, craning her neck to see past the group of girls surrounding Jem.

Lucy tried to motion that she would be out in just a moment, hoping no one had heard, but it was too late. Jem turned to see who was behind him. Their eyes met, surprise and confusion crossing his face. For one awful moment, Lucy thought she might cry. She felt the burn of tears at the corners of her eyes and pretended to adjust her sleeve, fiddling with the folds of pale-pink silk. He probably thought she was hovering in his shadow, hoping for a moment to speak with him, to reminisce over that evening on the porch.

Theresa politely forced her way through the girls surrounding Jem in a mass of glittering jewelry and little black dresses to where Lucy stood. "Got trapped back here?"

She nodded, not trusting her voice.

There was a short silence and she felt Theresa's gaze on her. "I'm not much for parties, myself."

"I did enjoy the orgeat." Lucy felt that she was being rude, obviously unhappy to be in the middle of the Strouds' celebration.

Her comment was greeted by a warm chuckle. "That's something, I suppose."

Lucy couldn't help the smile that tugged at her mouth. "Not just the orgeat, of course."

"Of course." Theresa patted Lucy's hand. "You know, Jane Austen has a lot to say about girls who hide in corners."

"Really?" Nothing Austen could say would make Lucy's heartache any less. She could see Jem clearly, more than a head taller than his admiring fans. He seemed bemused and flattered by the flirting directed his way.

"Perhaps not exactly, but something close. She said that there was nothing better than staying home, for comfort." Theresa cut a glance at the ever-increasing group of pretty girls in front of them, all doing their best to get Jem's attention. "For once, I don't think Austen is right."

Lucy tried not to laugh, but Theresa's dry wit combined with the Creole drawl was too much. Lucy felt it rise up in her throat and couldn't force it back. At the sound, Jem turned. His face wore an expression she couldn't quite define. The girls directly in front of Lucy and Theresa peered over their shoulders, wearing matching expressions of annoyance. One dark-eyed girl hitched her ruby-red lips in a tiny Elvis sneer as she flicked her gaze up and down Lucy's outfit, before turning her toned back on them.

"Enough hiding." Theresa tugged Lucy through a small gap between the myrtle tree and a slender blonde in a black bandeau dress. The band was playing an Irish-sounding folk tune, and the guests had started to drift toward the dance platform, spurred on in equal measure by melody and alcoholic beverages. Theresa greeted several people as they moved through the living room and then came to a stop near the punch table. She measured out a portion of pink lemonade and passed it to Lucy. "Nothing like a group of sweet Southern girls to block you into a corner."

Lucy felt the embarrassment fading with every

second that passed, and it was quickly being replaced with shame. She was a professional woman who had let a group of her sister's college friends make her feel inadequate. It shouldn't have taken an act of bravery to interrupt their squee-fest over Jem.

"I just didn't want to make a fuss," she managed, and hated herself for the excuse.

"Women can be vicious. They're probably real nice folks, but some of these girls never learned to take their manners out of their pockets and put them in their mouths." Theresa sighed. "Sometimes it's easier to not draw attention to yourself."

"No, it wasn't that. I have two sisters who never fail to tell me how terrible my hair looks, so a few dirty looks don't bother me a bit." Lucy didn't know Theresa that well but she admired her already. She didn't want Theresa to think she couldn't walk through a wall of college kids, no matter how many diamonds they were wearing.

Theresa shot her a look, blue eyes assessing. "You're avoiding Jem?"

"Not at all," Lucy said too quickly. "No."

"He's a wonderful young man. You would think he'd have such a big head about being blessed with those looks and having a medical degree, to boot." Theresa looked back across the room toward the garden. "I've seen him with his patients. He's truly kind in a way that only comes from being raised up right."

Raised up right. Lucy's aunt had said he was trailer trash and would never amount to anything. Lucy could never have believed it, but had allowed herself to act as if it were true.

Paulette strutted toward them, breaking into Lucy's train of thought. "You won't believe what just happened."

"Someone is wearing the same dress as you?"

Paulette rolled her eyes. "No, I went to the bar to ask for a mojito and that guy Johnny said he didn't make mojitos. Then he offered to make me a mint julep, in one of those silver cups and everything."

"Did you know they say the true cause of the Civil War was some Northerner adding nutmeg to a mint julep?" Lucy asked.

"Is that a joke?" Her sister glared. "I don't care what goes in a mint julep because I've never had one and I never will. They're totally uncool, and nobody drinks them except for old guys in seersucker suits and bow ties." Paulette's expression faded from anger to confusion as she glanced at Theresa and realized that she was speaking to the hostess, who was married to the only man at the party in a full seersucker suit and a bow tie.

"Oh, don't mind me," Theresa said. "I actually like a mint julep on a hot day. Crushed ice, sprig of mint. Almost better than sweet tea, if you've got nowhere to be and don't have to drive."

Lucy cocked her head. "Paulette, didn't you drive here tonight?"

Paulette shrugged. "One drink isn't going to hurt anybody."

"I thought I saw you holding something when I first came in . . ." Lucy broke off, searching her memory. Janessa didn't drink, and Lucy would drive her daddy home, so she wouldn't be counting his glasses. But Paulette wasn't the kind of girl who believed cautionary tales. She learned by experience, which, so far, hadn't been a total disaster, but it had the potential to ruin her life in a big way.

"I've only had two. Plus, it's a long party and I ate something before I drove here. I deserve to have a good time once in a while, and if Daddy doesn't care, why should you?"

For the first time, Lucy wondered whether Paulette followed their daddy's example, or if she acted this way to get his attention. Lucy's gaze dropped to the tiny, insanely expensive purse. Paulette was spending money as if it grew on a tree in their backyard, even though she knew their family was in mountains of debt. And still Daddy didn't pay her any mind. Lucy felt a stab of pity for Paulette that had, for once, nothing to do with the fact her sister had zero common sense.

Paulette nodded toward the garden. "I've got to get back out there. Maybe I'll meet the one tonight. I think Regan's found herself a new guy.

He sure looks better than the last boyfriend. He was a bouncer up at the Hoot 'n Holler Bar and had tattoos up both arms. She told me she thought he was so hot until he got his nipples pierced. She just couldn't get over that."

Lucy already knew the guy Regan had reeled in, and he was a far sight better than a pierced bouncer. "Please don't drink anymore. I don't want to have to take your keys."

Paulette was already walking away and waved a hand in response. Her sparkly cupcake purse glittered at her hip as she swayed across the room toward the French doors, long hair swishing over her shoulders.

"Do you want me to tell Johnny to hold off on her drinks?" Theresa asked.

"Would you?" Relief flooded through Lucy. The evening was hard enough without having to monitor Paulette's alcohol intake. "I'll make sure she's sober enough to drive at the end of the party, but I won't be able to stop her if she heads over there for another round."

"You're a good girl, watching after your sister like that." Theresa watched Paulette head out the door into the garden. "She's real pretty, but she might have a bit of growin' up to do."

"I think being the youngest is part of it," Lucy said, not wanting to be harsh. "And Daddy has always spoiled her."

"A spoiled woman is a dangerous thing. God

130

love her, somebody's gotta." Theresa shook her head. "Be right back," she said, and was gone.

Lucy let out a long breath and tried not to worry. She scanned the area, searching for her daddy. Maybe there would be a miracle and he'd be ready to head home early. She remembered he was on the deck, and she wandered close to the doors to find him in the middle of a long golf story, both hands gripping an imaginary club that he swung forward in a long arc. He was surrounded by friends and longtime business partners. Lucy admired the way he could hold the attention of a group, bringing the story to a perfectly timed peak, then driving home the punch line. She'd inherited none of his social flare, which had never really bothered her before.

A burst of girlish laughter sounded from Jem's group and she gritted her teeth. It was perfectly acceptable for Jem to have a good time. She just wished she didn't have to stand around and watch.

The band switched to a slow Cole Porter number, and Regan led Jem toward the dance floor. He seemed so tall, just a memory of the boy she used to know. He laid a hand on Regan's hip, but she slipped both arms under his jacket, pressing herself against him and swaying to the music.

Lucy felt a pulse pound in her throat. When she was little, Janessa would turn on a nature show and force Lucy to watch with her. Lucy hated the episodes where some newborn animal, maybe a gazelle calf, was chased across the savanna by a female lion, finally succumbing under the power and ferocity of the lion's savagery. In the end, when the baby had finally stopped moving its stick-thin legs and its tiny, black hooves were still, Lucy would let out a breath of relief. The suffering was over, the worst was past.

Watching Jem's arms wrapped around Regan, Lucy felt as if she were stuck in a never-ending loop of that tragic scene on the African savanna. Something precious was dying, and she wished it would just be finished so she could stop praying for a different outcome. Once it was settled, she would focus on repairing what was left of her heart. Until then, Lucy was frozen in time, seeing the way Jem bent his blond head, wishing she were the girl being held in his arms, being whispered to in the middle of a garden party on a perfect Southern summer night.

It was a sunny Sunday afternoon, the kind of day that made a person glad to be alive, but Jem slouched in his kitchen and stared at the cell phone sitting silent on the tiled counter top. Every Sunday afternoon, he called his mama. Loralee was full of news, near and far, and always good for a joke or two. They were geographically nearer to each other now than when he'd been in

Boston for so many years, but they'd always been close. The Sunday phone call was a tradition they'd started the week he'd left for college, and he usually looked forward to it. Now he wondered if she would call the National Guard if he didn't check in.

The sun shone through the window into the tiny blue kitchen with a particular fierceness and Jem decided to sit outside on the old porch swing. The rental house was clean and tidy, nothing fancy, but that porch swing was a bit of luxury. He settled his back against the warm slats and set the phone beside him. She was probably out gardening, or maybe she and her friends were down at the community center, helping out with some dinner or fund-raiser. She might not even pick up, Jem told himself.

Of course, she'd expected his Sunday phone call for the last ten years. Even when they'd spoken the day before, he'd always kept up the tradition. No, he didn't want to worry her. He would just get it over with as soon as possible. Hopefully she wouldn't ask too many questions and he wouldn't give too many details. He wasn't trying to hide what was happening in his life. He just didn't know where to start, or even what it was he felt.

"Yallow." Jem had to smile at the way his mama answered the phone. It was a mix of *yeah* and *hello* and there was no question in it.

"Hi, Mama." He said, working to make his voice as jovial as possible. "Having a great Sunday? How was Mass?"

There was a long pause. He cringed, imagining her expression. She wasn't the type to interrupt. She would never demand answers. But if he could see her now, he was sure he'd see an expression of calm assessment.

He hurried on. "St. James has got a nice choir, but the service seems a little short. Maybe I'm just used to St. Cecilia's. That organist always went for all seven verses of every hymn, and we'd be standing there singing way past the time Father Mike had gone down the aisle. You know, maybe I should try the early service . . ." His sentence trailed off. He dropped his head in his hand and let out a sigh. Babbling was a like waving a red flag. When he was little, she'd always known when he was hiding something. He'd start chattering and not be able to stop.

"Nothing better than a committed organist."

"We moved the clinic," he blurted out.

"I remember you said you were lookin' for something new." She was agreeing with him and asking for more, in her gentle way.

"Dr. Stroud found us a perfect spot. At least, lots of room."

"Good." Jem almost laughed at her response. That was his mama. She was a chatterbox until she knew something was on your mind, then, as if a switch were flipped, she listened to every word you said. And those you didn't.

"We moved to Crawford House."

There was only silence in response.

"She still lives there. I mean, I knew that. I was prepared for that," Jem said. "And I met her the day we looked at the area we would rent. It was fine, really. Everything was fine."

She didn't say anything for a moment. "Well, I'm glad."

"I mean, we didn't speak much. Not that day. But I've seen her since and it was fine then, too." He rolled his eyes. Repeating himself wasn't going to convince his mama that everything was normal. But if he admitted it wasn't okay, then he would have to face what he felt, and he wasn't even sure what it was.

"Is she married?" She sounded hopeful.

"No, not married. Her sister Janessa is, though."

"So . . ." He could feel his mama choosing her words carefully. "You know that I want you to be happy."

"Yes, Mama."

"And Lucy Crawford never made you happy, sweetie. In fact, she made you as miserable as a—"

"I remember it clearly." He wished he could head off this conversation, but she was too savvy, she knew him too well. "I didn't call to confess I was going to sign up for Heartbreak Part Two. I just wanted to let you know where we were, and I'd talked to her, and everything was fine."

"Oh, honey." Her voice didn't hold anything but sympathy. "I wish she was married, for your sake."

"I know," he said. And then he was letting go of the pretense, and spilling it all out, just as he should have done as soon as he called. "It's like there are two of me, Mama. The thinking part of me knows it's all over and is sure we can exist in the same area with no hard feelings. I do my job and see old friends and remember the good things about Tupelo. And then there's this other part that I'm not even aware of most of the time, planning and considering and hoping. I never know what this part is doing until Lucy shows up and then I think something crazy, like how I wish I could get her to laugh because I really love her laugh, or I want to ask if she still loves Langston Hughes, or I wonder what her boyfriends were like and why she didn't get married. And this part of me, this part I can't control at all, wants to know if it has anything to do with me."

He stopped to draw in a breath. "And the part I hate the most is this little voice that says maybe things could be different now that I have a medical degree and have a solid future, and I start to think of ways to impress her or get her attention." His eyes were squeezed shut and he waited for his mama to tell him how ridiculous it all was. He needed her to tell him how to close it off, how to get control of this traitorous part of him.

"Did I ever tell you I saw your father once, when you were about six years old?"

His eyes snapped open. "No." She had never talked about his father, except to say he wasn't willing to stand by her when she told him she was pregnant.

She sighed, and he could imagine the sadness on her face. His childhood was marked with that image, those lines of grief. "He was married and had a little baby. He recognized me right away."

"You'd think he would." Jem couldn't keep the bitterness from his voice.

"Oh, not really. We only knew each other for a few months that summer. Two young kids with too much time on their hands. And although I thought I was in love with him, I'm not sure I even knew him that well."

He had known Lucy for a summer and he would never have forgotten her, not ever. "Did you ask him why he left?"

"That's obvious, honey. He was scared. We both were."

"But you got stuck with the kid. That's hardly an excuse. You carried the burden—"

"Don't say that. You were never anything but a blessing for me." Her voice was pure steel for a moment.

Jem shook his head, not wanting to argue the

point. How an unplanned pregnancy could be a gift for an uneducated teen was something he didn't think she could explain. "I know your parents weren't happy about it." He didn't have many memories of his grandparents. Just a few and they were fuzzy. "A few decades earlier and you'd probably have been shipped off to one of those maternity homes where they hid pregnant teen girls."

"No, not in our family. We weren't rich enough to hide anything like that. But I know I hurt them. Good Catholic girls didn't have babies out of wedlock. It was about as big a scandal as it could be. I know you don't think this has anythin' to do with you, but it does. These things happen." The sadness was still there, even after all those years. She cleared her throat. "What I'm tryin' to say is that I was worried about you two."

Jem sat up straight. "You mean, Lucy and me?"

"Don't get defensive. You gotta remember how young you both were. Love is a powerful thing, sweetie. It's enough to make you forget what you shouldn't be doing, enough to make you forget you'll break your mama's heart when you have to tell her that she'll be a grandma too soon."

He frowned at the bright summer grass. Lucy and he had been as in love as two people could be, heart and mind, but they had been careful of how much time they spent together alone. They both had plans and had seen too many cautionary tales.

She'd told him that her mama had given her a speech about a girl's purity and honor, as if she'd never heard any of it before. He told her how his mama had lectured about respect and commitment. They'd heard it all, they understood how it happened.

Then again, he had never wanted anyone else as badly as he'd wanted Lucy. Her touch was like a drug. Just being near her was a physical pleasure. He tried to imagine what would have happened if they hadn't walked away from each other when they had to, how he would have reacted to the news that all their plans were ruined and they would be teen parents. Of course he'd have been scared, but Jem would have taken responsibility. They would have made it work, somehow, together.

"I never would have left Lucy, never. I'm not my father."

"I know that." His mother rushed on. "I'm not expressing myself real well here, but when I saw your father that day, I didn't feel anything for him. I mean, I felt sad that he didn't choose me, and that he left me alone, but I didn't feel what I'd felt before."

Jem was lost, but knew that his mama wouldn't have brought it up if she didn't think it was important to tell him.

"I don't think I really loved him, because there's something mysterious about love. You can't always point to one thing and say, 'I loved him because of the way he wore his hat,' or 'I loved her because of her laugh.' And if you can, then you probably better hope that thing never goes away."

Jem didn't say a word. He thought he knew exactly what she was trying to say, and he dreaded what she was going to say next.

"You and Lucy were different. You spent hours on that porch, talking and reading to each other. You didn't like her for the way she wore her hair or something that could be changed. Whatever it is you loved about her then is probably what you love about her now."

Jem flinched at the present tense. He didn't want to look too closely at whether or not he still loved her, but he could hardly argue with his mama's words. "But I don't want to," he said, more to himself than to her.

"I know, honey. But that crazy part of yourself? There's no way to turn that off. You loved her once and probably always will. You just have to accept it and go on."

Jem hung his head. This wasn't what he'd wanted to hear. His gut clenched at the thought of looking ahead to a life of running into Lucy, day after day, and not being able to control his thoughts, his emotions. He felt a flash of anger so bright it made him want to throw the phone. He'd been so stupid to think he could live in this town and not ache for her. "I wish I'd never come here."

"What's done is done. But give yourself time away from there. Maybe go on one of those river trips with your friend Lars."

He snorted. "Taking a river-rafting tour with Lars would make me happy to live anywhere, once I was sure I was going to survive."

"So maybe nothing that drastic," she said, but there was laughter in her voice.

"Besides that, you're saying I need to be careful. There's nothing else I can do."

"Yup." Her voice was soft and sad. "You should be really, really careful."

Monday morning had come too soon. Jem dragged himself out of his car and stood staring up at the white columns of Crawford House. He loved his job, loved his patients, but coming to work here every day might just give him an ulcer. He hadn't slept well. His dreams were long stretches of scenes in which he searched for his stethoscope while patients all shouted out their symptoms, punctuated by short flashes of Lucy's expression when he had made his speech at the Strouds'. He had finally rolled out of bed before dawn, sick to his stomach and feeling like the new kid on the first day of school.

He took the footpath around the north side of the house, barely glancing at the rose bushes in full bloom and the year-round cutting garden. The back porch stretched along the entire rear of the house, and he straightened a small sign posted near the stairs. The Free Clinic of Tupelo had some pretty fancy digs. He should be thrilled to be walking around in any part of it. But although his patients would receive better care in the new location, he would rather be setting up shop in the worst neighborhood in town.

A small sound caught his attention and he looked down at a tiny tabby cat, barely out of its kittenhood. It was thin and its eyes were rheumy, but it rubbed against his pant leg in a friendly way.

"Hey, buddy. I don't think you live here." Jem reached down and ran a hand over the kitten's back, feeling the knobs of its spine. He scooped it up easily in one hand and gave it a good once-over. A deep vibration started in the kitten's chest and seemed to travel all the way up Jem's arm. "Looks like you need a good cleaning. Where's your mama?"

The cat reached out a white paw and batted at the air. Jem lowered it to the ground, smiling a little at the way its tail stood straight up like a flag. But, sweet as it was, he had patients to see and wasn't keen on picking cat fur and who knew what else off his suit before the first appointment.

"I hope you're going to wash your hands," someone called out behind him.

"Hello, Olympia. Are you here to welcome our first patients?" As soon as he asked the question,

Jem was ashamed of himself. He was needling her. He knew very well there was no chance Olympia was going to speak with a patient of this clinic.

"I'm here to make sure the house isn't changed more than our agreement," she said. Her purple linen suit was accented with gold bangles that clattered on her wrists as she moved. "If we don't watch you people, pretty soon there'll be a flock of yard birds scratchin' at the grass and an old couch on the back porch."

"I hadn't thought of putting in a chicken coop." Jem pretended to consider the idea. "Fresh eggs would be very nutritious for a lot of families."

"And the cat has to go because we don't allow pets. They carry chiggers and poop all over the flower beds."

"The chickens would eat the chiggers. They could be free-range." He paused. "But not all-vegetarian organically fed if they're eating insects."

She didn't crack a smile, just rolled her eyes. "I'm so sick of vegetarians. Lucy is always trying to ruin a perfectly good dish by taking out the ham and putting in something green."

"Really? Like what?"

"Just the other night she made black-eyed peas. And guess what?" Olympia leaned in close, her expression deadly serious.

"It had peas?"

"It didn't have a bit of ham in it," she said. "I knew it right away. That wasn't ham hocks in that pot. The little pink cubes of something that were supposed to be ham were floatin' on the top like fleas on a dog." Olympia shuddered.

"It's true that the Southern diet is usually very heavy in meat and cholesterol." Breakfast had held no appeal an hour ago, but now his stomach was waking up to the idea of something slow-cooked in a cast-iron pot.

"Well, it's not just that. One day she cooked some kudzu."

Jem started to laugh. "Some leafy greens do bear a likeness to kudzu, I suppose."

Olympia straightened up, lips pursing. "I mean it. She grilled a Vidalia onion and stuck big ol' kudzu leaves in it. It was supposed to be nutritious. Can you imagine? I told her that she needed to learn how to bake a chicken like every other Southern girl and leave the weeds outside."

He could see it. Lucy had always been adventurous. She was always searching for something new, devouring everything she could learn about it, and then moving on. He'd thought it was fascinating, until he was the "something new" that she devoured and moved on from.

"I'd better get inside and make sure we're ready for patients. You're welcome to come in and look around." Jem moved toward the door and the kitten followed along behind him across the porch. He gently shooed it away with one hand. "Not you. Better head on home."

"I'll tell Zeke to take it out and dump it somewhere," Olympia said.

"Is Zeke back?"

"Sure is. That was the first thing Lucy did after y'all signed the lease. I told her to hire the Morgans' gardener for a few days a week. He's from Guatemala and they pay him five dollars an hour for a lot more work than Zeke does, but Lucy wouldn't listen." Olympia stopped by the door, waiting for Jem to open it for her.

If any good at all came from this arrangement, it would be having the old caretaker back in his rightful place in Crawford House. Letting Olympia pass through the door, Jem wiggled his shoe in front of the little tabby. It stared up at him and let out a tiny mewl. He let the door swing closed and watched it through the glass. It wasn't leaving. Jem hoped whoever had lost a kitten would come to claim it before he left tonight, because he didn't look forward to walking away from the hungry little thing. He had no idea whether his house allowed pets, but he wasn't looking to add to his family of one.

"Dr. Chevy, we got some calls early this morning," Leticia said, slipping out from behind the appointment desk. She held out a slip of paper and cast a curious glance in Olympia's direction.

Jem almost smiled. Seeing the receptionist of

the Free Clinic in the same room as his nemesis promised good things. Leticia was a middle-aged mom of three teen boys. She dressed her plump frame in semi-professional clothes and kept her dark hair cropped close, and her accent announced her Detroit upbringing in no uncertain terms.

"I need to see into those back rooms," Olympia announced. "The lease agreement said you would only paint and bring in furniture. If I find any nails or hooks in the walls, there will be trouble."

"Excuse me?" Leticia jerked upright as if someone had given her an electric shock.

"Jem, give me the tour," Olympia said, ignoring the receptionist completely.

"Nobody put nails in no walls so you won't be needing a tour, ma'am." Leticia was leaning closer now, her arms folded in front of her.

"It's fine. I can do it." Jem kept his face straight by pure willpower. If he had to take bets on these two, Leticia would win any showdown. She didn't survive the mean streets of Detroit's West Side by letting rich old ladies walk all over her. She was an excellent receptionist for a place like the Free Clinic, dispensing sympathy when needed and a verbal takedown when required.

"All right, Dr. Chevy." Leticia stalked back to her desk, letting her expression speak for her.

"I don't have all day," Olympia snapped, heading for the examining rooms. "Some of us aren't lucky

146

enough to have the State of Mississippi funding our every moment."

He took a moment to breathe deeply before following across the waiting room. It wouldn't do any good to fight with Olympia Crawford. It had been a long time since he'd been home, but he still remembered how to "yes, ma'am" like a good Southern boy.

Five minutes later, satisfied that the walls of Crawford House weren't being poked like pincushions, Olympia stood at the hallway that led to the kitchen area. "And remember, every-thing else is off-limits to you people. We don't want sick folk wandering through and making a mess on the carpet."

"We'll be sure to let the patients know that the entrance is around the back." Jem shrugged off the *you people* and checked his watch. He had barely enough time to grab his white coat and find a pen.

"Auntie?" The soft voice froze him in his tracks.

"Lucy, I was checkin' on the walls." Olympia shouldered her purse and leaned forward to peck her niece on the cheek.

Jem was suddenly aware of his hands, the heat of the summer morning thick on his skin. He nodded at Lucy, managing to avoid her gaze completely. She was wearing jeans and a Bulldogs T-shirt, but he couldn't help the memory that flashed through his mind of that pale-pink dress. His mama's words echoed in his head: *Be careful.*

"Go ahead to the kitchen." Lucy guided Olympia toward the hall. "There's sweet tea in the fridge. I just made it."

"Are you home again today? They must be cutting your hours at the center." Olympia didn't wait for a response. "I suppose I could stay for a glass before I meet Michelle at the Emporium. I've been invited to be on the planning committee for the next cotillion, and I promised to lend my expertise in organizing such a large party."

"Lovely. You go on head to the kitchen and get settled. I'll be right there."

Olympia gave a little shrug and left, the sound of her heels seemed to Jem like the bang snaps the kids like so much on the Fourth of July. The silence slowly expanded in the room and he felt Lucy's eyes on him.

"I'm sorry." Her voice was soft. "I'll do my best to keep her on our side of the house."

He nodded, glancing in Lucy's direction. "Is the interpretive center hurting for money?"

As soon as he asked the question, he wanted to take it back. Money wasn't the best topic to broach first thing in the morning, no matter the person. Add in Lucy's current financial issues, and it was downright rude.

"No more than usual. Struggling to procure funding is a reality of life at a battle site. We're not alone in that, I'm sure." She didn't seem to mind the question. Stepping toward Leticia, she held out a hand. "I'm Lucy Crawford."

"Right, sorry." Jem made quick introductions, feeling the burn of falling short of "good manners."

"This is your house?" Leticia asked, her eyes growing wide. "I could get lost in a place like this. I bet you got lots of bathrooms."

Lucy grinned. "Not as many as we should have. It's an old place. They didn't value the morning beauty routine the way they should have in 1855."

"You'd think they'd have needed a lot more time than we do." Leticia frowned. "Just getting ready with all those layers and buttons and things. I've seen those costumes. Dr. Stroud is always tryin' to get me to come to the reenactments. He said all I'd have to do is hold down the men while he pretends to hack off their legs." Leticia stacked a few papers on the desk and shook her head. "Now he's got my husband caught up in it, too. I found Eddie tryin' to knit some socks. He says he can't have nothing that's not handmade or from the Civil War, and of course there's no Civil War socks left, so he's got to make some himself."

"I think the men had it better, back then. Our last reenactment, I needed two hours and three helpers to get into my costume," Lucy said. "I wasn't even playing an upper-class lady. Just the washer-woman for the regiment."

"Why'd you want to play somebody like that?" Leticia gave Lucy a once-over. "You like slummin' it? I know a girl like that back home in Detroit. Her dad was the fire captain and she dressed like she live on Gratiot Avenue."

Jem opened his mouth to defend Lucy, but she was already answering. "There weren't many wealthy women on the battlefield, unless they were nurses, and there were even fewer African American women." She paused, as if not sure whether to continue. "I was thinking of doing something different this year."

"You're gonna be a nurse this time? Dr. Stroud'll be so happy to have you in his surgery tent," Leticia said.

"Actually, at the reenactment in September, I was thinking of dressing as a man."

"Like one of the regular soldiers?" Leticia asked.

"Sort of." Lucy took a breath. "There were some women, not a lot, that disguised themselves as men so they could go into battle. We just acquired the diary of a woman named Hattie Winter who went to war as a man."

"Wait, so you'll be a woman, dressed as a man? Who's gonna be able to tell?"

"Probably no one, really. Just like Hattie." The edges of Lucy's mouth turned up.

"But why she'd do that? You'd think a woman would want to stay where it was safe. I mean, nobody wants to be in a war."

Lucy glanced up at Jem, her dark eyes fixed on his. He wanted to look away, wanted to make his excuses and leave the room. But he was frozen to the spot, waiting for her to speak.

"Some women signed up to fight as men because they wanted to defend their communities, just like the men could, and some women disguised themselves so they wouldn't be separated from their husbands. But Hattie . . ." Lucy never dropped her gaze, but he saw her swallow hard. "Hattie was looking for the man she loved. He had been conscripted, and she couldn't bear waiting for him any longer, so she volunteered."

"Huh," Leticia said. "Did she find him?"

Lucy shook her head. There was the faintest sheen of tears in her eyes. "She never saw him again," she whispered.

"Well, that's downright depressing." Leticia sighed. "I don't know why you people are so hung up on the past. There's nothing we can do about it, and it seems to be all sorts of sad stories. You should focus on something real."

"It *is* real. And if we forget Hattie's life, we won't ever learn the lesson she left us." Lucy was speaking to Leticia, but her meaning was for him, her eyes only for him.

Jem heard his own words echoing back at him, from just a few nights ago: *If we simply forget the most painful episodes of the past, we might make the same mistakes over again.* He felt a stab, somewhere near his heart, right under his ribs, and almost clapped a hand to his chest, as if to ward off the emotion.

Jem wanted to reach out to her. He wanted to tell her that all was forgiven and it was all right to move on, because regret poisons a person as surely as jealousy. He should say something reassuring, about being friends and how he was over her, over everything that had happened . . . except that he'd be lying. The realization was like a kick to the gut.

"I'd better get ready," he managed. He turned on his heel and walked across the waiting room, heart in his throat.

"We've gotta prepare for the morning rush." Leticia sounded faintly apologetic.

"I understand. Nice to meet you, again." Lucy's voice was strong, as if she hadn't just been on the verge of tears.

Jem pushed open his office door and stared unseeing at the tidy desk. He'd have patients in a matter of minutes and he couldn't focus. His mama had told him to watch out and he was trying, but he couldn't very well refuse to talk to her. His life was slowly unraveling, just when he thought it was finally coming together. A girl had once broken his heart, and now she was threatening to bring it all back with a few well-chosen words.

He slipped off his jacket and grabbed his white coat, stuffing a pen and a prescription pad into his pocket. Nobody could ever accuse him of being a slow learner, but Lucy was a lesson he never seemed to grasp. He'd only been in Tupelo a month and already his mind was wrapping itself around the idea of her, nestling into all the familiar hollows of pain and regret. He'd only needed one summer to fall in love with Lucy, but it had taken ten years to get over her.

And darned if he was going to let it all happen again.

"I certainly am proud, too proud
to enjoy a welcome which depends
so entirely upon place."
—ANNE ELLIOT

CHAPTER EIGHT

"I was worried you'd forgotten me in here,"
Aunt Olympia said. Her iced-tea glass was empty.
She leaned back in her chair, arms crossed over
her chest. One foot wiggled impatiently, like a
metronome on high.

"Sorry." Lucy dropped into a chair and took a
deep draft of the slightly diluted sweet tea. It
wasn't even July and the heat was unbearable. She
felt the humidity weighing on her like a quilt,
suffocating and relentless.

If that party had been an exercise in humilia-
tion, then today's brief conversation with Jem was
the master class. She hadn't gone into the clinic
area with an idea of anything more than shooing
her aunt away. But she had stayed, and stayed,
until she was pouring out her heart in a kind of
coded message.

"Paulette said she was coming by this morning.
Maybe she forgot, too," Aunt Olympia said.

Lucy said nothing. She didn't understand herself anymore. It was one thing to plan on dressing as Hattie at the reenactment to satisfy some deep need inside to be someone else, someone strong and inspiring. It was another to blurt out those plans to Jem while standing in his waiting room, fighting back tears and praying that he understood.

She'd felt the emotion welling in her throat and willed it down. Jem had taken one look into her eyes and turned away. Politely, gently, but he had still left the room as quickly as possible. What more did he need to do? What did he need to say before she understood there was no chance of forgiveness? And the worst of it was that she didn't expect anything from him. Reconciliation was impossible. But a part of her wanted to tell him she was wrong, in any way she could. If only she could hear him say that he forgave her, maybe she could let it all go.

"Did you hear me?" Olympia leaned forward.

"She doesn't usually drop by on Mondays," Lucy said, snapping back to the conversation. Paulette liked to come around when she knew Lucy was at work because it was a lot easier to get a hard-cash loan from their daddy without Lucy's interference. "Is this about the wedding?"

Her aunt sat up straight. "What wedding? Whose wedding? I didn't get any invitation to a wedding."

Lucy went to the mail holder and brought back Rebecca's invitation. Her aunt read it over and shrugged. "That's real quick. I wonder if they're having a shotgun wedding."

"She's leaving for England in a few months for a sabbatical."

"Huh. I bet they come back with a baby. That's how those Northerners are. Even when they get married, they seem to have a baby just a few months later. They never do anything in the right order."

Lucy wanted to roll her eyes. She knew plenty of Southern girls who had their babies a little "early." *Babies all take nine months. Except for the first one. Those can come anytime,* her mama liked to say.

"And what is this Regency theme? Is she dressing like a princess? Brandi McQueen had a princess-theme wedding. There were the sweetest little glass-shoe party favors, and the cake looked just like the one in the Disney movie. She looked lovely comin' to the church in that white carriage, just like Cinderella, but her dress was so big it took four people to get her out of the little door."

"It's supposed to be like Jane Austen's England. I saw a picture of the dress and it's beautiful, but very simple."

"I don't think those two things go together at a wedding." Aunt Olympia frowned. "She's going to regret not putting time into her planning."

Lucy pulled out her phone. "Let me show you a picture she sent me. I'm going to be a bridesmaid, and my dress is in the same style." She scrolled through her texts until she found it. "See, it has a silk ribbon at the waist, and then it falls straight down, with a sheer, embroidered overlay. Mine is pale blue, but I'm not sure if all of us have a different color."

Aunt Olympia squinted at the screen. "She has to be havin' a baby. Nobody would wear that unless they were hiding a baby bump. It looks like a potato-sack dress."

Lucy hated the term *baby bump* but said nothing. "I think they look timeless and elegant."

"But there's no shape." Her aunt shook her head. "A woman has to be able to show off her figure in a dress. She should have asked Paulette to plan her wedding. She has great style."

Lucy shrugged and put the phone back in her purse. "So, if Paulette isn't coming here about Rebecca's wedding, what is she planning?"

"Well, she wants to have a dinner here. Her friend took a liking to Jem and they want to show him a good time."

Lucy didn't ask who the friend in question was. She had a perfectly clear mental picture of Regan, wrapped in Jem's arms, swaying together on the dance floor. Her aunt seemed to think it was just fine for a girl such as Regan to fall in love with Jem. Lucy wasn't sure whether it was because her aunt's opinion of Jem had changed or because Regan was white, and Lucy wasn't brave enough to ask.

"Why does it have to be here? They could have it anywhere."

"It's true that having a dinner here would be sort of strange, since he's in the house every day. But he doesn't come into this part, not even to the kitchen." Her aunt frowned, the metallic-blue shadow on her lids wrinkling up like folds on a paper fan. "Maybe a garden party is a better idea."

Lucy wanted to lay her head on the table. Garden party. The two most dreaded words in her aunt's arsenal. Dr. Stroud's party had been an indoor-outdoor party, where a guest might possibly find a place to stand, away from the guests and the noise and the dancing.

"Well, if she has it here, I'm sure I don't have to be part of it."

"Of course you do. Paulette is far too busy to plan everything. You can call the caterer and the bands, get everything set up. She'll send out the invitations."

"Paulette doesn't even have a job. How is she any busier than I am?" Lucy was surprised at the anger in her voice. What Aunt Olympia wanted, Aunt Olympia got, whether or not it made sense.

The older woman sucked in a breath and sat up straight. "Is this the way your mama taught you, to raise your voice to your elders? You used to be such a good girl, always helping around the house and making good grades. Now you're grown-up and you've got attitude."

Attitude. It's what someone said about girls who thought they knew better, when they didn't know anything. A wave of remorse washed over her. Olympia was her daddy's sister, shepherding the girls through the harrowing years after their mama's death. Whatever she had done wrong, she still meant well. "I'm sorry, Auntie."

Olympia sniffed. Adjusting the gold necklaces that lay against her blouse, she looked as if she might never get over the slight.

"Yoo-hoo," Paulette called as she came toward the kitchen. For once, Lucy was glad to hear her sister coming through the house. "There you are," Paulette said, launching herself at first her aunt and then Lucy. Her hair was newly styled in perfect waves that fell past her shoulders, light blond streaks highlighting the edges of each gentle curl.

"You look pretty," Lucy said. Paulette made her realize how much she needed a trip to the salon. A girl could do only so much with her hair before she needed the help of a professional.

"Oh, you should head down to Clarice's. It took five hours, but I brought my iPad so I could still work on my designs for Regan's new apartment. Clarice gave me a special price, only three hundred for everything, including all the styling products I needed."

Lucy had just started to sip her tea and coughed, choking on the ice-cold liquid. "Three hundred dollars?"

Paulette rolled her eyes. "Auntie, tell Lucy that a woman needs to look put together and that costs money."

"Sure, but maybe it could be your money and not Daddy's money," Lucy said. Anger made her chest feel tight and she pressed a hand to her forehead. Having the clinic move into Crawford House wouldn't do a bit of good if Paulette wouldn't stop spending.

"How do you know I didn't pay for it myself?" Paulette stuck a hand on her hip and pursed her bright-red lips. Lucy had to admit her sister was stunning, in an expensive sort of way. Her orange, tissue-thin T-shirt left one shoulder bare, the wide neck scooping low over her chest. Delicate silver chains hung in long loops, dotted every so often with tiny gemstones. She had undeniable style and a feel for trends, but her interior-design business was more of a pro bono service for all her friends than anything that could pay her salon bill.

"Anyway," Paulette said, "Daddy said he was happy I'm taking care of myself. Once you let yourself go, no man will look twice at you."

Lucy forced herself not to smooth down her

hair. She knew exactly what her daddy thought of his oldest daughter's appearance and her chances of marriage. She really ought to go to the salon more often, if only to make Aunt Olympia and Daddy happy.

"So, tell us your plans for the party. Should I call Bitsy's Catering? They make those delicious little shrimp soufflé puffs. Or maybe Danver's? They catered the Ferrises' party and the miniature bacon-wrapped sirloin-steak bites were delicious. Don't call Tasty Kitchens. Laura Malveaux had them do her party at Christmas and the appetizers had hardly any meat to 'em. She wanted a refund, but that Missy told them it was a no-returns deal. She comes from nothing special, but that woman has more nerve than Carter's got liver pills."

"No, no," Paulette said. "I'm not hiring a caterer. I'm cooking dinner." She beamed at them.

Lucy frowned. "Do you know how to cook?"

"Of course I do." Her sister was offended by the idea that she had somehow skipped that most important skill. "I cook for my friends all the time. Plus, I'm inviting someone very special. He just moved here from Memphis but his family has roots in Tupelo."

"What's his name?" Aunt Olympia's eyes were bright with interest.

"Marcus Gibbs. His grandpa is in Daddy's club."

"I know them. Fine people. La Ronda is on the cotillion board this year and has a real fine sense of floral arrangements," Olympia said.

"He's so handsome. I want to make a good impression." Paulette paused, as if remembering this was supposed to be for Regan's romantic prospects, not her own. "And this dinner will show Jem how Southern food should taste."

Lucy was thoroughly confused now. "But Jem is from Tupelo. He knows exactly how Southern food tastes. I'm sure he's had a lifetime of fried chicken and gumbo."

"No, I mean real Southern food." Paulette tugged her phone out of her purse and tapped the screen. "I went to Xander's for dinner and they served petit crolines with duck liver and a minted lamb purse that was to die for."

Aunt Olympia reached for the phone and stared at the picture. "That might be too hard for you, Paulette. What about a nice casserole?"

"I'm not cooking shepherd's pie for my friends. How hard can those things be?" Paulette leaned over. "The petit crolines are just puff pastry sheets with duck liver inside, and then the lamb purse is just, you know, a bit of lamb in some dough." She paused. "They're sorta the same thing, actually. Maybe I should throw in a side dish."

"A fresh salad would be nice," Lucy said. "Mrs. Hardy said the heirloom tomatoes are ripe. You could slice them and arrange them in layers on one of the platters with fresh basil and—"

"That is so country." Her sister rolled her eyes. "I promised Regan that we should show Jem how real Southerners eat."

"I'm sure he's perfectly aware of how real Southerners eat because he *is* one, Paulette."

"But he's been in Boston for almost ten years and only came home once. He said his mama flew up to see him at Christmas, but otherwise he just lived up North."

Lucy wondered if he'd loved Boston so much he didn't want to leave, or if he'd hated Tupelo so much he'd never wanted to come back.

"When he's done here, I hope he stays in the South. Maybe Atlanta or Memphis."

So he wasn't staying in Tupelo. Jem would never want to live in his hometown after he was done with the Rural Physicians Program. She had suspected that, but for some reason hearing the words still made her breath catch in her throat.

"Are you having the dinner this weekend?" Aunt Olympia asked. "You'd better ask your daddy what time is best."

Paulette lifted her chin. "I mentioned it to him and he said he'd rather eat at the club. He doesn't seem to think my cooking skills are up to par."

Lucy thought it was more likely that Willy Crawford didn't want to break bread with the new doctor of the Free Clinic. Some prestige came with a medical degree, but not enough to get over her daddy's prejudice about a poor white boy from the bad part of town.

She stood up and collected the glasses. Setting them carefully in the sink, Lucy fought back a deep sigh. The more things changed, the more they stayed same, so the saying went. Jem was being accepted by the better families of Tupelo, but he would never really be forgiven for coming from a trailer park. Of course she figured none of this meant much to Jem. He hadn't cared what people thought of him then, and he didn't seem to care much now.

Rinsing the glasses under the cool water, a flash of memory made her movements slow, then still completely. She stood, staring out the kitchen window, the water running over her fingers. It had been a humid, sweltering night ten years ago, but she couldn't seem to get close enough to Jem. They stood under the trees near his home, listening to the crickets. He'd held her tight, wrapping his arms around her, and when he talked, she felt his words like a rumble against her ear. He'd whispered into her hair, so quietly she strained to hear. He said it didn't matter what anyone thought, that as long as she loved him, nothing else was important.

Lucy saw the grass of her own backyard blur into nothingness. She made herself rinse each glass and set it on the drainboard. No one else had ever asked her to be brave, to be strong, to speak out. No, he hadn't asked her; he had *expected* it. He assumed she would stand beside him when he needed her and tell the world she believed in him, in them.

Turning off the water, Lucy straightened her shoulders. She'd been convinced to do something wrong, but the guilt was hers, and hers alone. She needed to move on from the past, and the best way would be to apologize to Jem. She wasn't sure how or when, but it had to be done.

As soon as she'd made the decision, Lucy felt a strange mix of panic and resolve. Whatever happened next, at least she wasn't just sitting back and dreading the next time they bumped into each other. She would come up with a plan, and a speech, and pray for the best. Lord willing, he might just accept her apology and she would be able to get a good night's sleep for the first time since Jem Chevy had come back to town.

"I do not think I ever opened a book in my life which had not something to say upon woman's inconstancy. Songs and proverbs, all talk of woman's fickleness. But perhaps you will say, these were all written by men."
—CAPTAIN HARVILLE

CHAPTER NINE

Jem sat in his car and stared up at Crawford House. It seemed a mythical place, the long white columns glowing peach, each window reflecting the blazing sunrise. No one would be awake yet, and that was just the way he wanted it.

Yesterday afternoon he had left as early as possible. The day's patients were the usual mix of old folk under the weather and little kids battling colds, but he had been off-kilter through each appointment. Lucy's eyes haunted him every moment of that day, and he'd left without transcribing his notes. He'd spent the evening walking, thinking over their conversation, getting a grip on his emotions.

Now, in the early-morning sunlight, Jem admitted he was no closer to a peaceful resolution to the problem. He would be here, in her house. She would be here, in his clinic. They would meet, face-to-face, and there was nothing he could do to prepare himself for what he felt.

Sliding out from behind the wheel, he closed the door of his car as softly as possible. Since it was so early in the morning, Lucy was less likely to be walking through the clinic waiting room. As a bonus, he might be able to avoid Olympia, too.

The gentle scent of tea roses followed him up the flagstone path, and Jem glanced over the landscape. Crawford House had always been a beautiful spot, even when tinged with pain and regret. Thick grass covered the sloping lawn, bordered at the far end by tall hedges and edged to the right by the entrance to the vegetable garden. Lucy's mama had loved that garden, planting pole beans, okra and corn. Jem could see the tall rows of early corn and the peach trees behind them, and he wondered who tended the garden now. A truck passed by on the main road and the sound echoed through the quiet morning. The city had grown while he'd been in Boston, but Crawford House maintained a certain isolation in the middle of it all.

He climbed the steps of the porch, keeping his footsteps light. Reaching into his pocket, he pulled out his keys, feeling like a thief. Jem gritted his teeth. He had a right to be here, but there was something about sneaking into the clinic while the entire house was asleep that was worse than walking in during the day.

Lucy's room was directly above the porch, or at least it had been ten years ago. Her mama had wanted her to take a room at the front of the house, but Lucy loved the view toward the ancient elm and the low hills beyond. Jem thought of her, upstairs asleep, and felt his chest constrict. This was worse than meeting her in the middle of the waiting room. He felt as if he were trespassing on her privacy. He had never belonged here and never would, no matter what time of day it was.

"Well, looky here."

Jem whirled around at the sound, scrambling for an excuse. "I didn't mean to . . ." His words faded away at the sight of the old man in front of him. Zeke stood at the bottom of the steps, holding a hammer and grinning. His hair was completely white now, but his body still looked strong and wiry.

Jem trotted down the steps and held out a hand. "Zeke, it's good to see you again."

Zeke shook his hand solemnly, looking up into his face and letting out a chuckle. "I always knew you'd come back here."

For a moment, Jem thought he meant back to Crawford House. "Yes, sir. I'm a Tupelo boy through and through."

"Miss Lucy missed you for a long while after

you left," Zeke said as naturally as mentioning the weather.

Jem searched for something to say, but everything that occurred to him was colored with regret. He glanced over Zeke's head and motioned to the garden. "Your corn crop's looking real fine."

Zeke nodded. "It's been a good spring, lotsa rain. Hard to keep up the weedin', but it be good soil. Not too much clay."

"You're headed to the garden?"

Zeke held up the hammer. "Miss Lucy wanted me to put in a coop. Just gettin' set up."

"A coop?"

"For chickens. Miss Lucy thought it might be nice to have fresh eggs available."

Jem thought of Olympia's comment about the clinic bringing in yard birds to scratch at the grass and grinned. "Can I help you at all?"

"Naw, son. You best not." He looked him up and down, noting his pressed khakis and button-up shirt. "You go on ahead inside."

Jem was already stowing his keys back in his pocket and rolling up his sleeves. "I have hours before the clinic opens. Where are you building it?"

"In the corner, between the butter beans and the pear tomatoes," Zeke answered, as if Jem were familiar with the layout of the garden.

"Is your wood already there?"

"It's in my truck." Zeke jerked his head. "Come on, then. I don't blame you for wantin' to be outside. I couldn't stand an office job myself."

"It's not so bad." They walked back down the path toward the parking area. "I'm moving most of the time. The paperwork is a pain though."

"You don't have no secretary for that?" Zeke asked.

"Not really. Leticia handles the appointments. I still have forms to fill out." Zeke's teal-blue Ford was parked at the corner of the drive. "Why don't you move the truck up a little closer?"

"This is close enough. Miss Olympia don't like my truck in the drive so I usually park down by the cedar trees." Zeke winked. "I plan on movin' it before she get here." He took hold of a length of two-by-four and pulled it clear of the truck bed.

"Let me carry these." Jem took the board from Zeke's hands.

"You and Miss Lucy are just alike, tryin' to make things easy on old Zeke. But I'm not dead yet." Zeke took another board from the truck and hoisted it onto his shoulder.

They headed back to the garden, side by side.

"Are they already cut to the right length?"

"My boy cut 'em for me last night. He has a real nice table saw. Clean and straight, he cut all this in a half hour. Makes me think of my daddy, built his own house, cuttin' all his wood by hand."

"How old were you then?"

"Oh, shoot, knee-high to a grasshopper. I remember the smell of the fresh-cut wood, and the sound of the old handsaw. He wore out too many to count. Broke the teeth off 'em and had to buy another. But they were right costly, so my mama went to work as a maid for Colonel Mason." Zeke passed through the garden gate and trudged toward the far end. A small clearing had been mapped out with sticks planted in the dirt at the four corners.

"Was she happy there?" Jem dropped his wood to the ground.

He shrugged. "She never said much about it. I know she missed us, but we saw her on Sundays." He took out a red hanky and wiped his forehead. "When you're dirt-poor, you make hard choices."

He'd been dirt-poor, but he'd never had to make those kinds of choices. Not personally. They started back toward the truck. "Sounds like you had a good family. My mama was the same way. When I was in school, she took two jobs, one during the night and one during the day, just so I could have jeans that didn't have holes in them."

"A good mama is better than a sack o' gold." Zeke pulled a plank from the truck and swung it up onto his shoulder.

Jem followed, thinking over those words, feeling the heat of the early morning on his skin. He had a lot to be thankful for, really. He could have been surrounded by a family that stood in his way. He had a flash of Lucy's aunt Olympia endlessly listing her complaints, Paulette's permanent sneer, and Janessa's self-centered chatter. Lucy seemed to think it was her responsibility to keep everyone happy, no matter the cost to herself.

As they passed the rose garden, a blur of brown and gray darted between his legs. Jem skipped a step and jerked to a stop, narrowly missing planting a shoe on the tiny kitten. "Hey, buddy. You were supposed to go home."

Zeke turned his head. "He was here all weekend. I didn't have the heart to let him starve so I snuck him a little chitlins. I guess he's a permanent resident now."

Dropping the wood next to the growing pile of lumber, Jem had to smile. Crawford House needed a little bit of life. The benches near the garden looked neglected, and the flowers were thin around the border near the front. It was a stately place, but it was missing a certain something, a bit of joy.

Humming a few bars, Zeke started to sing, *"I saw Texas go in with a smile, but I tell you what it is, she made the Yankees bile. Oh, it don't make a nif-a-stifference to neither you nor I, Texas is the devil, boys. Root, hog, or die."*

Jem snorted. "I never knew you hated Texans."

"Don't got nothin' against 'em." Zeke grinned. "I was thinking of the 'root, hog, or die.' That kitten can't live on air. He'll be looking for food and poor little thing won't stand a chance if he runs toward all that traffic they got headin' through here now."

"True." The kitten had followed them to the garden and was sniffing through the tomato plants. The sun was barely higher than the trees, but the heat was growing.

Zeke turned back toward the truck, his thin voice rising once again. *"A hundred months have passed, Lorena, since last I held that hand in mine, and felt the pulse beat fast, Lorena, though mine beat faster far than thine."*

Jem's heart dropped into his shoes. He knew the words to that mournful Civil War tune, knew it better than any pop song on the radio. Jem walked behind Zeke, watching the old man's boots ahead of him on the path and trying to block out the words.

"We loved each other then, Lorena, far more than we ever dared to tell; and what we might have been, Lorena, had but our loving prospered well." Zeke tugged a plank from the bed of the truck and paused, letting his voice carry up into the morning air.

He turned and headed toward the garden. Jem slowly pulled the last two planks toward him, hoping to put space between him and that song. Lost love, broken hearts and homesick men far from their families.

Zeke's voice was clear as the morning sky above. *" 'Twas not thy woman's heart that spoke; thy heart was always true to me: a duty, stern and pressing, broke the tie which linked my soul with thee."*

Letting out a sigh, Jem gave in and hummed along. Except that Lucy hadn't stayed true, as far as he knew. She had just gone on with her life, the same as he had. He wondered, not for the first time, what her boyfriends had been like. Educated, wealthy, traditional and handsome. He hadn't seen anyone around Crawford House, but that didn't mean a boyfriend wasn't on the scene. He could pop up any moment, putting his hand on the back of her neck, the way some men did when they felt they had the right of possession. The idea made him feel slightly ill.

Their voices blended together, one wavering with age, one robust. They trooped through the garden gate. *"There is a Future! Oh, thank God, of life this is so small a part! 'Tis dust to dust beneath the sod, but there, up there, 'tis heart to heart."* Jem sang the last words heartily, looking up at the last note.

That's when he noticed that Lucy stood in the garden, arms wrapped around her middle, her expression a mixture of things so complicated he couldn't decipher it. Her simple outfit of a pink, button-up shirt and black slacks should have been plain, but on her, nothing was plain. Even

174

though she looked tired and solemn, she was as stunning now as she had been at the Strouds' party.

She held his gaze as he came toward her, and the words of the song seemed to echo around them. *'Tis dust to dust beneath the sod, but there, up there, 'tis heart to heart.* If only things had been different. If only they weren't doomed to awkward moments and regret, with only heaven above as a promise.

"Mornin', Miss Lucy," Zeke said. Dropping his plank to the ground, he waved Jem closer. "Come lay it down over here. I'll build the frame in a bit. Gonna be a nice big coop, off the ground, with a little ramp in the front for all them hens to run up and down."

Jem maneuvered the lengths of pine into place and let them fall onto the stack. He brushed off his dress shirt, suddenly aware of the sweat on his face. He thought of walking away, knew he should give some excuse and leave the garden, but he couldn't quite make his feet move where he wanted them.

"I heard you singing." She was looking at Jem but was speaking to both of them.

"Sorry if we woke you."

She shook her head. "I was up."

A sudden rustling from a tomato bush caught their attention and the tiny kitten emerged, tail high.

175

"I believe this kitty launched an offensive with a vital strategic objective, and won. What a smart little thing," Jem said.

"It won? It's been hanging around all weekend, but I'd say it was a class-D battle." Lucy put a finger to her chin, as if in thought. "It achieved a limited tactical objective of reconnaissance and occupation."

"It's sure taken to Crawford House like it was born to be here," Zeke said.

"Maybe it's taken to the chitlins someone left on the porch," Jem said.

"Chitlins?" Lucy cocked a brow at Zeke. "Now the battle is upgraded to a class A. Indisputable victory on the field and termination of the campaign offensive. I guess the kitty stays."

Jem scooped it up and peered into its bright eyes. "I knew it. It needs a name. How about Jubal? Rosecrans? Beauregard?"

Reaching out toward the kitten, Zeke lifted its tail. "Huh. I thought you took yourself to medical school. You better think of a name more fittin' for a lady."

Lucy laughed and Jem looked up, unable to keep himself from smiling at the sound. He loved her laugh, how it rolled through several husky pitches. "How about Harriet Tubman? She knows all the little paths through the garden that nobody else does," she said.

"Or how about Rose O'Neal Greenhow? This

176

little kitty is silent as the grave. She'd wear the name of a famous spy with dignity." Jem held her in one hand and felt the rumble of her little body as she purred. She looked up at him and he could have sworn she smiled, whiskers out and ears up.

Lucy stepped forward, slipping her hand between the kitten and Jem. He felt her touch for a moment against his chest, then it was gone as she took her turn. "No, her name is Hattie." Her voice was soft and sure. "We'll name her after Hattie Winter, the woman who fought disguised as a man."

"I better move my truck before your aunt comes by," Zeke said, moving toward the gate. "She gonna be mad enough about the yard birds."

There was a beat of silence as Zeke walked away. The conversation that had been so easy now limped to a halt.

Jem cleared his throat. "So . . . chickens." As soon as the words left his mouth, he wanted to turn around and walk away. He sounded like an idiot. He couldn't find anything better to say than "chickens"?

She nodded. "I've been reading about sustainable living and how much of our food is delivered from far away, even when we are surrounded by farmland." She rubbed Hattie's head. "We have a garden, but it only produces for nine months of the year, and I thought chickens would be a good way to supplement it."

"So it's not just a way to annoy your aunt?"

She shot him a sly look. "Maybe that, too."

They stood there, smiling at each other until the moment stretched too long.

"I should—"

"We need to—"

Another awkward pause and Jem waved a hand. "Go ahead."

"I should let you get to work."

He blinked. He'd forgotten all about his paperwork. "Right." Reaching out, he gave Hattie a scratch. "Don't chase the chickens when they get here."

"She would never." Lucy looked up. "And, Jem?"

"Yes?"

"Thanks for helping. With the wood." Her eyes traveled past him, to where Zeke had walked through the yard to the parking spot. "I know I should have hired someone younger, but Zeke isn't just the handyman."

"He's a member of the family."

"Exactly." She seemed relieved that he understood. "It's not the most practical use of the money coming in, but I felt that if we had the chance to save this old place, it was all or nothing." She moved a finger under the kitten's chin. "Either we all stay here together, or none of us."

Jem nodded. "See you later," he said, although

he wasn't sure that he would. He turned and walked out of the garden, through the gate and up to the porch. He hardly noticed the steps under his feet and the wooden rail under his fingers. He was finally doing what he should have done five minutes ago. But now it was too late. A short conversation and he understood something about Lucy that he hadn't before: she was loyal. He had thought that she was flighty and fickle, but she was the opposite. It was true that she hadn't chosen him, hadn't vowed to be with him through college and beyond, but it wasn't so much that she had refused him, as she had chosen her family instead.

He took out his key for the back door and, after several seconds of fiddling, realized it was already unlocked. Jem shoved the key back into his pocket with a sigh. Avoiding Lucy completely wasn't going to work, although he needed to get his mind off her and focus on his job. His patients deserved someone who wasn't completely distracted. As he stepped into the dim waiting room and flipped on the lights, Jem tried to shelve his emotions. He'd think about it later, when he had time to sit and brood. All of the bitterness he'd held against her, for all those years, wouldn't fade away with one offhand comment. But he had to admit that he might have been unfair, just a little, in the way he saw her rejection of him when they were just teenagers.

Jem settled behind his desk and opened the files he'd left from yesterday. He stared at the words, pen poised, thoughts far away. She was anything but disloyal. Lucy was holding this family together. He had seen how she'd watched Paulette at the party, growing more worried with every drink she consumed. Lucy had come into the clinic to shepherd Olympia back toward the family area. Lucy was making the best financial decisions she could, trying to keep Crawford House out of foreclosure, even if that meant having her old boyfriend hanging around.

He dropped his head into his hands. Lucy had been forced to choose between him and her entire family. She'd broken his heart, but now that he was older, he saw it all more clearly. The Crawfords didn't deserve Lucy, it was true. And maybe, just maybe, he couldn't have expected her to leave everything and everyone she loved to be with a boy she had only known for a summer.

For the first time in ten long years, Jem wondered if Lucy had been right after all.

Lucy stood in the garden, morning sun beating down, the smell of the tomato vines and soil wrapping around her like a memory of her childhood. Hattie snuggled into the crook of her elbow, whiskers tickling her skin. Watching Jem walk toward the house made her chest tighten with conflicting emotions. For a moment they had almost seemed as if they were friends. She shivered, remembering the way his blue eyes crinkled when he laughed and the way he carried the lumber as easily as a man, but in his face was the shadow of the boy she once knew. She would never have thought they had anything left in common, but standing here in the garden with Zeke, they could have passed for something other than enemies.

Lucy lowered Hattie to the ground. She shouldn't have stepped off the porch once she'd realized Jem was outside, but the melody of the song pulled her into the garden. Such an old, mournful tune. She didn't remember Jem singing, not really. Maybe a bit of a pop song. She remembered the way he read a poem, and his laugh, and the way his face went stony when he was scared, but never him singing.

Hattie wound around Lucy's ankles and batted at the little buckle on the side of her flats. It was just like Jem to help carry the wood for the coop. He was the sort of person who was always ready to lend a hand. She wasn't surprised to see him, really, with a length of lumber over one shoulder and the sleeves of his dress shirt rolled up. He was so handsome she hadn't been able to look away, and it stole her breath to hear his voice rising with old Zeke's in that Civil War tune.

Lucy looked out past the garden, toward the old elm trees at the edge of the property. She had never forgotten him, and all it had taken was one bit of song to reopen her heart. With a mixture of dread and wonder, Lucy faced the truth: she loved Jem.

She had always loved him, and she always would.

The evening ended with dancing.
On its being proposed, Anne offered her
services, as usual; and though her eyes
would sometimes fill with tears as she sat
at the instrument, she was extremely glad
to be employed, and desired nothing in
return but to be unobserved.
—ANNE ELLIOT

CHAPTER TEN

"No, this dinner has nothing to do with me. I already told you I'm going out." Lucy stuffed her keys in her purse and yanked on her shoes. She had managed to avoid Jem since that morning in the garden three days ago, and she was hoping to make it all the way through the weekend without another encounter.

"You have to help me! Everyone will be here in less than an hour and there's nothing to eat!" Paulette was waving her hands in the air and her voice was reaching a pitch that only dogs could hear.

"This was your idea, not mine." Lucy shouldered her purse and went for the door. If she could get out of the house, she'd be safe. No way was she going to sit through a dinner with Jem and Regan, no matter what kind of disaster Paulette had created in the kitchen. It wasn't her problem.

"Mama would have wanted you to help me," her sister said, tears muffling her words.

Lucy tried to keep walking but the guilt was too much. She paused, resting her forehead against the front door. "Maybe Mama would have wanted you to cook something easier than lamb purses or whatever you just burned to a crisp."

"I'm telling you, the recipe must have been printed wrong. I did everything the way it said to. I walked away for a second, and it just burst into flame." Paulette was back to being angry.

"So, what about the other dishes?" Lucy turned, arms folded over her chest.

"I'd planned these tiny bacon-wrapped scallops topped with black truffle butter, but the bacon must have been bad quality. It was supposed to cook just a little, then I was going to wrap it around the scallops, but it turned crispy in no time. So, then I thought I'd just cook the scallops, but they went from totally raw to little, chewy erasers. Now all I've got left is the truffle butter, and nobody can eat straight truffle butter for an hors d'oeuvres."

Lucy sighed. "What else do you have?"

Paulette chewed her lip. "I made some smoked-salmon mousse."

"So, just serve that on crackers and make some

sandwiches or something. It will be fine. Pretend it's a picnic." Lucy turned back to the door.

"But we can't eat the salmon mousse. I blended it with the sour cream and cream cheese and onion and dill and lemon juice and caviar . . . but I used *raw* salmon instead of smoked." Paulette started to cry in earnest. "When I realized it was the wrong thing, I thought maybe I could cook it, but it just turned brown and started smelling up the kitchen."

Lucy shook her head. "I don't know how to help you. I'm not even sure what's in the pantry."

"Tons of stuff." Paulette grabbed Lucy's hands and pulled her toward the kitchen. "Mrs. Hardy keeps it stocked. Just whip something together and I'll be so grateful."

"Maybe I could make some macaroni and cheese if there's enough milk in the fridge."

Her sister stopped, frown creasing her face. "Mac and cheese? That's not very fancy."

"Look, do you want me to help you or not?" Lucy wanted to reach out and give Paulette a good shake. The girl was so used to getting her own way that she didn't even know when to stop giving instructions.

Paulette let out a huff. "Fine. I'll go get ready. I brought my dress and makeup because I didn't want to cook in my nice clothes."

A moment later she was gone, and Lucy was standing alone in the kitchen. *Lord, You have quite a sense of humor.* Here she was, the one place she didn't want to be, cooking for the people she didn't want to see, and cleaning up for the sister who treated her like the hired help. But what Paulette had said was true: their Mama would have expected Lucy to lend a hand. A good Southern girl didn't walk away from a crisis, especially one involving food and guests.

Lucy slipped on the red-checkered apron that hung behind the kitchen door and grabbed two large pots. The garden was in high gear and she could find plenty of good produce. Whether Paulette's friends would be impressed by any of it was another matter altogether.

Hattie met her at the entrance of the garden, tail high. Her tiny meow was like a rebuke.

"Sorry, sweet pea. Can't stop to play. How about we look for tomatoes?" Lucy searched through the vines, tugging off the ripest ones as the kitten wound her way under the leaves and through the squares of the tomato cages. The green-bean row was next, then the cucumber patch. Lucy carried one pot to the porch and headed back to the garden. Hattie trotted beside her.

She would dearly love to cook a fabulous Southern meal and show Paulette that lamb pockets weren't the way to impress a guest, but the need to get the food prepared in a short amount of time was bigger. Lucy thought that if everything went perfectly, she could make an edible dinner and get out of the kitchen just as the guests arrived.

In the rows of corn she selected the most tender of the white, sweet variety and deftly twisted ears off the stalks. Carrying them to the corner of the garden where the compost moldered, she husked them as quickly as possible. Rubbing the ears between her hands, she cleaned the silk from between the uniform kernels.

Hattie sneezed and Lucy giggled at the strings of corn silk hanging from the kitty's ears. "Very fancy, but I think you look pretty just as you are," she said, brushing them away. Arms full, she deposited them on the porch and headed back to the garden, mentally ticking off ingredients.

When the second pot was filled to the brim with fresh vegetables, she lifted it, her back straining. She wasn't used to this kind of exercise. Sitting at a desk and reading through old diaries was making her softer than she should be. Maybe a little weight lifting in the mornings would be a good idea. Lucy felt her shoulders protest as she trudged toward the porch. Hattie was already at the back door.

"Nope. I can't have you underfoot." She tried to close the door, but somehow the kitten squeezed through an impossibly small gap and scooted underneath the old oak table.

Lucy blew out a sigh. "Fine. Just don't sit on the counter. You don't have any pants and that's highly unsanitary." She laid the colander in the sink and started to wash batches of okra, big leafy handfuls of kale and tiny cherry tomatoes. The clock was ticking and she felt the minutes slipping away, but her body relaxed into the familiar rhythms of kitchen work. She hummed as she worked, letting the smells of fresh herbs and just-picked produce work their magic on her frayed nerves.

Lifting down the copper pots from the ceiling rack, Lucy flashed back to her mama's gumbo. Mama had loved to cook, but not alone. She liked Lucy to keep her company in the kitchen, perched on one of the old oak stools. Mama would sing and Lucy would watch the dance of a woman who cooked from a recipe that was generations old.

Mama would take collard greens and lay them over good bacon and add a little water and cider vinegar, letting them simmer for hours. Most folks hated the smell of collards cooking, but Mama had learned from her mama, who had learned from her mama, that a cook should add a whole pecan to the pot so it wouldn't stink up the house.

Once that was started, Mama would work on the gumbo, whisking flour into the grease from some spicy sausage. She never left the pan, stirring and watching. It seemed to take hours until it turned a nutty brown and the scent filled the kitchen. Every now and then Mama would talk, but it wasn't clear if she was speaking to Lucy or the food. *Bouki fait gombo, lapin mangé li,* she'd say as she stirred, and Lucy would laugh, loving the old stories of the dumb goat and the trickster rabbit who always ate his gumbo. Mama had so many stories of that rabbit that Lucy started to believe she wrote them herself. Nobody could remember all of those, surely. As Lucy got older, she realized that a person held on to what was important and forgot the rest, and to Mama, those stories were as important as the lipstick she never went without.

Lucy paused, hands full of green beans, her memory flashing back to the giant pots of crawfish on the stove. Mama would squint her green eyes into the steam, her hair pulled back, frowning in concentration. The salted water was flavored and ready to receive the "mudbugs" out of their burlap sacks. *Other than an onion or maybe an ear of corn, if it wasn't alive when you threw it in, then it shouldn't be in the pot,* she'd say. Did Mama mind that Lucy didn't cook those old family recipes? Was she turning her back on her culinary heritage as surely as Paulette was?

Lucy snapped the ends of the beans faster, glancing at the clock. This whole dinner was breaking Mama's cardinal rule: don't hurry. She thought if a cook was in a hurry, you might as well just make a sandwich and go on your way, rather than risk destroying a good roux or burning a pecan pie. But Lucy didn't have the luxury of time today.

Both stoves were covered with pots, large and small, in different stages of coming to a boil. The ovens were warming. Lucy scanned the counter and blew out a breath, saying a few words of a prayer. It was a big kitchen with plenty of counter space and two working stoves, but there was only one cook. She needed about three more hands, and Hattie wasn't going to be able to fill that particular need, even as cute as she was. Everything had to go perfectly, no disasters allowed, or this meal wasn't going to happen.

She knelt down and peeked into the cabinet. There was a jar of muscadine jelly in here somewhere, she was sure of it. The kitchen was bright enough when the morning sun shone through the windows that faced east, but this late in the evening, Lucy wished for a few more overhead fixtures. Sighing, she started removing bottles and jars, moving farther and farther into storage space. Soon, her head and shoulders were deep inside, her hands reaching for the last few jars in the far corner.

A sound at the hallway door made the air stop in her lungs. She felt her eyes go wide, knowing that Paulette would never tap on the frame that way. And neither would Regan or any of their other friends. Lucy scooted backward, awkwardly shuffling along the ground, like a kitchen postulant making a backward pilgrimage on her knees. It took several more seconds to stand up and turn around. She put a hand to her forehead, feeling the sheen of sweat and the strands of her hair frizzing in the humidity.

Jem stood in the doorway. A pulse pounded in her throat. To him, this moment probably wasn't any different from the last times they'd met. For her, it was the first time she'd seen him since she understood her own heart, that no matter how much time passed, she would always be in love with him.

His light tan suit and matching vest were perfectly pressed, and the white shirt underneath was crisp and fresh. He was holding a small potted plant. Lucy raised her eyes slowly, finally meeting his gaze. He wasn't smiling. It seemed the memory of their easy banter in the garden with Zeke was long gone.

Jem looked around the kitchen, along the counters filled with produce and at the stoves crowded with bubbling pots. "I didn't realize you were cooking tonight."

"Neither did I. Paulette had a small problem with her original menu." Lucy waved a hand toward the garbage, where the charred remains of the lamb pockets were visible.

His lips tugged up in the barest version of a smile. "And you volunteered to help out."

"Not exactly." She smoothed the old apron over

her hips. "Can I get you some sweet tea? Paulette is getting ready. You could wait in the living room until she comes down."

The smile disappeared. "Do you need help?"

"Oh, no. Just throwing stuff in pots. Not hard at all." Her gaze darted at the old clock on the wall. It wasn't hard but it would take time.

He stepped into the kitchen, set the plant on the table, slipped off his jacket, and set it on the back of a chair. He started to roll up his shirt-sleeves. "I'm sure you could use another pair of hands."

Lucy said nothing. That was just what she'd been praying for, but maybe she should have been a little more specific as to which people she wanted in the kitchen.

He indicated the plant. It had a pale teal ribbon around it. "Hostess gift. I'm sure I should have brought a bottle of wine, but I was thinking about what you said in the garden."

She waited, unsure of what he'd brought her. It looked a bit like clover, with small yellow flowers.

"You probably already have peanuts," he said.

"Actually, we don't. They don't grow well in the heavy clay." It was pity. Peanuts were one of the best sustainable living crops.

Instead of being disappointed, Jem smiled. "Those are probably the Runner or Spanish peanuts. They both need sandy soil. This is a Tennessee

Red Valencia, specially bred for the soil we have here."

"Really?" Lucy's eyes went wide. She hadn't ever looked for another variety because she'd heard that peanuts didn't grow without a lot of work and soil cultivation. Neither she nor Zeke had the time to prepare a raised bed. But maybe they could grow a small crop of these. "That's a wonderful gift, thank you."

He nodded, posture relaxing the tiniest bit, as if he'd been worried about his gift. As he washed up at the sink, she noted how tan his skin seemed, the dusting of blond hair and how his forearms were muscled. The vest and the white shirt reminded her of men in old black-and-white photographs. For a moment she felt as if she were looking at a man from another era, long ago. When they were teens, he'd been tall, but sort of scrawny. He was a man now, practically a stranger. That she still loved him made no sense, but she couldn't force her heart to shut him out.

Lucy pointed to the pile of cucumbers. "I was going to slice those with some Vidalia sweet onions and—"

"Add white vinegar, salt and pepper?" He pulled a chair from the table and sat down, positioning the garbage bin between his knees. Grabbing a cucumber, he started peeling with long, swift movements. "My mama makes that dish every summer."

Lucy watched him for a moment, feeling a strange sense of déjà vu at the scene. Jem had never sat in her kitchen and certainly never peeled vegetables for dinner, but something about this moment was familiar.

She dried off the small red potatoes and brought them to the cutting board. "How is she?"

"Who?"

"Your mother." Maybe it was too personal of a question.

"Doing fine. Loves Birmingham." He placed a skinned cucumber on the counter and reached for another. He looked up at her and seemed unsure about what to say next. "I was sorry to hear your mama passed away. I know you were close."

Lucy nodded, chopping a red potato in half, then quarters. "Thank you. One moment she was frying some bacon for breakfast, singing 'In That Great Gettin' Up Mornin',' and the next she was dead." Lucy knew she sounded harsh, but she didn't think she could bear his pity right now. He would never be anything less than truly sympathetic, but she wished he would make it easier for her to keep her heart at a distance.

"That must have been real tough on everybody. Is that why you came home? To help your family adjust?"

She focused on her chopping, not wanting to explain, but not sure how to avoid the question.

"You can't convince me you flunked out," he said.

She snorted. "No, there was no flunking out." She scooped the pile of potato quarters onto a foil-lined pan and drizzled on swaths of olive oil. "It didn't take long before there wasn't the financial ability to pay for the tuition."

"But you could have gotten a scholarship, right?"

She sprinkled sea salt over the pan and popped it into an oven. She turned to look him in the eye and said, "My daddy refused to fill out the paperwork. He didn't want to turn in his tax statements, he didn't want to show his income and he certainly didn't want anyone to know his daughter was on a scholarship."

Jem's face had gone hard. "So he let people think you had to leave for academic reasons."

Neither of them said anything for a moment. It was completely unfair, she had to agree, but nothing could be done about it now.

"It doesn't bother you?" He stood up and seemed much taller than she remembered. Maybe it was the close quarters, or how his eyes had gone dark with emotion.

"Of course it does." She shrugged. "What could I do?"

He stared at her, as if trying to decide whether she was serious. "You could have become independent, tried to get in by yourself on a scholarship, something." His voice had risen and he ran a hand through his hair, making it stand up straight in the front.

"And where would I go in the summer? What about Christmas?" She crossed her arms. It was easy for Jem to play the what-if game now. At the age of nineteen, she had broken her own heart and lost her mama in the same year. Lucy hadn't been thinking about declaring her independence. She had just been trying to survive.

"You could have made new friends. They would have become your family."

She shook her head. "Nobody *becomes* your family. It doesn't work that way. You're born into a family, and you'll be part of it until you die."

Something flickered behind his eyes. He shrugged. "Maybe you're right."

Lucy turned back to the stove, checking the pots and fighting to regain her footing. Why did chopping vegetables have to turn into a deeply emotional review of choices made ten years ago? She felt tired, as if she'd run too far, too fast.

"What next?" His tone was subdued, and when she glanced at his face, the animation was gone from his eyes. He was carefully polite now, like any other summer-evening dinner guest helping out in the kitchen.

She swallowed back a wave of pain. She didn't want to talk about the past, but working side by side with Jem without saying anything meaningful was worse than fighting. "I've got to boil the macaroni and get the cheese grated."

"Macaroni and cheese, roasted red potatoes, cucumber salad, sweet corn . . ." He ticked them off one by one, his mouth turning up in a smile. "This is quite a feast."

"Don't forget green beans, blackberry cobbler, heirloom tomatoes. Paulette won't be happy because it's not fancy food, but it's better than raw-salmon mousse." Lucy couldn't help but mirror his smile as he took in her words. Maybe the way to a man's heart truly was through his stomach. It seemed as if their disagreement was forgotten the moment he focused on the cooking. "We've only got about half an hour left. I'll put the green beans and corn in now. If you'll grate the cheese, that would be a big help."

Jem had his head in the refrigerator before she was done speaking. She put the grater on the counter and took out the cast-iron skillets.

He glanced over and asked, "Cornbread or biscuits?"

Her throat went tight. She'd been thinking that cornbread would be easiest, but now that the moment was here, she couldn't imagine making that dish in front of Jem.

"You know I like cornbread. Preferably with cracklins." He gave her the barest hint of a wink.

Lucy thought her heart would pound out of her chest. Was he flirting with her? He couldn't be.

Could he? She cleared her throat. "I was thinking of biscuits."

He nodded. "That sounds good, too."

They worked in silence for a while. Lucy gathered the mustard, paprika and pepper for the macaroni and cheese. Her thoughts were tripping over each other, filling her with confusion and the barest hint of hope. That garden-party nightmare from so many years ago was one of the defining moments in their relationship. Her family had snubbed him, and she had failed to stand by him, physically and figuratively. Only days later she was telling him good-bye and that it would never work out between them. She had been persuaded to believe that they were from two different worlds and their love was doomed from the start, all because of a social misstep in a foil-covered pan. The cracklin' cornbread memory was irredeemably painful for both of them. Wasn't it?

If Jem could laugh about that cornbread episode, then maybe he didn't hate her after all. She was afraid to hope that what lived in her memory as one of the lowest moments of her life, flawed with prejudice and failure, wasn't the same for him. She took a breath, wondering if now was the right moment to tell him she was sorry, that she regretted that moment with all her heart. Maybe it was possible that he could forgive. Maybe he already had and all she needed was to say the words before he told her he was past that horrible night.

"I'm looking forward to your presentation next week," he said.

Lucy let out a breath. Sadly, the Civil War was a much safer subject between the two of them. "It certainly brings out the history buffs. I don't like speaking in front of a crowd, but I do enjoy meeting the people who collect the paraphernalia as a hobby. You probably know more about battlefield medical care than I do."

He started to slice the large yellow heirloom tomatoes, layering them carefully on a platter. "Not really. I suppose I know a bit about it because of the reenactments, but I won't be able to tell you the difference between the metacarpal knife and the amputation scalpel unless they're the same instruments we use today."

The idea of having to actually use those tools on a patient in any era made her stomach turn. She watched him slide the sharp kitchen knife through the tomatoes, gently but confidently. She wondered what training he'd had in surgery and how much he'd had to work with cadavers, then wished she hadn't thought about it. She shivered even though the kitchen was sweltering. "You always did have a strong constitution."

He shrugged. "For medical procedures, sure. But everyone has a weak spot."

She dropped vegetable shortening into a bowl

full of biscuit ingredients and said nothing. She wondered what his was, then was irritated at herself for wondering. She supposed her real weak spot was Jem. Life would be as steady and dependable as it could be, but as soon as he appeared, she felt as if she were sitting on an emotional time bomb. For every moment he was near her, she felt it tick-tick-ticking away until just the wrong word or a playful wink sent her into a tailspin.

"Do you know a lot of the reenactors?" he asked.

"Sure. A great group of guys. It's a source of pride that they're as historically accurate as possible. Jimmy Hewitt made his own uniform last year and his ego got taken down a peg or two. He sewed a black cord on the side of his trousers instead of a flat black ribbon. He was careful to make sure the hem and cuffs of his captain's uniform were orange for an artilleryman, but the horsehair plume on his hat was red."

Jem raised an eyebrow.

"For his rank, the plume should match the cuffs," she explained. "So, poor Jimmy had the hat of a colonel, the coat of a captain and the trousers of a major general. They kept asking him how many men he had to rob to make one outfit."

Jem chuckled and Lucy dropped her eyes to the bowl. He was a good-looking man on an ordinary day. He'd been blessed with all the traits of the classically handsome, but when he laughed, everything changed. The lines around his eyes, the way his smile wasn't a bit halfhearted, and the indents on either side of his mouth that weren't quite dimples, it made her want to weep.

She mixed the dough, forcing herself to take deep breaths. "Could you hand me the milk?"

He reached into the fridge and passed her the jug. "Civil War buffs are more dedicated to the costumes than any other group, I think."

"Maybe so, but my cousin is getting married next month and having a Jane Austen reception. We'll all be dressed in those high-waisted gowns. My aunt says we'll look like we're wearing potato sacks."

"I'm sure you'll be beautiful. . . ."

She shot a look at his face and handed back the milk jug. He said it so easily that either he was throwing her an empty compliment or he really did think she would look nice. She wished she knew his "tells," the little movements that betrayed his true feelings. She'd known them once, long ago.

"As for me, I'll be standing around in a Mr. Darcy outfit."

Shock went through Lucy, and for a moment she couldn't find the words. "You're going to be in Rebecca's wedding?"

Jem nodded. "Tom was a friend of mine in high school."

"Tom, Rebecca's fiancé? Was your friend in

high school?" She knew she was repeating him, but none of this made sense.

"He works in Miami now, and his girlfriend is from DC, but she teaches at Midlands. They thought they'd—"

"Meet in the middle." Lucy finished for him, almost to herself. They would be witnessing the marriage of a couple who had overcome everything they hadn't. "I'll be a bridesmaid."

"And I'll be a groomsman." He glanced at her face, his blue eyes shadowed, then looked over her shoulder at someplace on the wall. His brows were drawn together. "Small towns. You know what they say."

She wasn't sure what they said, but she knew that it was just her luck that Jem would be in the wedding party.

"What about this?" He held up a bundle of fresh parsley.

She nodded, trying to refocus on the dinner. "Maybe use the kitchen shears. I was going to add them to the potatoes when they came out of the oven. And then you could cut the sage, too. I thought I'd fry some in a pan with butter for the corn."

Dusting the cutting board with flour, she turned out the dough and started to knead it. He reached across her for the shears and she took a step back, but not quickly enough. He smelled clean, with just a hint of cologne. She cleared her throat and wondered how she smelled. Probably like garlic and dirt from the garden, if she was lucky. The steam from the pots was coating the kitchen surfaces, and she knew she must be a sweaty mess.

Seconds later, she realized he was awkwardly cutting the parsley, shears held in his right hand. "Wait, there's another pair." She indicated the drawer with one dough-covered hand.

"These are fine."

"I know, but Mrs. Hardy is left-handed, too."

He looked up, surprised. She wondered if his expression was because the Crawford family cook was a southpaw or because he thought she'd forgotten that he was left-handed. He pulled out the left-handed shears. "Better." He flashed a smile.

"I told Mrs. Hardy that left-handers are more likely to be artists or musicians. She said she couldn't carry a tune in a bucket with a lid and couldn't draw a circle to save her life. I think she might have been exaggerating."

There was that laugh again. Lucy was caught between reveling in the sound and wishing with all her heart he wouldn't make it. "I think that's a myth. I'm as scientifically oriented as they come."

"But you're also creative." She kneaded the dough a few times and decided it was ready to roll out.

"How so?" He seemed honestly confused.

"You don't . . . I thought . . ." She half turned, one hand cupping a bit of flour. "You used to love open-mike night at Gary's."

"Oh, well, spoken poetry is different. Everybody likes that."

"No, they don't." She hoped her tone was offhand. She didn't dare look him in the face. They had met there, in a dark room filled with a small group of people glorying in the power and beauty of words. "Not here."

"Did you know when they had the national poetry-slam competition in Boston the tickets sold for hundreds of dollars and the stadium was filled to capacity?" He scooped the parsley into a bowl and reached for the sage. "We had to camp out in line for two days just to make sure we got tickets."

Lucy searched through the drawer for the biscuit cutter. He hadn't camped out in line alone. He'd been with friends. Maybe a girlfriend. Her throat went tight. She hadn't been to a poetry slam since he'd left. Her friends had invited her to open-mike night at Cantab Lounge when she was at Harvard, but she couldn't bear to go.

"We were packed in, shoulder to shoulder, like a bunch of poetry-loving sardines, breathing in the same words." He shook his head. "I'd never known so many people loved poetry. In this town it was like having a third eye. Something you kept under your hat if you could, until you were around the other folk who were just as weird as you were."

She twisted the biscuit cutter, using her wrist the way her mama had taught her, repeating the motion over the wide slab of dough. What was so unique to Jem, what had brought them together, was common in a big city such as Boston. She wondered if that was how he saw her now. Maybe there were a thousand girls like Lucy out there. Now he knew better than to think she was anything special.

"Is the Red Hen still open?" he asked.

"I think so." Her heart skipped a beat at the name. It was the place he had first asked her out. He said it as if it meant nothing to him, as if it were just another club.

"I loved that place." He set the bowl of chopped sage beside the parsley and went to the sink to rinse the shears. "Friday nights were wild. You'd think ten poets in a contest wouldn't take five hours, but I remember it'd be one in the morning before they crowned the winner."

She remembered walking home with him, under a half-moon, ears ringing with leftover words and heart aching with the beauty of it all. "My daddy accused me of hanging out in a jive joint."

"Like a blues hall?" Jem was smiling. "Well, that would have been fun, too."

Fun. She laid the biscuits on the greased sheet and slid them into the oven. She should have been glad that he wasn't harboring bitterness toward her, but she wished just for a moment that their summer together had been more than fun.

"Are you almost done? They're going to—" Paulette, who had been talking before she even made it into the kitchen, broke off at the sight of Jem. Although the soft curls of her updo gave her an effortlessly sophisticated look, her red dress was so tight Lucy thought she could see Paulette's belly button. Paulette's mouth dropped open and she looked from Lucy to Jem and back. "What on earth?"

Jem wiped his hands on a kitchen towel. "I'm sorry I'm so early."

"No, that's not a problem at all. I'm just shocked that Lucy made you help in the kitchen."

"She had her hands full in here. I was glad to help." He looked around and started to roll down his sleeves.

"Jem brought us a peanut plant for the garden," Lucy said, pointing to the tiny pot.

"Peanuts?" Paulette cocked her head and stared at it. "I didn't know they grew on a bush. I thought they came from a tree."

Lucy caught Jem's eye for just a moment and almost laughed. His expression was part shock and part confusion. She wanted to tell him that Paulette really was that ignorant, and not just about legumes, but that would be unkind.

"Well, thank you for the plant. I'll be sure to put

it in a sunny window." Paulette flashed a brilliant smile and waved him through the doorway. "Go ahead to the living room. I'll bring out the drinks."

As soon as he was down the hallway, Paulette, eyes wide, turned to Lucy and hissed, "What are you thinking?"

"What did you want me to do?" Lucy grabbed the butter and dumped it in the skillet with the sage. The kitchen seemed to shrink, the steam and mess pressing in on her as soon as Jem had gone.

Paulette took a tray from the cabinet and set six martini glasses on it. "Something. Anything. I can't believe you gave him a job like he was a kitchen slave."

Lucy paused, briefly closing her eyes and counting slowly in her head. She hated when Paulette threw around words like *kitchen slave* as if they had no connection to her race or her family history. "I think everything is almost done. I'll drain the corn and put the top back on so it stays hot. The cheese is grated so I'll mix it up and stick it in the oven as soon as the biscuits are out. Then I've got to go."

"You can't leave yet. I'll be entertaining in the living room and can't be running back and forth to the kitchen. Daddy says a good hostess stays with the guests." Paulette looked furious. "You said you would help but the table isn't even set."

Lucy poured milk into a bowl and grabbed the bag of flour. "I'm mixing up the cobbler. When the potatoes are ready, put them in a serving bowl. Put in the cobbler and set the timer for an hour. It should be done right around the time dinner is over."

"Wait, I can't remember all this," Paulette said, sounding panicked.

"You just listen for the beeping."

"I don't know why you said you'd help if you're going to leave me in this mess. The man I invited tonight might really be the one." Paulette sucked in a shaky breath.

"If this guy is the one, he's not going to care if you have to take something out of the oven."

"Daddy said he'd come back early from the club and meet him. I want everything to go perfectly, and you're trying to make it a big disaster." Paulette was near tears. "Oh, I get it. You're mad because I showed up and Jem realized he didn't have to stay here in the kitchen."

Lucy just shook her head. Melted butter, sugar, a pinch of salt. She focused on the ingredients in the large white bowl in front of her instead of the words coming out of Paulette's mouth.

"You have to stay at least until I get the drinks served. I can't do both at the same time." Paulette reached into the fridge for a bag of cut pineapple and strawberries.

Lucy shrugged. "If it takes less than five

minutes, I'll be here. Otherwise, you'll have to figure it out."

Paulette let out a grunt of anger and left the kitchen, bag of fruit under her arm and the tray of glasses balanced in her hands. Lucy grabbed a bag of blackberries from the freezer and stood for a moment, letting the cold air billow out in white clouds, chilling her flushed skin. A few more minutes and she could sneak out the back. She'd done her duty, and now it was time to get as far away from this dinner as possible.

Thus much indeed he was obliged to acknowledge—that he had been constant unconsciously, nay unintentionally; that he had meant to forget her, and believed it to be done. He had imagined himself indifferent, when he had only been angry; and he had been unjust to her merits, because he had been a sufferer from them.
—CAPTAIN WENTWORTH

CHAPTER ELEVEN

Jem stood at the long window and looked out at the rose garden. He could never have imagined when he left Tupelo that he would stand in this spot, waiting for dinner, being served drinks in the living room. He'd thought moving the Free Clinic to Crawford House would be as bizarre as it could get, but he'd been wrong.

"Do you like martinis?" Paulette went on without waiting for his response. "I just love a good martini. Would you rather have a Deep Blue Sea or a Gummy Worm?"

He turned, glancing over the liquor bottles and fruit-juice containers. "I'm not much of a drinker. If you have water—"

"No, this is a party," she said, laughing. "My daddy says you should always have party drinks. I'll make myself a Glamour Girl and you can taste it. I can double the peach schnapps for yours if you like it." She mixed ingredients in a shaker, listing a constant stream of drink descriptions like a commercial voice-over to the action.

A few minutes later, she was done, popping a maraschino cherry into the light-pink drink. "Here. Try it." She held it out to him.

Jem shook his head, trying to force his face into a friendly smile. "Go ahead, if that's your favorite."

"True, you probably don't want to get caught holding one of these. They're not very manly." She giggled. Taking a gulp, she set it back on the sideboard. "Let me make you something else."

He wandered to the bookshelf while she worked, half listening to her descriptions of the bars around Tupelo and the bartenders she liked the best and which bouncers were the cutest. He looked over the titles, pausing to touch the spine of a worn copy of W. H. Auden poetry.

"This is probably more your style." She handed him a bright-blue drink with a triangle of pineapple stuck jauntily to the top. She glanced at the shelf and shook her head. "Better not touch those. Lucy will string you up from the nearest tree."

"She doesn't like anyone else to read them?" He

frowned at the books. They looked old, for sure, but leather books could last hundreds of years with good care.

"I needed a few pages for this project and she freaked out." Paulette rolled her eyes and popped a maraschino cherry into her mouth.

"A few pages?"

"I saw the cutest thing on Pinterest where you took a marker and blocked out words to make a poem. I thought if I used a poetry book, it would be easier because, you know, it's already a poem."

"So, how did it work out?"

"Um, well." Paulette took another sip and shrugged. "It's hard to make a poem out of just a few words, so I left maybe half of them, just the ones I liked. It didn't look as pretty as the picture I saw, even though I chose this one book because the paper was nice and yellow."

Jem felt his eyes go wide. "You didn't make a copy? You marked up the page right in the book?"

"No, I took the page out first, silly." She laughed a little, as if he weren't catching on. "Otherwise the pen would leak over everything else. Anyway, I don't understand why Lucy had to get so upset about it. She acted like I'd stabbed someone. She acts like old things are better than anything modern. Our daddy doesn't care about any of these old books. I don't know why she should."

"Which book was it?"

She frowned into her glass. "I can't remember.

But the poem I used was about a girl walking in beauty and about stars in her eyes."

"'She Walks in Beauty' by Lord Byron?" Jem could almost see Paulette happily taking a Sharpie marker to the pages of a hundred-year-old poetry book. And he had no trouble imagining Lucy's response. He wanted to laugh but it was too awful, in the end, to think of that kind of treasure defaced.

There was a knock at the door and Paulette rushed to open it. Regan passed through, pausing for hugs, and they exclaimed loudly over each other's hair and clothing. Regan wore a long, flowing skirt paired with a barely there halter top and jeweled sandals. She looked beautiful. Her skin was perfectly smooth and tan, and when she turned for a moment, he saw that the halter was backless. At least she wouldn't be too warm. He thought of Lucy in the kitchen, working over the steaming pots in a T-shirt and jeans.

Regan handed Paulette a small package. "Just a little somethin' for you."

Paulette tore off the paper and admired the patterned luggage tags. "I love Peachy Fontaine Boutique. Oh, and they have my initials on them. You are always so thoughtful. You pick the perfect gifts."

There was the sound of another car. "Here's Marcus," Paulette exclaimed, waving madly out the door.

A movement caught Jem's attention and he saw Lucy at the living-room doorway, trying to slip unobserved toward the side table that was crowded with drinks. He tried to catch her eye, but her head was down, gaze scanning the area. He wondered what she was doing, then glimpsed a small purse on the floor, which Paulette must have dropped to make room for the martini ingredients.

Regan came toward him, smiling. "I'm glad you could make it." She leaned forward and Jem moved his glass, putting out an arm to give her a half hug, but she slipped her hands under his jacket and kissed him on the lips.

"You hardly return my calls and I'm worried you're working too much." Regan pouted, her perfectly plump bottom lip pushed out.

Jem tried to step back, but his heel hit the bookshelf. He hadn't answered her calls because she said she wanted to chat and it hadn't seemed a high priority. Plus, he remembered her chatter from the Strouds' party. He could only take so much. Regan smelled good, but her perfume was overpowering, sort of like everything else about her. He shifted, trying to lift his drink into her field of vision. "I don't want to spill this on your outfit."

"Oh, I'd forgive you." She gave him a little squeeze and then let her hands rest at his hips for a moment.

Jem felt his face go hot. He wasn't a prude, but

Regan was making him uncomfortable. If she thought this was flirting, she was wrong. If he acted like this with his receptionist, he'd be fired. If he acted like this with *any* woman, he'd be a first-class jerk.

A deep voice cut through the awkward moment: "Is the party already started?" Jem saw a handsome African American man in the doorway, surveying the room as if he'd been given the deed to the place. He wasn't tall, but he was well built and wearing a pressed polo shirt. He looked as if he'd just walked away from a round of golf with the mayor.

"It has now," Paulette said, giving him a peck on the cheek. "Come on in and I'll make you a martini."

Lucy had paused in her search and stood watching Marcus enter the living room. Something about her expression made his chest go tight.

"Hi, Regan, good to see you again." Marcus received a kiss on the cheek, looked past her to Jem and held out a hand. "And our new doctor. It's a pleasure to meet you. I admire your dedication to the poor of the area." Marcus's accent was purely local, but his bearing spoke of wealth and education.

"Jacob Stroud has worked with the Free Clinic for almost twenty years. That's real dedication, and I'm honored to work with him."

"I know the Strouds. I missed the fund-raising party. My father asked me to fill in for him on an important business meeting in New York City."

"Oh, I've always wanted to go shopping on Fifth Avenue," Regan sighed. "Did you pick up anything nice?"

"I'm afraid it was business only"—Marcus glanced back to Paulette and smiled—"but there may be a pleasure trip in my future."

Paulette beamed at him.

"I almost forgot. A little something." He handed a large bag to Paulette.

"Hmm. All the good gifts come in small boxes," she said as if joking, but it was clear to Jem that she was serious. It couldn't be a piece of jewelry in a bag that large. He realized that his peanut plant was not even close to an acceptable hostess gift. It had made sense at the time, actually seemed almost perfect, but now it seemed like something a country kid would bring his grade-school teacher.

Paulette peeked into the bag and gasped. Pulling out a canvas, she held it up. "Look, it's me!"

The photo was an overly Photoshopped version of Paulette, with much larger eyes and perfect skin about five shades lighter than her real self.

Marcus said, "There's a company that will make a canvas from your Instagram photos. So I thought, what better gift for you than one of your pretty selfies?"

Lucy made a sound that was part snort, part laugh, and covered her mouth with her hand.

"And this is . . . ?" Marcus cocked his head and waited to be introduced to Lucy. Her T-shirt had a small stain on the sleeve and her face still bore a sheen of sweat, but she was beautiful despite it all.

"Oh, that's my sister." Paulette handed Marcus his drink and quickly crossed to Lucy. She grasped her wrist and whispered in her ear. Lucy rolled her eyes and said something Jem couldn't hear, pointing to the table. Paulette trotted over and grabbed Lucy's purse.

"And does your sister have a name?" Marcus asked, laughter in his voice.

There was an awkward pause, where Paulette pushed the purse at Lucy instead of responding.

"I'm Lucy. I just forgot my keys were in here. I'll be out of your way now. Have a good dinner." She gave a polite smile and turned toward the hallway, not meeting Jem's eyes.

Watching her walk away without even acknowledging her generosity seemed wrong. "Lucy cooked the meal," Jem said.

"I'm Marcus Gibbs. And you're leaving us? You have somewhere to be?" He managed to sound welcoming in a way that Paulette would never achieve, no matter how many cotillion classes she took.

"Thank you, but I should go." Lucy shouldered

her purse and flashed a smile, this one a little more sincere.

Marcus crossed the living room. His accent seemed to deepen as he spoke to Lucy. "And I think I recognize you from Brice's Crossroads."

Surprise flashed across her face. "I'm the curator."

"I haven't been there myself, but our company owns the state travel magazine, and I saw the article about y'all last month. I hear there's a new exhibit coming about the women who disguised themselves as men so they could fight."

With just a few words, Marcus had ignited a spark in Lucy. Her gaze was bright with interest as she said, "By the end of the month we'll have it set up. We've acquired original photographs, letters and a very important diary."

"I can't wait to see it." Marcus stood about six inches taller than Lucy and they looked perfect together, like a couple from a website advertisement for singles. She was curvy and perfectly proportioned, matching Marcus's wide shoulders and muscled build. Both casually dressed but undeniably attractive.

Jem was suddenly aware of his vest and white button-up shirt, wishing he had chosen something less formal. A cold lump settled in his gut. He would never find the right note for these parties. You had to be born into it to understand when you came dressed in a polo shirt and when you came in a three-piece suit. There was a code to every move they made, and this poor boy from the run-down trailer park across the tracks would never crack it.

"Stay for dinner. I won't be able to eat if you leave after all your work," Marcus said.

"Well . . ." Lucy paused.

"We won't have enough. Right, Lucy?" Paulette looked alarmed and moved to place herself between Marcus and her sister.

Jem knew he should say there was plenty. With the pot of corn and dishes in the oven, there would be plenty for five people. He was ashamed of himself, but he didn't want Lucy to stay, not now. He said nothing.

"We can split a plate," Marcus said. "I had a late lunch at the club."

Paulette nudged Lucy closer to the doorway.

Jem was suddenly reminded of how many times he had felt subtly shut out of the nice places. How much worse it was for Lucy to hear it said so plainly, in her own living room. Jem felt his cheeks go hot with shame. He had his own reasons for wishing that she would leave, but he couldn't stand by and smile while she was so badly treated.

"There's plenty. Lucy could feed a small army with what she managed to make in one hour," Jem said.

Lucy looked up, surprise in her eyes.

"See? It's all decided." Marcus beamed.

A faint beeping sounded and Paulette sighed. "If you're staying, you'd better go get the food out of the oven."

"Let me help." Marcus was already headed down the hallway before Lucy turned and followed.

Jem watched them until they were out of sight. His gaze fell on the cold martini in his hand. The garish teal color reminded him of the Popsicles he'd loved when he was a kid, but hardly ever got to have because even quarters added up fast for a poor family without a dad. The gas station on the corner sold them out of a little white case in the front of the store, and on the first Sunday of the month he would take the money he earned doing chores around the trailer park and buy a blue one. His mama asked him every month if he wanted to try another flavor, but he never did. He knew the blue was good, and he didn't want to waste his quarter on something that he might not like.

Regan let out a huff of air and put a fist on her hip. "Well, that stinks."

"Totally not surprised." Paulette crossed the room. "She has zero social life. As soon as he mentioned Brice's Crossroads, I knew she would never leave."

"But they don't have anything in common," Regan said. "He's a businessman and she works in that old museum."

"She's real good at making people like her when

she wants to. She just doesn't care enough to make an effort, usually. Maybe she's decided to finally get a husband." Paulette drained her glass.

Regan slipped her hand through the crook of Jem's arm. "It's just wrong that she stole your date. That's not a very nice thing for a sister to do."

If Jem hadn't been completely sure before, he knew now that Regan was laying claim to him. This was a double date . . . except that now Lucy had disappeared with Paulette's very eligible catch.

"I'm not going to pitch a fit. I'm a better person than that. The right guy will come along. My daddy says he can't wait to see me happily married, and that day is going to be the best day of my life." Paulette smoothed her hair and lifted her chin. "Aren't you going to try your drink?" she said to Jem, apparently realizing for the first time that he hadn't even sipped his martini.

He glanced down and nodded. "Sure am." He'd spent his childhood making perfect choices because there was no room for error, but he wasn't eight years old anymore. It didn't matter if he bought the orange Popsicle and hated it. He could always buy another.

Letting the liquid slide down his throat, he winced at the burn and the sickly sweet aftertaste. When he was a teenager, Jem had settled on the idea of Lucy and never looked elsewhere. But he was a man now and he should look around more, even date a few women who might not work out.

He smiled down at Regan. She was pretty, in an overly cosmetic sort of way. Being her date for this dinner wouldn't be as bad as sitting here alone, watching Lucy "turn on the charm" for Marcus. He didn't have to be careful with her, didn't have to be on his guard at all. Falling for Regan would take a lot of work. Although it wasn't quite what his mama had meant, Jem was sure that spending time with Regan was safer than anything else he could do.

He swallowed the rest of the martini in a gulp. No, he had spent too much of his life being cautious. He was almost thirty and was still playing it safe. Maybe Regan was right about working too hard. Maybe it was time to stop being so serious and have a little fun.

When the evening was over, Anne could
not but be amused . . . nor could she help
fearing, on more serious reflection, that,
like many other great moralists and
preachers, she had been eloquent on a
point in which her own conduct
would ill bear examination.
—ANNE ELLIOT

CHAPTER TWELVE

"Thank you for helping carry the food," Lucy
said. She tried to ignore the fact she was wearing
a T-shirt that probably had a little bit of every dish
on it and did her best to be gracious. Of all the
people she thought she'd meet tonight, she hadn't
planned on the Southern version of the Old Spice
guy. Figured.

"Not a problem." He flashed that smile and she
focused on putting one foot in front of the other.
"We'll get these on the table and then you can go
change."

She appreciated his thoughtfulness. It was
going to be a little awkward to sit at a dinner she
hadn't really been invited to, but it would be even
worse to sit there in her grubby clothes. She shut

off the oven timer and opened the door. Waves of cheesy-smelling goodness wafted into the kitchen. Using her mama's red-checkered hot pads, she carefully pulled the casserole dish from the oven and set it on the stove. The top was browned and perfectly crusty. Lucy's stomach rumbled and she realized she hadn't eaten since breakfast.

Taking a platter from the cupboard, she started to lay out the corncobs. Marcus held out one hand and she let him take over. She slid the cobbler into the oven and set the timer again.

"Is the fried-sage butter for the corn?" Marcus leaned over the little dish and inhaled. "My grandma makes it this way, too."

"Really? I thought it was just a low-country-Louisiana dish."

"She was from Cane River," he said, grinning.

Lucy's eyes went wide. "So was my mama."

"There you go." He leaned against the counter and regarded her. "I knew we'd have a lot in common."

Lucy could have pointed out that Marcus would have had this in common with Paulette, too, but she didn't. She mirrored his grin for a few seconds, then realized they weren't getting much done in the kitchen. She turned back to the stove, still smiling.

"I think we'll need to take a few trips," he said. "Let me carry the platter."

Paulette seemed to be working on a steady

stream of martini concoctions and barely acknowledged them as they passed the living room. Within a few minutes they'd transferred all the dishes to serving bowls and set them on the long table in the formal dining space. The polished mahogany reflected the light from the chandelier and was decorated with enormous floral arrangements of tropical flowers. Lucy wasn't sure if they were real or fake, but she knew that they would make it hard to see over to the person on the other side.

The airy room was stuffy and she wondered why Paulette didn't have the dinner out on the covered porch. The fans there kept the air circulating, and the view of the garden was refreshing. Then again, the lush decor was more Paulette's style.

"I'll be right back," Lucy said to no one in particular, but Marcus threw her a smile. Seconds later, as she ran up the stairs, she wondered how he had known she lived here, but then she shrugged it off. Paulette must have told him. She rooted through her drawers and closet, spilling clothes onto the bed. She didn't have many clothes, but what she did have were firmly in one of two camps: vintage formal wear from the attic, and simple office clothes. She let out a sigh and forced herself to think. Was it better to wear what she had on? It wasn't flashy, but then, she was never really fashionable.

The sudden vision of sitting at dinner between

Paulette and Regan decided it. Jem was heart-stoppingly handsome in that vest, and she couldn't stand the thought of sitting there in a business skirt and jacket. Lucy grabbed a hanger out of her closet and held up one of her mama's old dresses from when she was in high school. A sleeveless, button-up shirtdress with a Peter Pan collar didn't seem so fancy, but the miniature rosebuds on a teal background added a bit of romantic whimsy. Lucy touched the little pearl buttons and smiled. She'd never seen her mama wear the dress, but Lucy could imagine how it set off the green of her mama's eyes.

Taking the dress into her bathroom, Lucy stripped off her clothes and did a five-second version of a bath, praying she didn't smell like sweet onions and sage. Slipping the dress over her head, she buttoned it up and gazed at herself in the mirror. The sheer overlay on the top was carefully sewn with tiny pintucks and fit her perfectly. She couldn't do anything for her hair. It had been ages since she'd been to the salon. She'd meant to go, but never seemed to get around to it. She wetted it down and ran her fingers through it, letting it curl naturally into small ringlets. Swiping on a bit of sheer lipstick and some mascara, she took a deep breath. It wasn't fancy, but it would have to do.

When she arrived in the dining room, she tried not to notice how close Regan was sitting to

Jem on the settee. He certainly didn't seem to mind the way she rested her hand on his thigh. Lucy felt her jaw clench and hated herself for caring. She glanced away, but not before an expression crossed his face that seemed shuttered and angry.

Marcus glanced up and let out a low whistle. "That there is a mighty fine dress."

She smiled at the compliment. "It was one of my mama's. I think she sewed it herself."

Paulette made a sound in her throat. "Lucy is concerned with recycling products. She feels the world is being crushed under a mountain of trash."

"No," Lucy said. "I just don't think we should throw out anything that can still be used."

"Even if it's fifty years out-of-date." Paulette smirked.

"They say all styles eventually come around again." Marcus pulled out a chair and motioned Lucy to sit. "And some women can wear anything and look fabulous."

"I already have everybody arranged," Paulette said, rushing over. She pointed to the chair at the very end for Lucy.

Lucy slid into her place, half smiling at how she was separated from the group by an empty chair on each side, just like that darker brother sent to the kitchen in the poem. Poetry really did seem to fit every occasion, at least in her life.

Paulette settled Jem and Regan side by side near the windows, with Marcus at one end and herself to his right.

Paulette surveyed the dishes. "I guess this is the best we could do under the circumstances, but sometime soon I'll have to have you all back for a real dinner."

"I haven't had a home-cooked meal like this for months," Marcus said. "My mother is on the Tupelo City Hospital board and she's always at some meeting. Our cook is good, but she's from somewhere in Mexico, and even though she says she follows the recipes, they're not quite the same."

Lucy took a sip of her iced tea and glanced at Jem. He was waiting for something and she scanned the table, watching the others scoop out green beans and pluck ears of corn from the platter. Then she realized he was waiting for grace.

"Should we pray?" she asked.

Paulette froze, her fork halfway to her mouth. Marcus obediently folded his hands.

Regan moved her fingers back from her biscuit and nodded. "Well, of course. Jem, will you say grace?"

"Sure." He made the sign of the cross and recited a short prayer about gifts about to be received from God's bounty, made another sign of the cross, and it was over.

Lucy fought back a laugh. Apparently Regan wasn't familiar with Jem's religious background because her mouth was hanging open. Paulette pretended as if nothing strange had just happened, but the smile fixed to her face seemed a bit too wide. Lucy was very sure that no other Catholic had ever offered grace at the Crawford House table in her lifetime.

"So, you're Catholic." Marcus nodded as if he'd made an important discovery. "That must have been hard when you were growing up."

"How so?" Jem asked.

"You probably felt sort of lonely, left out." Marcus looked to Paulette for support. "I'm sure there aren't many Catholics in Tupelo."

"There are a few. In high school, my friend Lars went to the same church I did. He's running river tours on the Sampit River and lives in Greenwood. He comes back here every now and then." Jem took a bite of a biscuit and smiled. "These are perfect. Lucy, you did a great job. I haven't had food this good since I came back to town."

"You're very welcome," she answered, hearing the breathiness in her voice. She cleared her throat. She needed to remember that she was a professional woman. It seemed as if all it took was a compliment on her biscuits and a smile from Jem and she was thrilled to pieces. It was hard to fight almost thirty years of training to be a good Southern woman, but she was determined to be admired for more than being a good cook.

"I can make biscuits." Regan tossed her hair over one shoulder and frowned in Lucy's direction.

"Of course you can," Paulette said. "It's not hard. You just mix them up and stick them in the oven."

Lucy almost rolled her eyes. This was the woman who was panicking at the idea of having to get the biscuits out of the oven when the timer went off.

"And I can fry up bacon, too." Regan thought for a moment. "Bacon and biscuits. That's a meal right there."

Marcus reached for an ear of corn. "So, tell us about your clinic, Jem."

He looked up. "You mean, the hours of operation and how many patients we treat a day?"

"Well, I was just thinking it must be hard to deal with all the teen moms on welfare. I'd be tempted to hand out job applications." Marcus shook his head. "I don't have a lot of patience for people like that. And they've learned these habits from their parents and grandparents. Have babies, live off the government, never get a job, everything is free. It must be frustrating."

"My mother was on welfare most of my life," Jem said.

There was a long silence where no one seemed to know what to say.

"She couldn't make ends meet, even with her two part-time jobs," Jem said. "The trailer we lived in had roaches and a plywood floor in the bathroom, but it took most of her income. So I understand where most of them are coming from and try to help without making assumptions." He paused. His voice was soft. "I don't always succeed."

Lucy sat frozen, her fork in her hand. She wanted to say how much she admired him, how she was sure he was doing just fine, but she couldn't seem to make the words leave her mouth.

Regan looked as lost as Lucy and scanned the table for some other topic. "These are lovely flowers, Paulette. Did you get these from Penny's on Hanson Street? I just love their Hawaiian Sunrise. They have the tropical flowers over-nighted as soon as you put in your order. You pay a lot more than anywhere else, but they're so fresh."

Paulette launched into a description of how the florist had sent the wrong arrangements and how she'd ordered these orchids to match the linen napkins she'd picked up on Tuesday, but the orchids had come a shade more orange than the fabric, even though she'd brought the napkins into the store to check. Lucy let the words wash over her and focused on her plate. Spearing a green bean, she brought it to her mouth. She'd been so hungry, but now her stomach felt unsettled and nervous. Shooting a glance at Jem, she noted the set of his mouth and the way his shoulders seemed too straight, as if he was forcing himself to stay at the table.

Had he mentioned his mother was on welfare that summer? She was almost sure that he had mentioned it, and she hadn't really thought much about it, except to feel sorry for him. She swallowed, feeling the tightness in her throat, the wave of self-disgust. He must have confided in her, but at the time it hadn't been important. She'd been in love with everything about him. The way his hair stood up a bit, that slow way he smiled, his easy laugh, the way he could recite poetry so the words offered up a whole new meaning. She'd loved him, but she hadn't understood him.

Lucy watched his face. He nodded, smiled and buttered a biscuit. He was playing along and not really part of the conversation at all. Is that how she'd seemed to him? Present, but wrapped up in her own world? Paulette's story had inspired Regan to describe her own recent woes with a local salon owner who had promised that her highlights wouldn't turn brassy, but after a week they had gotten a strange orange tint. She had demanded the owner come in on a Sunday morning and fix it because she could not live another day looking like that.

Jem glanced up and caught Lucy's gaze. She

forced a smile, and for a moment he looked as if he wanted to speak, but then he turned to Regan. Leaning close, he said, "Orange hair or not, you look beautiful."

Lucy felt his words like a kick to the gut. And then hated herself for it. There was nothing wrong with his complimenting Regan, nothing wrong with his being a good date. She took a sip of sweet tea and tried to look as if she were enjoying the meal. But inside she knew that Jem was playing a part, and it took her breath away. Jem, who had always been fearless about his past and his present, was for some reason pretending that any of this mattered, that any of it would be in his future. He had never cared what the wealthy people of Tupelo thought before, but maybe he was different now. Maybe this is what he'd learned during medical school and during his years in Boston: how to smile when the conversation drifted from the inane to the absurd.

"You should see me on Halloween." Regan leaned into him, pursing her lips. "Last year I wore a kitty costume that had cutouts here and here." She ran her hands down each side from her ribs to her thighs. "I couldn't wear any panties and it was cold." She gave a little shiver.

"I hardly ever wear panties," Paulette said, shrugging. "You can ruin a perfectly good outfit with panty lines, you know?"

Lucy stared at her sister. They couldn't possibly

be related. No good Southern woman talked about her panties at the dinner table, let alone in front of guests.

"My friend Tom's wedding will be a little like Halloween, except the groomsmen will look like Mr. Darcy and the girls won't look like kitty cats. Right, Lucy?" Jem wiggled his eyebrows at her. "Lucy gets to dress up with me."

Regan shot her a look. "Why are you going?"

Lucy resisted saying that it was none of Regan's business. "Because I'll be a bridesmaid." She poked her green beans with the tines of her fork. There wasn't much more to say. "The girls are going to be in Regency dresses."

"Tom called me twice, just to make sure I hadn't changed my mind. I'd already agreed, I was really happy for him, but he thought I might bow out when I heard what the men had to wear."

"Oh. White stockings and fancy slippers?" Lucy thought she might be tempted to drop out, too, if she were a guy and had to wear tights.

"No, thank goodness. We're going to be in blue jackets and riding boots." Jem shrugged. "Tom has zero interest in Regency costumes, but it's amazing what men will do for the women they love."

Lucy nodded, dropping her gaze to her plate. She wished she knew firsthand what a man would do for her, but she didn't, and she had only herself to blame.

"I think Mr. Darcy is so handsome, especially when he's coming out of the lake in that movie. I love how you can see his nipples through his shirt." Regan gave a little giggle. "Maybe after the wedding, the groomsmen can take a little dip in the pond."

"Ooooh, good idea," Paulette said. "That would be amazin'. A whole *bunch* of Darcys."

Lucy gripped her fork to keep from throwing a biscuit at her sister's head. There was a fine line between an elegant Regency wedding and a tasteless nod to a movie scene.

The faint sound of the oven beeping caught her attention. "I almost forgot the cobbler," she said. "Excuse me."

It was a relief to leave the table and head toward the kitchen. She forced herself to take long, slow breaths. The kitchen was stifling and she slid open a window to let out the hot air. Grabbing the pot holders, she slid them on and opened the oven. The cobbler was perfectly browned at the edges, dark-purple blackberries dotting the surface, melting into the batter with a lighter shade of pink. Lucy carefully set the pan on the stove top and took a pinch of sugar, sprinkling it over the whole thing. It smelled like summer and her childhood and her mama. Everything good was wrapped up in the smell of this dish straight out of the oven, but Lucy felt drained and sad.

A meal this good should have been the focus of

an evening of friendship and family, but between her sister and Regan and Jem, she had no appetite.

She shut her eyes for a moment and whispered a silent prayer. *I made my choice a long time ago, and it's not Jem's fault that I regret it. I don't like Regan, but that doesn't mean that she wouldn't make him happy. Help me to be happy for him.*

"Can I carry anything?"

She turned to see Marcus filling up the doorway. He seemed bigger, somehow, than he had in the living room. The sleeves of his polo strained over his biceps. He smiled, completely at ease in the kitchen. She couldn't help returning his smile just a little bit. The dinner was a disaster of complicated emotions, but she was glad to see Marcus.

"I think you have an ulterior motive for coming in there," she said, keeping her face straight.

He frowned. "And what would that be?"

"Stealing all my recipes, of course." Dropping the oven mitts into a drawer, she put a hand on her hip. "Admit it. Your mama sent you here to spy on the Crawford family cooks."

He laughed out loud. "I'll have you know that my mama has her own arsenal of recipes, and she's not afraid to use them." Coming closer, he leaned over the cobbler, inhaling deeply. "But that should be considered a secret weapon. You could bend any man to your will with this cobbler."

"Really now?" She looked up at him, letting a sly smile touch her lips. It felt good to flirt, just for a moment.

His eyes went half-closed and he shifted closer. "Mmm-hmmm. But I think you do just fine on your own. You should only bring out the cobbler as a last resort."

A second too late she realized he meant to kiss her. Lucy felt his hand touch her back and he leaned forward. She turned, his lips landed at the corner of her mouth, and she froze. Her mind was waging a battle between her Southern upbringing and the knowledge that Marcus had her backed against the stove, not even giving her a chance to agree.

"Wait a minute," she said, putting a hand to his chest.

He didn't respond, but moved his mouth across hers. Marcus wrapped his other arm around her and pulled her closer still. She pushed against him, feeling the bar of the oven door against her hip, the sharp pinch of his teeth pressing against the lips she had clamped shut. Lucy felt a spike of panic. The others would be chatting over dinner and have no idea that she was fending off this stranger in the kitchen.

"Lucy?"

At the sound of Jem's voice, Lucy felt a wave of pure relief, followed by absolute despair.

It was another second before Marcus raised his

head. "I think we took too long to get the dessert." His voice was full of laughter.

Lucy swallowed, gaze darting between Jem and Marcus. If they'd been alone, she would have read him the riot act. A man doesn't just grab a woman and push her against the stove. But then as her eyes met Jem's, she remembered a kiss from long ago that was just as unexpected and was entirely welcome.

"Paulette asked me to tell you to bring the dessert plates," Jem said, his eyes locked on her face.

"She could have told me that when I left," Marcus said.

"But you said you were going to the bathroom." Jem's gaze went to Marcus, and Lucy saw a flicker of disgust.

"Oh, true. But I decided to stop here on the way back." He winked at Lucy. "I think your sister is the jealous type."

Lucy didn't know whether Marcus meant Paulette was jealous of her or of him. Only an hour ago he'd implied that he'd be bringing Paulette on a trip to New York, but now he was in the kitchen, kissing Lucy. Either way, Paulette's jealousy was warranted.

Lucy went to the cabinet and reached for the dessert plates. Her hands were shaky and she felt sick to her stomach. Women talked a lot about setting boundaries and not being taken advantage of and standing up for their personal space, but kicking a stranger on the street was a whole lot easier than to perform self-defense in one's own kitchen against one's own guests. Add in Jem's presence and she was completely unnerved.

Just as she was setting the tiny stack of plates on the counter, they slipped from her hands with a crash. She let out a cry, blinking at the shards of china that had once been part of her mother's wedding set. The dogwood blossoms on a cream-colored background, the shining gold edges, were now shattered beyond repair.

"Are you all right?" Jem was beside her, reaching for her hands, scanning her palms for any cuts.

"I'm fine." She took her hands back, feeling the sweat on her skin. Her eyes filled with tears, and she wasn't sure if it was because she'd broken her mama's china or because Jem was worried about her hands. That said everything about him and the kind of man he was. She didn't think there was another man in the world who could walk in on his ex-girlfriend making out with some guy and then, seconds later, be compassionate enough to make sure she wasn't hurt.

"I think I only broke the bottom two. Maybe I can find replacements." Her voice wavered on the last word but she kept her gaze down.

"Let me rinse these off. We don't want anybody to ingest bits of porcelain." Jem carried them to the sink and started to run them under the water one by one. She set the broken pieces in a pile on the counter and sighed.

"That's too bad," Marcus said, shaking his head. "A real shame."

Lucy wanted to respond, but when she looked into his face, all she felt was anger. She would never have dropped the dishes if Marcus hadn't forced that kiss on her. Even though it was Jem's arrival that had made her want to cry, Marcus's behavior had started it all.

She turned without a word and carefully brought down two more plates. "Could you carry the cobbler to the table, Marcus?"

"Sure can." He retrieved a few hot pads from the drawer and a moment later was gone.

She glanced at Jem and saw the tight line of his mouth. She didn't know what to say. Thanking him wasn't quite right since he hadn't done anything except arrive in the kitchen.

"Do you have a clean dish towel?" he asked.

She took a tea towel from the hook and started to dry the plates. Now she should tell him how she hadn't wanted to kiss Marcus, but the words were stuck in her throat. Every time he handed her a plate, his face grim and shuttered, she lost her nerve. It didn't matter anyway, not really. Jem probably thought she was stealing Paulette's date, and if she tried to explain, it would only seem as if she were embarrassed at being caught.

"We'd better get these to the table," she said,

and was proud that her voice was clear. Her face felt heavy with unshed tears and her chest was tight. If she could just make it through the dinner, she could crawl into bed, pull the covers over her head and pretend the world did not exist. But for now, she was still expected to sit down at the table and eat some blackberry cobbler. She would sit quietly, avoiding both of them. She didn't think she could meet the eyes of the man who'd kissed her against her will, and then the eyes of the man that she still loved, but could never have.

He considered the blessing of beauty as inferior only to the blessing of a baronetcy; and the Sir Walter Elliot, who united these gifts, was the constant object of his warmest respect and devotion.

—SIR WALTER ELLIOT

CHAPTER THIRTEEN

Jem clenched his fists in his lap. The alcohol in the martini was working its way through his system, pushing him toward actions he would never have considered otherwise, and he wished he'd never touched the stuff. He wanted nothing more than to drag Marcus outside and punch his handsome face. He hadn't liked the guy before, but when he'd seen Marcus kissing Lucy, Jem had felt hatred rise up in him, hot and powerful. It wasn't a kiss between lovers, or even between people who had just met and were attracted to each other.

Paulette was in the middle of a story about an Italian purse that was ripped on the inside and how she'd convinced the seller to replace it and throw in a complimentary wallet that cost almost as much. Jem let Regan carry the weight of the other side of the conversation and tried to slow his heart rate.

When Marcus had announced he was headed to the restroom, Jem had seen him turn right, not left. His mama had warned him to stay out of Lucy's way, but this was different. He'd known Marcus was going to the kitchen and shouldn't have cared, but something about the guy's slick smile and the way he played the women in the room had set off all Jem's alarms. He'd made some excuse and followed . . . just in time to see Lucy backed up against the stove, turning her face, eyes open wide in fear.

The memory of her expression flashed bright, and all his muscles tensed. He wished his head were clearer. His control wavered every time he thought of her face. *God, I don't want to hurt anybody. I want to be a man of peace.* His mama hadn't raised him to "take it outside and settle it." She had raised him to think first and fight only when necessary. Even though he wanted to put his fist through Marcus's shiny smile, now was not the time. He was a guest in this house, and if Lucy wasn't asking Marcus to leave, there was no reason to drag the guy down the front steps.

But, oh, he wanted to.

He put a bite of cobbler in his mouth and chewed, hardly tasting the soft berries and sweet cake. Lucy had been turned, her shoulder against

Marcus's chest, elbow raised. She should have used her knee, stomped on his instep, bitten his lip, anything. He wondered whether she knew self-defense and whether it was possible to bring up the topic. She was so beautiful that surely she had encountered unwanted attention before. Then again, she'd stayed close to home. She was known and respected here, probably didn't have to fight off men in the kitchen very often.

He shot a look at her face. Her gaze was on her plate, and she turned her fork over and over in her fingers. He wanted her to stand up and yell at Marcus, tell him to get out of her house and never come back, but she sat silent.

"I think Daddy's home," Paulette said, and leaned over to peer out the window.

Jem saw a bright-red Miata park in the driveway. Willy Crawford took several minutes to get his feet on the ground and edge out of the car. Jem wondered if he'd been drinking. It was common for the members to drink at the club and then drive home. Most of the town knew it and tried hard to stay out of their way.

The slow steps of Lucy's father were like the thudding of Jem's heart. He'd met the man a few times. None of those meetings had ended well. Maybe Jem had changed enough that if they came face-to-face now, Willy Crawford wouldn't even recognize him.

"Well, what do we have here?" Willy appeared

in the doorway, surveying the scene. His eyes were red, but he seemed steady on his feet.

"Come on in, Daddy," Paulette said. "I want to introduce you to some friends of mine." Marcus stood up at the same time that Jem did.

"I remember Regan real well." Willy flashed a smile. "Hard to forget a girl as pretty as you."

Regan beamed, one hand touching her blond hair. "How are you doin', Mr. Crawford?"

"Just fine." His eyes took in Marcus at the head of the table and Lucy at the other end. Jem could see him consider the implications, and a small smile touched Willy's mouth.

Paulette introduced Marcus and the men shook hands. Willy said, "Your family owns Global Pleasures Travel and Vacation, is that right?"

"Yes, sir. Started right here in Tupelo, but we've got call centers in twenty states and our Internet site does more business than Orbitz." The statistics were impressive, but Marcus managed to look humble.

"And you're part of the business now?"

"Yes, sir, I am. Just graduated from Duke with a master's of business administration."

"It's good to see a local boy come back home after getting his education." Willy nodded his approval. "I saw your daddy at the club a few weeks ago, but I was pressed for time. The next time I see him, I should let him know that Crawford Investments could bring a lot to the table if we entered into a partnership. We're a solid business, long history."

Out of the corner of his eye, Jem saw Lucy lift her head, but she said nothing. He wondered how Willy Crawford thought any of the businessmen in Tupelo had missed that he was near bankruptcy.

"Daddy, this is Jeremiah Chevy. He's working with the Free Clinic, the ones who've leased out the back of the house," Lucy said.

Willy raised his chin. "Oh, I think I remember you. Kid from that trailer park, came to one of our parties once."

In the awkward silence, Marcus raised his eyebrows and a smile spread over his face.

"Yes, sir. That was me." There was nothing to do but acknowledge that he had once brought a foil-covered dish of cornbread to a catered formal party.

"Daddy, that was a long time ago," Paulette said, sighing. "Jem is a doctor now."

"Good for you." Willy headed toward the hallway. "You're a testament to hard work. If you made it to college, anyone can."

"Daddy," Lucy started to say, but he didn't turn to look at her as he passed through the doorway.

Lowering himself into his chair, Jem tried to shake off the slight. He hadn't expected a hug and the keys to the car, but the backhanded compliment was irksome.

Marcus sat back down. "Your father is a real fine man. You can tell he comes from good stock. Paulette, didn't you say your great-grandfather fought in the Civil War?"

"I think so. Right, Lucy?"

Everyone at the table turned to look at her, and Lucy glanced up. "What?"

Paulette sighed. "Marcus was wondering if our great-grandfather fought in the Civil War. Didn't he get the Purple Heart?"

Lucy looked confused and Jem almost smiled. Paulette brought clueless to a whole new level sometimes, and it was hard to know where to start when you had to answer her questions. "The Purple Heart wasn't really around until the 1930s. Our great-great-grandfather was in the Fourth US Colored Troops and fought at Chapin's Farm. He was given the Medal of Honor." Lucy looked down at her plate for a moment. "He didn't need to enlist. He was the son of a wealthy man, but he wanted to fight."

"I've never understood that," Regan said. "If I had the choice to fight or to stay home, I'd stay home. It's just bloodthirsty the way so many men run to sign up when there's a war. Maybe it's all the video games and violent movies, but you'd think they'd have more sense."

Lucy put a hand to her head and squeezed her eyes closed. She looked as if she was counting to herself, or praying. She looked up, her lips turned up in a grim smile. "I'm getting a bit of a head-ache. I think I'll go lie down."

Paulette didn't acknowledge Lucy's statement, but nodded vigorously to Regan. "I know. And then when you think about women joining the army or whatever, it just makes no sense. They must want to be men deep down. No real woman would want to wear a uniform and learn to shoot a gun."

Lucy stood up abruptly and took a breath. "Nice to meet you, Marcus. Nice to see you again, Jem and Regan." She didn't meet Jem's eyes as she left the table.

Jem half stood, but she was already gone. He sat slowly, staring into his plate. There was a limit to politeness. He completely understood her frustration, especially as she spent her days researching the men who fought and died for their families, their freedom and their communities. He swallowed hard. It was a dishonor to run when your country was in danger, and Regan couldn't see that. Her vision was so narrow, her heart so small, that she couldn't imagine how a man would willingly walk into live fire, knowing he might not make it back to his loved ones. There were times a man was called to make sacrifices. A soldier agreed to be separated from his wife and children, from his parents and friends, so that others might have freedom.

Lucy had chosen her family over him, the boy

she loved. Jem had thought that it had been easy, that she was flighty and shallow. But like a man heading to war, she had chosen to sacrifice herself for her home and her family. Jem didn't think they deserved it, but it wasn't his opinion that mattered. For years, his vision had been so narrow, just like Regan's, that he couldn't imagine how Lucy could have walked away from him. It was easier for him to believe that she was making the easy choice.

Jem let the conversation carry on without him. He'd wanted to like Regan, to have a lighthearted diversion. She was pretty and flirtatious. But he had loved one girl, and one only, for a long time. No amount of denial, bitterness, or blue martinis could change that fact.

CHAPTER FOURTEEN

"You said when you were done, you'd take a walk outside." Alda poked her head inside the doorway. Today she had green streaks in her blond hair and tiny guitar earrings. "Come on. No more hiding in this office."

"But I'm not finished. I have this stack of letters to organize—" Lucy broke off at the look on Alda's face. "I guess I could use a little air."

"Let's walk the trail. It'll only take a little while. You'll be perky and fresh for the presentation."

"More like tired and sweaty," Lucy grumbled, but she tucked the fragile papers back into the archive box.

"I'm not fixin' to walk the whole thousand acres and the seven sites on the battlefield, girl. Just the first loop." Alda held Lucy's office door open and waited, making it clear that she wasn't hearing any more excuses.

Minutes later they were walking down the narrow path toward Bethany Cemetery, the light breeze giving a bit of relief to the heat. Lucy inhaled deeply, noting the smell of growing things and the fertile soil. It truly felt good to get out of her office. If only Jem weren't due to arrive in an hour, she might actually be enjoying herself. She focused on slowing her heart rate and clearing her mind.

Alda was quiet, gaze focused on the trees ahead, walking slowly. Lucy matched her pace, hoping she didn't sweat too much. Her summer dress was simple but dressy, the pale-blue cotton sheath adorned with one vintage pin of her mama's. The white, enameled petals were edged with gold and silver balls gathered in the center. Paulette called it an ugly monstrosity and so far out of style it would never come back. She'd told Lucy that a modern woman should wear something that makes a fashion statement.

Lucy had reminded her that a vintage pin definitely made a statement. Paulette huffed that only grandmas wore magnolias, that it was cliché and passé and backward. Lucy didn't care. She wore it because she needed to feel close to her mama today, and if it made her look like an old lady, then so be it.

Lucy glanced at Alda and had to smile. Alda certainly never cared what anybody thought of her style.

They walked in silence for a while and Lucy felt her shoulder muscles relax. She tried to imagine, just for a little while, that there was no past and no future, just this quiet moment. They reached the cemetery and stood, looking at the ninety six Confederate gravestones. An old elm stood guard over the white markers, and the flag on the pole moved gently in the soft breeze.

"Do you know why I moved home to Tupelo?" Alda asked.

"You came home to watch over your grandma, I think." Lucy remembered Alda's saying that she'd loved Memphis. The lights and the energy of the city made her feel as if she'd found her place at last.

"That's just what I told everybody." Alda stared out at the graves, her eyes filled with sadness.

Lucy said nothing, just watched Alda's face and waited for her to continue.

"I was supposed to get married. We had a spring wedding all planned out. Catering, flowers, dress, the whole shebang." She paused. "He decided he wasn't ready. He wanted to see the world, wanted to get a record contract, work the Memphis clubs."

"I'm sorry," Lucy said, and hated how hollow the words sounded.

"So was I." Alda touched her earrings, gaze faraway. "I knew it was just an excuse because he could have done all of those things with me. I still miss him. I thought I would hate his guts, but I loved him for years after he dumped me." She turned, a half smile on her face. "Isn't it weird that you can't just stop loving someone when they don't deserve it anymore? He was such a jerk, and it's like my heart didn't get the news flash."

Lucy nodded. She knew what it was like to have your heart act independently of your head.

Alda turned back to the gravesite, gaze fixed on the leaves moving at the top of the trees. "He had the most amazing voice." Her tone was so soft that Lucy had to listen closely. "I never knew that music could make you feel so much until I heard Harlon sing."

Lucy thought of Jem, and the way he could read a poem in a way that gave it a whole new meaning. She wondered if she had understood poetry at all before she met him.

"I heard he got a record deal a few months ago. He might be famous soon. I might get to hear him on the radio all the time." Alda rolled her eyes. "Won't that be wonderful?"

She laughed, but Lucy felt a twinge of concern for Alda. Having Jem around Crawford House all the time was a whole new kind of pain. She hadn't known it could be so hard just to know he was somewhere in the house, even if she couldn't see or hear him. He was close, and everything in her yearned to be near him.

Alda shrugged. "I don't mean to whine. It's just

hard to stand here and look at these graves without thinking of all the sadness in the world, to know they were loved and loved others. All gone in a day."

Lucy could have sworn that the grief of a hundred families lingered over this place. The spot was green and peaceful, but the ninety-six markers were a stark reminder of the finality of death. The mass grave of thirty more anonymous dead at the far end was even more powerful. The same sacrifice, but not even a stone to remind the world of their names. Lucy wasn't sure anyone ever really read through the whole roll that was framed at the center. She'd seen the tourists wander through with their fanny packs and giant styrofoam cups of fountain drinks, enjoying the momentary glimpse into the past, not pausing to read the names of men who had lived and breathed and loved.

"I don't think it was all just erased because they died."

"You mean, because they went to heaven or something?" Alda shrugged. "I know you believe that there's a God and if we're really good, we're going to a happy place after this is all over, but I just don't. I think this is all we get."

Lucy grimaced at the idea that Christians only behaved so they could go to a happy place. "I do believe in heaven, but I was thinking more about their sacrifice, and what comes after. Jesus said there was no greater love than to lay down one's life for one's friends." She looked at the tombstones, blackened from a hundred years in the elements, some leaning to one side. "Some were forced into service, but a lot of men volunteered. They were trying to protect their families and fighting for what they thought was right."

"It's weird to hear you talk like that when they were fighting to keep slavery legal," Alda said.

"Of course I think they were wrong, but I admire the fact they were willing to die for something. So many people don't really care about anything. They just can't be bothered. They skim along on the surface of life, just giving the bare minimum. They're not paying attention." Lucy thought of how much time some people spent watching TV, as if they were just passing time until they reached the end of their lives. They were afraid to be bored, but didn't have anything good to fill the time except chatter and noise.

"So, you think it matters how much they *cared?*" Alda didn't sound convinced.

"Sort of. Thoreau said most men lead lives of quiet desperation. I know he probably meant that people didn't get to choose their path and never got a chance to do what they wanted, but I think so many people are afraid to be passionate about anything. Maybe they want to paint, but they're afraid to fail and make something ugly. Instead they ignore that desire and just pass the time, doing nothing." Lucy thought of Dr. Stroud and his reenactments. She thought of Theresa and her love of Jane Austen—of the sisters united in their love of stories from two hundred years ago. "And those people who are passionate, if you ask them, there's usually someone who inspired them. It comes from somewhere. And it turns into a long, linking chain of people."

Alda sighed. "A chain of people who refuse to lead a life of quiet desperation, like Harlon. I could have cared less about country music before I met him. Now I love it. I love singing it, thinking of stories that could turn into poems that could be songs. Love and hate it, really, because it reminds me of him."

"That's what I'm trying to say, I guess, that these men were so passionate their memory lived on long after they were gone. Just because they died didn't mean their families stopped loving them. Love stays with us, whether we want it to or not."

"So, you think maybe they were all amazing men who inspired everyone around them to be better people when they died? I s'pose that could be, if we ignored the whole slavery part."

Lucy glanced up at the old elm tree, sorting out her thoughts and searching for words that fit the certainty inside. "I don't know what they were passionate about, or how they spent their time. I'm sure they were extraordinary in their own way, but they were also just regular men. They probably held grudges, made enemies, had their petty moments. Heck, they probably wouldn't have had a conversation with me if we lived in the same era."

Alda snorted. "True."

"But just like someone with a passion, their sacrifice sparked something in other people, maybe a lot of people. And when they were gone, that spark lived on. Those people were left to use that love somewhere." The breeze ruffled Lucy's hair, and for a moment she imagined the touch of a lover, the kiss of a son, the gentle pat of a father.

Lucy thought of her mama's care of her, of her singing and her laugh. She had such joy and life in her that when she was gone, the world seemed empty and cold. She hadn't died for a cause, but her love lived on. Lucy had done her best to look after her sisters, to make sure Daddy was happy, to keep Crawford House in the family.

Jem's face flashed through her mind. She spoke to herself without thinking it through. "I don't think the person needs to die for us to carry that love around. It still makes us who we are. We just need to apply it somewhere. If we let it stay inside, it will turn into something bitter and cold."

Alda put a hand to her mouth, face creasing in pain. Tears squeezed out from under her lids and slid down her cheeks. Lucy reached out and hugged her close.

After a few minutes Lucy said, "I'm so sorry. I didn't mean to hurt you."

"No, you're right," Alda gasped. Her voice was rough and her breath hitched with every word. "I've been trying so hard to get rid of what I felt for Harlon. And I shouldn't."

Lucy rubbed Alda's back, a feeling of panic tightening her chest. She was the last person to give love advice. She hadn't done anything but pine for Jem since he'd gone, and done nothing but pine for him since he'd returned. She hadn't taken her love for him and put it anywhere at all.

Alda looked up, eyes red. "I need to take that love and spread it around. What a waste to just keep it tucked inside."

She leaned into her, squeezing Alda tight. The girl was brave and made Lucy want to do something other than roll into a ball and cry. "You inspire me."

"I can't imagine how." Alda wiped her eyes. "All I did was run home to lick my wounds. I guess I can't sit around and mope forever."

"Moping isn't all it's cracked up to be, that's for sure," Lucy said.

Alda paused. "I haven't wanted to ask."

"About what?"

She let out a breath and wiped her eyes. "You've been different lately. Real sad, just like I was when my Harlon dumped me."

"I wasn't dumped." Lucy tried to smile. "I've just had a lot on my mind."

"Really?" She looked skeptical.

"Really. I have absolutely zero prospects in my romantic life, so it would be impossible to be dumped." Lucy was fudging the truth a bit, but there wasn't any way to explain that she was wallowing in a decade's-old broken heart. It would take a few hours that they didn't have. "We'd better get back. I've got to freshen up so I look nice for all the reenactors coming to watch my presentation on battlefield amputations."

They turned back to the path. "I always wonder about those reenactor guys. Do they have wives? Girlfriends? Do they have any life besides playin' dress-up?"

"I'm pretty sure most of them have healthy social lives."

"With other dudes who like to sleep in ditches and pretend to die an ugly death in battle," Alda said, snickering.

"Dr. Stroud is married to a very nice woman. I met her a few weeks ago at a party. Of course, she's sort of obsessed with Jane Austen, so maybe that's why they get along."

"I guess everybody's gotta have a hobby," Alda said. She pointed toward the interpretive-center parking lot. "Look over there. Do we have people arriving already?"

Lucy's stomach dropped and she searched the

line of cars for Jem's silver four-door. There it was, at the far end, under a shady tree. Her mouth went dry and her step faltered.

Alda glanced up at her, concerned. "Are you nervous? You don't look good."

"Thanks—just what every girl wants to hear before she makes a public speech."

"You know what I mean." Alda touched Lucy's arm. "Did you eat lunch? Do you need to sit down? It's pretty hot out here."

Lucy shook her head. "I'll be fine."

They were close to the doors now and Alda reached for the handle. "I'll go bring out the kits and the photos."

She nodded, not trusting herself to speak. Through the glass, she saw Jem. He had his back to her, talking to a short man in a bow tie, but she recognized him. His blond hair was always a bit ruffled, his shoulders a little hunched as if he'd grown up fast and felt too tall for the room. He turned at the sound of the opening door and met her gaze. A smile spread over his face.

He was wearing rough gray pants, worn leather boots, a white shirt and suspenders. He wasn't quite in Civil War attire, but he wasn't wearing modern clothes, either. She blinked, and for a moment she saw him as a man from long ago. His gaze traveled down to the pin on her dress and his eyes went soft. He said something to the short man in the bow tie and walked toward her.

260

"Hi," he said. "Good to see you again."

She heard same sort of greeting dozens of times a week, but his words made her cheeks go hot. "It's only been three days."

"But it was a long three days." The corner of his mouth went up.

Lucy swallowed hard. He was flirting with her. Just as in the kitchen as they cooked, he was sending a little message of interest, but he had also flirted with Regan, letting her lay a hand on his thigh or lean into him at the table. Lucy looked past him and searched for something to say. "Did you come here with Dr. Stroud?"

"No, he's at the clinic. As soon as the nurse from the County Health arrives, he'll run over."

She frowned. "So, this is your day off?"

"Sure is. I usually don't wear suspenders to work." He hooked his thumbs through them and rocked back on his heels. Lucy couldn't help smiling at the sight. He looked happy, relaxed.

"Well, I hope we make it worth your while and you don't regret giving up your free day."

"Never." There was that shy smile again. He paused, as if choosing his words. "Lucy, I was wondering if you would want to—"

"There you are." A voice cut into his sentence and they both turned to see Marcus a few feet away. He was in a suit with a boldly patterned tie that matched the silk handkerchief in his jacket pocket. He looked like the gentleman he'd never been. Lucy felt herself go cold.

She nodded in his direction, but didn't move to greet him. She had lain awake that night, going over and over what had happened in the kitchen. She berated herself for not being more firm, then burned with anger at the way his fingers had gripped her arms, and minutes later she'd cycle back to shame for not having pushed him away.

"You look amazing. I love this new style," he said, reaching out and looping a dark, glossy curl around his finger.

"Thank you," she managed, and stepped away. She had let her hair dry naturally, with just a bit of mousse to keep it from frizzing. The soft curls framed her face, and although Aunt Olympia would be horrified at her lack of sophistication, it felt pretty. Or, it had until Marcus had mentioned it. Now she wanted to pull her hair back into a ponytail and hide it away.

"I should get ready," she said, and glanced at Jem, wishing he would finish whatever he'd been about to ask. Jem's expression was closed and hard. She felt a stab of shame. He had never said anything about the kiss he'd seen in the kitchen, and she had hoped he would forget all about it. But the sight of Marcus had brought it back because Jem's friendliness had evaporated into silence.

"Do you need any help? I can carry boxes." Marcus pretended to flex his muscles.

"No, thank you." She managed to keep her voice light, but there was no way she was going to let herself get backed into another corner by Marcus and his helpfulness.

"Go ahead, we'll be here," Marcus said cheerfully.

Without another glance, Lucy slipped away to her office. As soon as she closed the door, she leaned against it and whispered a prayer: *Help me get through this, Lord, and to focus on these men who died, not on Jem or Marcus.*

She turned to the desk and lifted the small boxes, determined to put her own pain aside and honor the dead.

"I do regard her as one who is too modest for the world in general to be aware of half her accomplishments, and too highly accomplished for modesty to be natural of any other woman."
—WILLIAM ELLIOT

CHAPTER FIFTEEN

Jem watched Lucy walk away, feeling the sweat on his palms. It had taken him all weekend to get up his nerve, and then Marcus had to stick his nose into the conversation. Jem had been a few words away from inviting her to coffee, just a small gesture of reconciliation, but it had taken all his courage. Once burned, twice shy, as they said. His college friends would tell him he was a fool for even considering a friendship.

"She shot you down, didn't she?" Marcus let out a bark of laughter. "Dude, you need to make your move with more confidence. It was real obvious you expected her to say no."

Jem swiveled to stare at him. "More confidence? Is that what you call your behavior in her kitchen?"

"That's right." The guy had the nerve to look smug. "She liked it, no doubt about it."

Jem felt his pulse thudding in his ears and forced himself to breathe slowly. "And she got your number from her sister and called you right away? She said she really wanted to see you again?" It occurred to Jem that he might be asking a question he didn't want to hear the answer to, but if he were a betting man, he would lay money on the fact that Lucy hadn't been liking any of Marcus's moves in the kitchen.

"Nah, but she will. She's just playing it cool." Marcus adjusted his tie. "I like a girl who doesn't come on too strong. It gets real old."

"I would think you'd enjoy it." Jem didn't think Marcus was the kind of guy who wasted any opportunities.

"Of course I take what's offered, if you know what I mean, but for the long term, no real man wants used goods."

Jem's fists clenched. He knew exactly what Marcus meant and it made him sick. "A real man doesn't concern himself with whether the goods are used or not."

Marcus blinked. "Maybe I hit a little close to home there, huh? No offense, really. I got a buddy who married a girl who had a kid. I asked him whether he minded that she's got a baby daddy, and he said as long as the other guy pays for the diapers, he doesn't care."

"Just in time." Stroud and his wife walked toward them. Jem tried to put on an expression that was far from the disdain and fury he felt toward Marcus. Stroud's bow tie was a little crooked and he still had a stethoscope around his neck, but he was a welcome sight.

"She hasn't started yet," Jem said, although that was obvious. The room was filling with people and several rows of chairs were filled. The low hum of chitchat made the piped-in Civil War ballads barely audible.

Marcus reached out to shake Stroud's hand and headed for a group of well-dressed men in the corner. Jem was thankful that he was gone. He didn't know how he could have kept his temper any longer.

"Good. Did you tell her you're going to be my patient for the demonstration?"

"I didn't get a chance, but she must know by the costume." Jem waved a hand at his shirt and trousers. Lucy had given him a long look but hadn't asked any questions.

"I'm going to the powder room," Mrs. Stroud said. "Save me a seat."

"Will do, honey." Stroud glanced over at Marcus. "Strange to see him here. I didn't know he was particularly interested in the Civil War."

"He came to a dinner at Lucy's this weekend. I think he's more interested in her than anything else."

"Oh, really?" Stroud let out a chuckle. "He'd best be polishing up on his history, then. I can't

266

imagine Miss Lucy choosing anybody who didn't have his battles straight." Stroud took another long look. "Then again, he's a handsome man. I've always wondered when she would find her match. A beautiful woman like that, with her heritage and education, seems odd she's never settled down. She must have had more than her fair share of good prospects."

"She's still young." Jem didn't want to talk about Lucy's marriage plans. Even though his mama had said that Lucy's being married might save him some grief, right now he felt that seeing her with a husband would be more painful than dealing with all their unresolved issues.

"Certainly, but I've never seen her with a boyfriend either. We've been to plenty of the same parties. Her sisters always have someone on their arm, but never Lucy." Stroud smoothed his white mustache. "Come to think of it, she never really stands around talkin' to people, either. Maybe she's a shy one, although she seems comfortable enough here."

"I'm sure there's been someone. She might not parade them around like her sisters do."

Stroud shrugged. "Probably. You know, Nick Riven over at the National Center for the Preservation of Civil War Battlegrounds told me he asked her out and she turned him down. He got the impression there was someone else, but she didn't say."

Jem frowned, wondering what this Nick looked like, where he came from and who his family was. Then Jem wondered who the other "someone" was. It occurred to him, all at once, that Lucy could have a boyfriend. Someone her family didn't approve of and didn't invite over, someone who didn't attend all the nice parties. They could be content together, in their own private world, keeping everyone else out of their happy bubble.

Stroud clapped a hand to Jem's shoulder. "Listen to us, a bunch of old gossips. Worse than the ladies."

Jem forced a smile. "Should we take a seat?"

"Right. My wife will wonder what we were thinkin' if we get stuck standing. Miss Lucy sure seems to pull in a good crowd to these presentations."

They found a place and Jem settled on a metal folding chair. A moment later Mrs. Stroud joined them. There was a hard knot of unease in his chest. Could Lucy have someone that she kept private, not wanting to risk the ire of her family?

After a few moments, he dismissed the thought. Lucy was all or nothing. She wouldn't sneak around in the dark. He didn't know everything about her, but what he did know told him that Lucy didn't lie in word or deed. She spoke her mind and faced the consequences.

But even if there wasn't a secret lover, what made him think that Lucy would want to give him the time of day? She surely didn't care about the medical degree he had now. She had broken up with him because he didn't fit in, because her family could never accept him. As his mother had said, what he'd loved about her wouldn't have changed, and in the same way, the things that had kept them apart were still just as real. Just because she didn't want Marcus didn't mean that she wanted Jem, either.

He let his mind wander while Stroud talked about various medical tools. Jem was glad he hadn't finished his sentence, no matter what he was feeling. He needed to keep his mouth closed before he got another taste of rejection.

Jem listened as Lucy spoke, mostly from memory, with only a small batch of notecards in one hand. "Robert E. Lee's Army of Northern Virginia met the Army of the Potomac under George B. McClellan at Antietam Creek near Sharpsburg, Maryland, on September 17, 1862. Antietam was the bloodiest single day in American military history, with almost twenty-three thousand casualties. Dr. Jonathan Letterman, the medical director of the Army of the Potomac, developed systems of casualty management that are used today."

Lucy's voice was firm and clear. She looked relaxed, with an ease to her movements. She didn't mind speaking in front of this kind of crowd, but Jem's palms were already sweaty with the idea of playing an unconscious soldier.

"At First Manassas in 1861, it took a week to remove five thousand casualties from the field. Dr. Letterman pushed for changes to handle the logistics of treating the wounded. His model became the standard by an act of Congress in 1864. Put into practice at Antietam, the twenty-three thousand casualties were removed from the battlefield in twenty-four hours. Our entire medical triage system evolved out of the military."

She hadn't glanced Jem's way, but made eye contact with several people who stood on the sides. Jem resisted the urge to see where Marcus was standing.

She gave a quick overview of the kind of medical training a doctor might have and how few trained surgeons were available at the start of the war, then brought into focus the main subject of her talk. "Amputation became the primary surgical skill of the Civil War battlefield surgeon, resulting in about six thousand such surgeries.

"We have Dr. Jacob Stroud here to give us a demonstration, using a Civil War battlefield kit. He has graciously allowed our center to display several of his best medical kits, and today he'll be reenacting a battlefield amputation with one of the most unique medical kits in existence. The four-tier, sliding US Army models by Snowden and Brother from Philadelphia were quite common, but today he's brought with him a very rare kit. Made by the George Teimann Company of New York, it was owned by the Sixth Massachusetts Volunteer Militia surgeon Norman Smith, MD. With it, he documented and performed one of the first amputations of the Civil War in the Riot at Baltimore. The soldier, one Lieutenant Herrick, survived and was discharged a few weeks later."

Stroud nudged Jem with an elbow, their cue to stand up.

"Today Dr. Stroud will be demonstrating the run-of-the-mill amputation performed on the battlefield. We need a volunteer . . ." Lucy's voice trailed off as she looked over at them. Her brows went up. "I think Dr. Jeremiah Chevy has been convinced to play the patient."

A smattering of applause greeted her statement, and Jem followed Stroud to the front of the room. A long table was set up in the center, with a smaller, raised table to the side. Stroud motioned to Jem, and he carefully settled himself, hoping the conference table would bear the weight of a grown man.

"Welcome, everyone," Stroud's voice boomed out into the room. "Miss Crawford has done a real fine job of giving the history of battlefield medical care, and now I'd like to draw a more personal illustration of what went on back then. We're going to use this fine specimen of manhood to bring home the point."

271

A wave of laughter greeted this statement. Jem felt his face go warm. He could always count on Stroud to play to the crowd.

"Civil War surgeons knew about germs, but hadn't made the connection that microorganisms cause disease." Stroud selected several small tools from the kit. "When a soldier was brought in from the field with a bullet wound, which of these do you think he might use to investigate the wound? The curved probe? Or perhaps this exploring needle?" He waved a sharp metal tool the size of a pen.

He waited while several in the crowd shouted out their guesses.

"Nope. Y'all would be bad Civil War surgeons." Stroud wiggled a finger in the air. "This is the probe of choice."

Laughter greeted his answer, with a few exclamations of surprise.

"Remember that the connection between infection and germs wasn't clear yet, so most of the doctors only rinsed their hands between patients." Stroud looked down at Jem's legs, frowning. "We never decided which parts we were gonna remove. Should we take a vote?"

The crowd answered with loud calls of "Leg!" and "Arm!" and Stroud pretended to count the responses. Jem forced himself to keep a straight face. The man could make the most gruesome presentation seem like a party.

"A man in the Civil War era might have an easier time without a leg. Even a gentleman needed his hands, what with holding the reins to a carriage. If Jem here was a regular man with a small plot of land, he might need his hands to chop the wood for winter, direct the ox-drawn plow, or harvest his crops. Imagine, for a moment, that he survives the war, but arrives home with one arm. His family would need to carry the burden of the farm tasks now. That usually was a wife or a child if he had one old enough.

"A battlefield surgeon couldn't do without his assistant." Stroud glanced around the crowded room as if searching for the perfect candidate. "Miss Crawford, I need you." Stroud said, waving her closer.

Jem froze. It was one thing to play a wounded soldier in front of her, but he hadn't counted on her joining him.

She moved into his view, her face tense. Her dark eyes were wider than normal and he wondered if she was disturbed by the topic. She hadn't seemed to mind talking about it. Stroud pointed to a spot beside him. She took her place, just inches away from Jem. He could smell her perfume, could reach out and touch her hand if he wanted.

Stroud retrieved a band of strong canvas and a metal tool. "This is the tourniquet. A temporary may have been applied on the battlefield, and this one will keep the patient from bleeding out during the operation.

"An amputation could take as little as two minutes in the best of conditions. If the surgeon had help, then he could perform the surgery and leave his assistant to finish the job. Miss Crawford will play that role."

Withdrawing a small rag from the kit, Stroud held it in the air. "Chloroform. Takes effect faster than ether and is nonflammable. Amputations happened without knocking out the patient, but we'll show you the good side of Civil War surgery today."

The crowd chuckled a little. They seemed to understand that Civil War surgery had no good side.

"I'm going to hold this over Jem's face, and in less than a minute he'll be out." Stroud pretended to press it to Jem's nose and mouth. Jem turned his head to the side and closed his eyes, letting the tip of his tongue loll out of his mouth. The laughter in the room almost made him grin, but he kept his face relaxed.

He felt Stroud's hand lift his arm. "As soon as I've stuck my finger in the wound and assessed the damage, I realize the bullet has shattered the bone and the arm can't be saved." He pulled Jem's arm vertical. "My assistant will unbutton the patient's shirt and prepare the arm while I find my instruments."

Jem felt her fingers at his wrists, fumbling with the buttons on his cuff. The shirt was simple coarse cotton, picked up at a reenactment in Kentucky. Jem heard Lucy's breathing, and the sound seemed to coincide with the beat of his heart. Finally, she released the button and rolled up his cuff in quick movements.

"Farther. Let's amputate Dr. Chevy's arm right above the elbow." Stroud spoke loudly enough for the room to hear. "Remember, we won't be using any of these delicate extractors or locators because we've decided to remove the limb, not the bullet." Stroud was describing several tools from the kit. Metacarpal saw, large forceps knife, ligature needle.

Lucy rolled the loose fabric up to Jem's shoulder. Her hands rested there briefly, and he felt the trembling in her fingers. He wished he could turn his head and see her face, but he was supposed to be completely unconscious. Jem could hear the small clink of instruments as Stroud removed, named and replaced the tools so the audience could see how he was going to proceed.

It occurred to Jem how odd it was for Lucy and him to be here, in this spot, ten years later. He always thought he'd live somewhere like Memphis or Atlanta, but now here he was in Tupelo, about to be dissected in front of an audience with Lucy as the assistant. As teens they had bonded over spoken poetry, literature, the great Southern writers, but it wasn't enough to keep them together. What had brought them back together was the Civil War. On the surface they were opposites, like a magnolia tree and a hemlock, but their roots ran deep, intertwined in the red Mississippi clay. All their differences faded before their mutual love of kinfolk, Southern soil and history.

He wanted to stop the presentation, turn and speak to her now. Was it possible that they could start over, get a second chance? He forced his breathing to slow and relaxed his muscles. Everything he had in him wanted to jump off the table and try to explain what he knew for sure, so clearly, right now. They were meant to be together, despite all their differences. And he had always loved her. Always.

Lucy felt the stiff smile on her face become even more strained. She should have known Jem was going to be part of the presentation. The rough leather boots and simple shirt were all signs she'd missed because she was too distracted by his flirtatious comment.

She rolled his sleeve to the shoulder, feeling the warmth of his skin under her fingertips.

"All right, Miss Crawford, if you would place your right hand in his and extend the arm," Dr. Stroud said.

She didn't have the right to touch him, to grip his hand and raise it high. She hoped he couldn't feel the way her hand trembled, and she tried to breathe slowly. She looked at the hand in hers and wondered if it had always been that big, or if he had grown more after leaving for college. His palms were soft and warm. She loved the way his veins stood out in relief against his skin, the way the muscles of his forearm were so much bigger than hers.

A sudden wave of nausea caught her by surprise. This was a nightmare. She had never been good at the gruesome aspects of the Civil War battles, but to hear Stroud preparing for a fake amputation on Jem was too much.

"The knife is used to quickly cut the muscle," Dr. Stroud said, making exaggerated movements diagonally across Jem's biceps, above the elbow, and Lucy's stomach flipped over in unison. "Then an amputation knife is used prior to cutting the bone with a saw." He mimed an exaggerated pulling motion on Jem's shoulder area, as if to pull the muscle upward. Grabbing a long, sharp knife, Dr. Stroud held it up.

Lucy sucked in a sharp breath against her teeth. There were spots in her vision and she swallowed hard. Jem's fingers squeezed hers tightly and she focused on their hands. She turned her head slightly, not able to see the square saw, with a long row of sharp teeth, near Jem's skin. Focusing on their intertwined fingers, she clutched his hand close to her. She'd read somewhere that locking your knees can bring on a faint, and she bent her legs a little, forcing herself to stay calm.

Jem's thumb rubbed against the back of her hand. She could hear her short breaths and hoped she wasn't hyperventilating. Janessa had once said that Dr. Stroud made her queasy with all his battlefield conversation, and Lucy had rolled her eyes. Now she understood. When it was in the distant past, it was regrettable but necessary. Now, she wanted to throw herself over Jem's body and refuse to let Dr. Stroud go through with his make-believe amputation.

"A ligature needle is used to pass a thread through the muscle or around an artery during suturing," Dr. Stroud said. "By now the patient has been unconscious for less than five minutes, but they've been brutal and life-changing minutes. He will return home, if he survives the field hospital and recuperation without dying of gangrene, where he will need to adapt to a life without his left arm."

"At least it wasn't his right," a man called from the front row.

"Except that Jem is left-handed," Lucy responded.

A wave of sympathy sounded through the crowd, and Dr. Stroud glanced at her. "Good point." He released the tourniquet on Jem's upper arm and waved a hand. "All done. Thank you for allowing me to show off my battlefield prowess, and I promise if you ever come to the Free Clinic of Tupelo, none of these instruments will be used."

More laughter echoed in the room before the visitors began to applaud. Jem opened his eyes and sat up. He looked at her, his expression a mix of concern and something else she couldn't name. "Are you all right?"

"Fine. Really, it was just a little more explicit than I was expecting."

"You've seen these tools before," Jem said. His eyes were still shadowed with worry.

"Yes, but it's different when you see them against skin and muscle and . . ." Her voice trailed off. Her hand still gripped his. She let go and shrugged. "Sorry, historians tend to get all wrapped up in the research, and we take everything personally. Plus, it's been sort of a long day."

He nodded and opened his mouth as if to say something else, but decided against it. He rolled down his sleeve and buttoned the cuff.

"Thanks to both of you," Dr. Stroud said, laying the last tool in the red velvet lining and sliding the four tiers of the box together.

"Anytime. You have a gift for public amputation." Lucy managed a smile. "I thought I was going to have to grab that little vial of ammonia and hold it under my nose."

He laughed, his white mustache twitching. "I think you're stronger than you think."

279

Theresa arrived at her side. "You did a wonderful job, all of you."

"Thank you," Lucy said. "I don't think I could do this all the time. I felt a little light-headed."

"That's why I love Austen. The worst medical emergency is a few falls. Nothing even close to what I just witnessed." Theresa smiled. "You need an afternoon with a good Regency love story to make it all better."

"I think you might be right." Lucy had never thought she had a weak stomach.

Dr. Stroud frowned down at her. "I'm sorry to hear all the medical talk was unnerving. The clinic is growing so fast we can't keep up, and I was just going to put out a call for volunteers. You're at the top of our list."

"Oh, I couldn't," Lucy said. "I don't have any training."

"None required. Just wiping down toys, handing out paperwork, maybe answering the phones when Leticia is in another room." Dr. Stroud leaned forward. "No blood, guts, or gore. None at all."

"Really, it would be such a help. I've got the Ladies' Auxiliary from the First Methodist Church coming by a few afternoons a week, but we still need more," Theresa said.

Alda's words came back to her. *I need to take that love and spread it around. What a waste to just keep it tucked inside.* Lucy couldn't stop loving Jem, but she couldn't keep it wrapped up inside either.

Jem hopped off the table and stood with his hands in his pockets. Against her will, her gaze traveled from his boots to his face. Lucy didn't want to look to him for direction, was afraid to see the expression on his face. Would he grimace at the thought of her being around the Free Clinic? He was looking out across the folding chairs, watching someone in the back of the room. Nothing showed in his eyes but politeness.

Lucy felt a rush of relief. He probably wouldn't even be there when she was, or if he was, they wouldn't be in the same room. "Okay. I can do that. I have Thursday afternoons off, if that works for you."

Dr. Stroud beamed at her. "Sure does. What do you think, Jem? Miss Lucy is coming to help out at the clinic."

"Great idea. We need all the help we can get." There was a smile on his face but it didn't match the hint of strain in his voice.

Lucy shook off the sharp pain of disappointment. What had she expected—that he would be thrilled to work in the same office with her? She was doing this because of him, but nothing could come out of it except the blessing of spreading that love around.

Her chance to be with Jem was long gone. All that was left was love, and she wasn't going to let it go to waste.

A persuadable temper might sometimes
be as much in favor of happiness,
as a very resolute character.
—ANNE ELLIOT

CHAPTER SIXTEEN

Lucy stood at the Strouds' glossy green front door
and wondered what she was thinking, spending an
afternoon watching a romance movie. As if she
didn't have enough heartache in her own life, she
was going to live someone else's for a few hours.
But she'd promised, and it was too late to back
out now. She lifted a hand and knocked. Seconds
later the door swung open and revealed Theresa
Stroud, Regency style. She was wearing a soft,
floor-length dress with a little jacket. Her hair was
up in a bun, with curls framing her face.

"Come on in, honey," Theresa called, reaching
out her hands to Lucy.

"Was I supposed to dress up?" Lucy asked,
suddenly aware of her simple slacks and a
sleeveless shirt. She'd made sure not to wear her
running shoes, but she hadn't bothered with
makeup, either. She was hoping this movie wasn't
going to be a tearjerker, but just in case she didn't

put on any mascara. It had been two days since she'd held Jem's hand at the presentation, but she felt his touch almost as warmly now as in that moment. As if her skin had memory, it was holding on to his touch, replaying it over and over. Her heart felt bruised and weary from the constant reminder.

"Oh, no, I just like to get in costume before I watch the show." Theresa waved her into the living room. "I've made us some Austen goodies."

Lucy had a flash of giant slabs of venison or a whole roasted pig, but the table held just a few china plates and an elegant decanter with lemon slices.

"These are Bath buns from the 1769 recipe by Mrs. Raffald. She didn't call for salt, but I think they're bland as dirt without it." Theresa held up the plate of little brown rolls. "Take one. Tell me what you think."

Lucy sniffed it, inhaling the scent of caraway seeds. Her first bite was just a nibble, but the flavor was delicious. The second bite confirmed it. Buttery, sweet, soft and like nothing she'd had before. "These are wonderful. You'll have to teach me how to make them."

Theresa clapped her hands together. "An Austen cooking day! Wonderful idea." She pointed to another plate. "Here we have tiny jam tartlets, Cassandra Austen's original recipe for baked custard, miniature rum cakes, and, finally, lemon ice is chillin' in the freezer for right after the movie."

"It all sounds delicious. You went to a lot of trouble."

"Not at all. I love these recipes. I don't want them to be forgotten. Just the other day I tried out a parsnip-and-carrot pudding. Jacob wasn't thrilled with it but I told him it was a lot healthier than a doughnut."

Lucy grinned. "I suppose if we can eat carrot cake, carrot pudding might be just as tasty."

"Exactly." Theresa pointed to the beverages. "Now, I usually have a perfectly steeped cup of tea with a syllabub dessert, but the weather has been so hot. I thought an orange-and-raspberry shrub would be good for today." She poured a glass of bright-orange liquid and passed it to Lucy.

The first sip was refreshing, but Lucy blinked. Sweet and strong, it had a kick. "Do you make it fresh?"

"I made it just this morning, but the vinegar will keep the concentrate from going bad for weeks. Sometimes they add rum to four cups of blackberries and then pour it over ice with lemon juice and water."

Lucy smiled. It wasn't often that she was faced with so many completely unfamiliar details. Everything that Theresa said took a moment to sink into Lucy's brain. It felt good to let go of all her work at the center, all her worries over

Crawford House and her sisters and all her heartache over Jem and just focus on something new. "The idea of a refreshment consisting of rum-soaked blackberry mash sitting for weeks in the warm weather makes me wonder how the Regency-era ladies got anything done at all."

"Amazing, isn't it? But Jacob says that Chatham Artillery Punch has become watered down with every new generation. I guess we just don't have the hearty constitutions they did."

"But I think our life spans have grown, though."

Theresa said, "We're weak and boring—"

"—but live to a ripe old age," Lucy added.

They looked at each other and laughed, having had the same idea at the same moment.

"I'm not sure if that's a good thing, or not." Lucy set down the glass and pulled out her phone. "Oh, I've been meaning to show you this. My friend Rebecca is having a Regency-themed wedding in a few weeks. This is my bridesmaid's dress."

Theresa peered at the screen and clapped a hand to her chest. "Oh, honey. You are so lucky. I heard Jem talking about his costume." She glanced up. "It must be the same wedding. Don't tell me there are two Austen weddings this summer. This poor old lady would just faint with happiness."

"No, it's the same wedding. And this sounds odd, but Rebecca said she wanted more Austen experts there. She planned the wedding so quickly that her Regency-geek friends are almost all otherwise occupied. Would you be able to come?"

"I can't just invite myself to someone's wedding, dear," Theresa said, laughing.

"Of course not, but if you're willing, I know she'd be glad to have someone shepherding the guests through the dances and answering questions about the food or costumes."

Theresa seemed to consider it for a moment. "But I don't know her, or her husband-to-be."

"Her fiancé seems to be a great guy, but he's more into football."

Theresa grimaced. "Football. Never understood the attraction. Huge, grunting men chasing each other all over the place and then crushing each other to the ground."

"Hmm, maybe I shouldn't tell you that I'm a die-hard Bulldogs fan. Just wait for the season to start and you'll never hear the end of it." Lucy laughed at the expression on Theresa's face. "I'll call her tonight and tell her I've found someone who will know how to wear her gown and curtsy just the right way."

Theresa shook her head a little, but she was smiling. "I would never give up the chance to support another Jane fan, and I'd certainly never give up the chance to go to a Regency party. I went with Jacob to an Austen dance last year out in the old Wrigley barn right off the highway. It was the best time we'd ever had at a party together." Her eyes were soft with the memory. "They had a wonderful band of folk musicians, and the dances were just magical. I can't imagine how many couples fell in love that night."

Lucy felt her heart contract at the words. There wouldn't be any falling in love for her at Rebecca's wedding. She was more likely to be doing her best to avoid Jem. The idea of watching him dance with girls dressed in beautiful Regency dresses made her stomach ache.

Theresa reached for a plate, choosing a Bath bun and a tart. "We better get on the stick or we'll never watch the movie. I'm partial to the older version, with Ciarán Hinds, but my niece says this is her favorite. The movie is real long since it was a BBC miniseries, so we might only watch the first part or two today." She glanced up. "You don't mind coming back, do you?"

"Not at all. I'm so happy to be here. You've given me something to look forward to all week." Lucy followed Theresa and settled near her on the couch.

"Oh, I can never figure out this channel changer. The other day I couldn't get it to show anything other than a blue screen, and I was madder than a wet hen in a tote sack," Theresa grumbled. "If we were like Jane, we'd just read to each other."

"That sounds wonderful." Jem was the only person who'd ever read to her. She loved the cadence of his voice, the way he gave just the right amount of weight to each word. When he'd asked her to read to him, she'd been embarrassed at first, but soon she lost herself in the words. It wasn't anything like reading to herself.

Theresa pushed a button and the TV flashed to life. "Most people start with *Pride and Prejudice*. Miss Elizabeth and her sassy self are just a kick. Even *Emma* has a lot of humor in it, when she's sparring with her Mr. Knightley. But *Persuasion* is my favorite. Not a lot of humor, for sure, but the best story."

"Why is that? Is the plot very complicated?"

"Oh, not at all. It's very simple, really. But the way she brings these two back together is really a work of art." Theresa glanced at her. "There's no cliff-hanger or suspense or mystery at the end. We know they're going to get back together, of course."

"Just like a romance." Lucy cleared her throat. "I have to confess I don't really read romances. Or watch them. I like nonfiction. And poetry. And football."

Theresa let out a long laugh. "Girl, I just love everything about you."

Lucy felt her face go warm. Was Theresa serious, or was this that backhanded compliment that Southern women did so well?

"No one can call you boring with that list," Theresa said. "And I'm going to wager that you do love a good romantic story. You just don't know it yet."

Lucy thought to her bookshelves. Hundreds of books couldn't be wrong. "Could be true. Maybe I'll be a romance junkie by the time you see me next. I'll be trolling the supermarket aisles, looking for my next bodice ripper."

Theresa cocked her head. "Maybe we're misunderstandin' what I mean by romance." She thought for a moment. "What poetry do you like?"

"Short list? In no particular order?"

"Right. Give me some names."

Lucy stared at the tin ceiling. "Sara Teasdale, Byron, W. H. Auden, Thoreau, Langston Hughes . . ."

"Good. Now give me your favorite poem from one. Any of them, or maybe just that first one." Theresa had a smug look on her face, little wrinkles creasing at the corners of her eyes as if she were trying not to laugh.

"That's really hard," Lucy said, but words were already running through her mind. "For Sara Teasdale I think it's 'But Not to Me.' " She glanced at Theresa and started to laugh. "You want me to recite it?"

"Sure do." Theresa settled back against the cushions and waited expectantly.

"Okay. Well . . ." Lucy took a breath. She hadn't recited poetry for years. Not since Jem. *"The April night is still and sweet with flowers on every tree. Peace comes to them on quiet feet, but not to me. My peace is hidden in his breast where I shall never be. Love comes tonight to all the rest, but not to me."* Her voice was husky by the end.

Theresa said nothing for a moment. The laughter was gone from her eyes. "I was going to use that poem against you to show how you're a romantic at heart. But I think you already know that."

Lucy opened her mouth but Theresa went on, "In *Persuasion*, an admiral's wife says that no woman expects to be in smooth waters all her life. What she meant was that women are tough and we know that hard times will come. You are right in the middle of the stormy sea."

"True. Crawford House has been in danger of—"

"Not the house. I was thinking of Jem."

Lucy sucked in a breath. "Who told you?"

"No one. I have eyes." Theresa sighed. "I look old with all this gray hair, but I remember being young and in love."

"But I'm not, we're not." Lucy rubbed her temples. "Not now, anyway. It was a long time ago."

"I thought it might be something like that." Theresa sighed. "He's such a friendly guy, laughing and telling jokes. My husband loves havin' him around, and I've enjoyed his company, too. But when he's near you, he's quiet as the grave."

Lucy frowned. She wanted to point out that Jem had done just fine at the Strouds' party. He'd danced with Regan and flirted with a group of pretty girls. At the dinner, he'd laughed over a blue martini and complimented Regan on her hair. "He probably feels uncomfortable around me. It didn't end well."

"It rarely does," Theresa said. "I'm sorry for that. I hope you two can reach a place of peace, knowing that the past is long gone and all we have is right now."

"I want that. But I don't know if it's possible." Lucy wasn't sure it was possible to watch Jem date someone else, knowing she still loved him.

Theresa squeezed her hand. "I'll be praying for both of you."

"Thank you," Lucy said, and felt tears well in her eyes. She brushed them away, irritated at herself for becoming emotional. When Rebecca had offered to pray for them, she'd felt a rush of defensiveness. There was no hope, so she shouldn't even ask God for help. But now that Lucy knew herself better, knew her heart had never let Jem go, she was desperate for that prayer. She was at the end of her emotional rope and was finally at that place where she welcomed those prayers. It was the place she should have been in the beginning, but was too busy fighting the truth.

"Let's get this movie started. There's nothing like a little Austen to soothe the wounded soul," Theresa said.

Lucy nodded and inwardly steeled herself. Spending so much time with Jem had left her feeling raw, as if her emotions were exposed to the world. Watching a romance about lost love might be more than she could handle.

"Here we go." Theresa sat back, looking over at Lucy. "Thank you, again."

"For being fed and pampered and relaxing on your couch?" Lucy asked, laughing.

"For making a lonely old lady happy."

Lucy didn't know what to say. Loneliness might be their common bond, really. It had nothing to do with age or marital status or employment. Sometimes, you just needed a friend to sit on your couch and watch your favorite movie.

They smiled at each other for a moment, then the strains of instrumental music drew their attention to the screen. A dark-haired young woman trotted through a mansion, checking off items on a clipboard, directing servants, adjusting the white sheets. As she moved from one era to another, Lucy felt her stomach drop. Anne Elliot was doing what Lucy had narrowly avoided: making sure everything was ready for her to leave. The music swelled as Anne gazed over the furniture, unrecognizable under the protective covers, and Lucy felt Anne's loss more deeply than she could have imagined.

She gripped her chilled glass of orange-and-raspberry juice. When Rebecca had talked about Austen, she'd mostly mentioned Mr. Darcy or Mr. Knightley. Lucy hadn't thought of the doe-eyed, pale-skinned heroines.

On the screen, Anne Elliot walked down a long hallway, glancing just once at the covered paintings, her mouth a grim line. Lucy thought Jane Austen would start the story with the romance, or the loss of it, but instead the tale seemed to begin with Anne's home, and having to make difficult decisions. Maybe this writer from two hundred years ago knew how everything important met at the intersection of family, home, love, and loss. This was something Lucy understood with every fiber of her being.

The final frame of the episode faded away and the credits began. Lucy heard a sound and glanced at Theresa, preparing for tears. Instead, the older woman's head was resting on the back of the couch and she snored softly.

Lucy smiled, forcing herself to take a deep breath and unwrap her arms from around her middle. She'd been so engrossed in the movie that she hadn't even noticed Theresa had fallen asleep. The story was heartrending, but something had hit her harder. Every time she saw that cold, shuttered look on Captain Wentworth's face, she saw Jem. Old hurts and bitterness were so clear in his eyes that it took her breath away. She closed her eyes for a moment. *I know I was wrong, but don't let him hate me.* Maybe it was too much to ask, but grace was powerful, and someday they might be able to forgive each other.

Anne hoped she had outlived the age of blushing; but the age of emotion she certainly had not.
—ANNE ELLIOT

CHAPTER SEVENTEEN

"I can't believe this is only the beginning of July. It feels like the middle of August." Leticia wiped her forehead and adjusted the little fan at her desk. "I'm startin' to think I'd better move back to Detroit."

Lucy tossed the used sanitary wipe into the wastebasket and took another. The smell of the bleach stung her nose, but the toys in the clinic waiting room would be free of germs for the next group of little kids. The afternoon had been so busy she hadn't had a chance to sit down, but with the momentary lack of patients, she'd planted herself in the kids' play area. "Did you like it there?"

"Like it?" Leticia gave her a look. "Like hearing gunshots all night and bein' afraid my husband was gonna be robbed on the way to work? No, I didn't like it. When we knew we were having a baby, he wanted to move home." She sighed. "I wasn't convinced it was the right thing. I mean, the South is the last place a Black person wants to live, right?"

Lucy smiled. A sort of a "reverse Great Migration" was happening, and Leticia's story was just one of dozens she'd recently heard. As the Northern cities struggled under bankruptcy and poverty and crime, families were moving South, searching for a place to raise their kids. "But you changed your mind."

"I sure did. There's a real sense of family here. And the kids are taught to respect their elders. They have expectations here that I didn't see in Detroit." Leticia paused. "And the food is amazing. Everything is fried or buttered or cooked in a cast-iron skillet, unless it's right out of the garden."

"We've got a bumper crop of corn and beans this year. You take some when you leave, okay?"

"I sure will, but I might have to fight your kitty to get in there."

Lucy snorted. "She's a tiger. A really tiny, harmless tiger."

"Maybe she's jealous that people are taking her green tomatoes and okra. Maybe you should show her what the end product is like so she'll let us through."

"I don't know if Hattie would enjoy deep-fried okra, but I can try. It's better than the chitlins Zeke

295

is giving her. Poor thing is going to have clogged arteries before she's a month old."

"I'm not a fan of chitlins, but I don't think they'll hurt Hattie," Jem said from the doorway. "If we're discussing people food, I don't care what it is, as long as Lucy makes it. She can really cook." He was wearing a white lab coat that had DR. CHEVY embroidered above the pocket.

"Thank you." Lucy stood up, suddenly feeling as if she didn't know where to put her hands. She hadn't seen him in his doctor's coat before and he looked different, more official and less like the boy she once knew. She hadn't seen him since the presentation, and although she'd thought it would be a relief not to run into him, she'd missed him. No matter how many times she told herself not to get attached, she felt a rush of happiness to see his smile.

"Zeke said your peanut plant is growing real well."

She nodded. "It is. Thank you again. I think we could make our own peanut butter if we get a good crop next year. Or peanut brittle. Or maybe boiled peanuts for a treat."

"So many options. What do you say, Leticia?"

"My neighbor made me some boiled peanuts. I never had anything so disgusting in my life. So slimy and salty." She shuddered. "Anything but boiled peanuts would be fine."

"You'll need a lot for peanut butter. I have an idea," Jem said. "You should sing to them."

Lucy started to laugh. "And why would I want to do that?"

"Helps them grow. It's scientifically proven." He rubbed his chin. "But these are authentic Mississippi heirloom peanuts. They'll need just the right song."

"Like some Elvis? Or B.B. King?" Leticia asked.

"Nah. We need a Confederate soldier song, a folk tune."

Lucy put her hand to her mouth to hide her smile. She knew what was coming. The only thing better than hearing Jem sing this song was going to be watching Leticia's face when he did.

His voice was clear, and the jaunty melody filled the little area. *"Sitting by the roadside on a summer's day, chatting with my messmates, passing time away. Lying in the shadows underneath the trees."* He paused to wink at Lucy. *"Goodness, how delicious, eating goober peas. Peas, peas, peas, peas. Eating goober peas. Goodness, how delicious, eating goober peas."*

Leticia shook her head, her mouth open in disbelief. "What on earth are you singing? 'Goober Peas'?"

He just grinned and kept singing. *"Just before the battle, the General hears a row. He says, 'The Yanks are coming, I hear their rifles now.' He turns around in wonder, and what d'ya think he sees? The Tennessee Militia, eating goober peas."*

"I thought it was the Georgia Militia," Lucy interrupted.

"I've heard that version, too. But I think the original had Tennessee Militia because they were the last to declare secession."

"But it's a reference to the Battle of Griswoldville, where the Georgia Militia fought so bravely. It doesn't make as much sense with Tennessee," Lucy said.

Leticia stared from Lucy to Jem. "I can't believe you two are arguing about this song. It's a nonsense song. I can't even tell what you're talkin' about."

"It's not nonsense." Jem looked shocked. "It's part of our Southern heritage, right, Lucy? Everybody should know 'Goober Peas.'" The corners of his mouth went up. "Plus, it's just a good song."

He crossed the waiting room and held out his arms, one hand upright and the other curved as if there was a person inside that space. Lucy blinked up at him. "I don't know the dance to it. I didn't know there was one."

"There's no dance. Come on, it's easy." He took her left hand and wrapped his arm around her waist. She could smell soap and something like freshly mown grass. He started to move in a slow waltz as he sang, *"I think my song has lasted almost long enough. The subject's interesting, but the rhymes are mighty tough. I wish the war was over, so free from rags and fleas. We'd kiss our wives and sweethearts, and gobble goober peas."*

"You two are plum crazy," Leticia said.

Lucy joined in on the chorus, laughing into the words. *"Goodness, how delicious, eating goober peas. Peas, peas, peas, peas. Eating goober peas. Goodness, how delicious, eating goober peas."*

She started to let go of his hand, but Jem held tight, moving smoothly into another step. "Did you know there's a stanza they sang at the Union prison on Johnson's Island?"

Lucy shook her head. It was hard for her to think straight when he was so close to her. His voice had lost its cheery tone and his eyes were somber. They moved easily together around the waiting room, and everything faded away as he sang, *"But now we are in prison and likely long to stay. The Yankees they are guarding us, no hope to get away. Our rations they are scanty, 'tis cold enough to freeze. I wish I was in Georgia, eating goober peas."*

He sang the chorus, but she didn't join in. The words were slow and sad now, nothing like the jaunty folk song it had been when he'd started. She glanced up. His hand was warm in hers, and she felt his arm strong against her back. He held her just as surely as Marcus had. But where Marcus's strength set off warning sirens in her head, Jem's made her forget the world. There was nothing but him and her and this sunny waiting room on a Thursday afternoon. The lines of his face were so familiar, the way his mouth tilted up on one side.

"I sure wish it was cold enough to freeze. I don't know why these old places don't have air-conditioning," Leticia said.

Her words seem to filter in to Lucy from somewhere far away. She stood motionless, Jem still holding her hand, their gazes locked. Her pulse thudded in her ears. The look in his eyes wasn't bitter or cold or anything she had seen before. He seemed to be caught somewhere between fear and hope.

Leticia cleared her throat. "I hate to interrupt the moment, but we've got company."

Lucy sprang away from Jem, her gaze darting to the doorway that led to the hall. She expected to see Aunt Olympia there, a furious expression on her face. But the area was empty. She looked around, confused.

Jem was watching her, eyes narrowed. He dropped his hand to his side. "Just a patient, Lucy."

Turning to the glass doors that led to the deck, she saw a young, pregnant woman carrying a baby on one hip. "I wasn't . . . I just thought . . ." Lucy's face went hot. She'd been scared senseless at the idea of being caught with Jem, and he knew it.

He walked away without another word, holding the door open for the young mom. Lucy felt her stomach drop into her shoes. She had failed him. Again. She'd prayed they could be friends, but it would never happen. Jem was wonderful and funny and sweet, but they could never be friends because Lucy was a coward. She swallowed back a sour taste in her throat. All it had taken was the suggestion of Aunt Olympia's disapproval and she'd snapped ten years into the past. She was still the girl who was afraid of her daddy's disapproval, the one who didn't want to lose his love because she was too stubborn, too strong-willed.

"Kaniesha, is everything okay?"

She shook her head, her braids shaking from side to side; her face was tight with worry. "Dr. Chevy, Tina sounds so bad. She had a cold and she was coughing, and now she's not coughing as much. But listen." Kaniesha held the baby up. The infant's dark eyes were heavy lidded and she let out a feeble squawk. Her tiny voice was hoarse.

Jem took the stethoscope from around his neck and quickly pressed it to the baby's chest. "She certainly sounds congested. Come on back. Leticia will grab the paperwork and you can fill it out in a few minutes."

Seconds later they were gone and Leticia was bustling around, pulling intake sheets from the drawers. Lucy numbly went back to the plastic container of disinfectant wipes. She had begged for some sort of peace between them and it had seemed as if God had answered her prayer. It was too bad that she had ruined it, again.

Tears filled her eyes and she blindly wiped a bright-yellow airplane and set it back on the shelf. She had thought if she could only have one more chance, then maybe things could be different. But she had to face that no matter how many chances she got, no matter how many times Jem forgave her, she wasn't strong enough to be the woman he needed, the woman he deserved.

She'd thought Regan was the worst person he could be with, but Regan would never be ashamed to be with Jem. Regan might be shallow and petty and ignorant, but she was not afraid.

Lucy had never felt so disappointed in herself in her whole life.

The door swung open and a man with two small children walked in. He looked dirty and tired. He crossed the waiting room, dragging a little girl in each hand. "Excuse me."

"Yes?" Leticia stacked forms and slipped them onto a clipboard.

"My girls are startin' school after the summer. The teacher says they need to get their vaccinations."

"Have they had any before?"

"No, ma'am." He shook his head. "I always had them brush their teeth, though. They got real good teeth."

Leticia smiled at the two girls, who each hid behind one of their father's legs. "Well, let's get you all set up for a checkup. Do you live near here?"

"Pretty close. We took two buses."

Lucy tried not to show her surprise and turned away. Two buses was close? She thought fifteen minutes in her own car was too long some days.

"I'll ask Dr. Chevy, but I'm pretty sure he'll just want to do a basic checkup today and then we'll start to schedule the vaccinations." Leticia leaned down to the girls. "So, no shots today, okay?"

One girl leaned out and flashed a wide smile. "Can we play with your toys?"

"Sure, go ahead."

Both girls scampered toward Lucy, tiny pigtails bouncing. They stood for a moment, surveying the brightly colored puzzles and plastic push toys.

"Wow," one breathed. She looked up at Lucy. "Are these all your toys?"

She smiled. "No, they belong to the clinic."

The other girl nodded. "I knowed that. Nobody got that many toys."

Lucy looked at the small shelf. It was so easy to forget that there were children right in her own hometown who couldn't imagine owning five toys and a puzzle. She crouched down and held out her hand. "I'm Lucy. What's your name?"

"Linnie. And this Winnie." They wore identical

smiles, their bright black eyes sparked with curiosity. "Are you the doctor?"

"No, I'm just volunteering."

"I knowed that, too." Winnie gave her an exaggerated shake of the head. "Girls is never the doctor. They's the nurses."

"Oh, no, what about Dr. Clare? Huh? The lady doctor who took care of Grammy in the hospital when she broke her hip bone?" Linnie asked.

"Yeah, but she was a white lady. They can be doctors." Winnie looked at Lucy. "Right? There are white lady doctors. I seen 'em."

Lucy felt her eyes go wide. Were there children who still believed your gender or color dictated your career? "There are white lady doctors, Black lady doctors, white man doctors, Black man doctors."

They stared at her.

She thought for a moment. "And there are white man nurses and Black man nurses, too."

"Now you're just bein' silly," Linnie said, and let out a laugh. Apparently Lucy had gone too far and the girls had decided she was pulling some sort of prank.

Jem appeared in the waiting room, brows drawn together. "Leticia, I'm setting up Tina with a nebulizer, but I can't find the infant masks."

"Top drawer at the end," Leticia answered, not looking up. She was helping the twins' dad fill out paperwork.

Jem nodded, then turned to Lucy. "I know this isn't part of your job description, but I was wondering if you could help back here for a moment?"

"Of course." She stood up and followed him down the hallway into the last room. The young mom sat in a straight chair, the baby sleeping on her lap.

"Kaniesha, this is Lucy Crawford. She's helping out around here."

Kaniesha nodded, but didn't say anything. It was clear that Kaniesha didn't want her in the room, but since Jem had asked, she felt as if she should stay.

"You said you needed to use the restroom. Lucy could hold Tina for you while I get the nebulizer set up." He was unwrapping tubes and plugging in a machine while he talked. He clearly thought Kaniesha would jump at the chance.

Lucy saw her debate the idea, chewing on her lower lip. "Fine," she finally said. "If I didn't have somebody kicking me in the bladder, I could wait a bit longer, but . . ." She scooted forward on the chair, lifting her arms.

Slipping her hands under the little girl's sleeping form, Lucy lifted her close and gently stepped away. Kaniesha stood up with a groan. "Oh, man. I never should have drank all that water. They tell you to drink eight glasses a day, but my eyeballs are floatin' and I'm livin' in the bathroom."

Lucy moved to the side so Kaniesha could pass, and she waddled from the room.

"Go ahead and sit down. This will take just a moment," Jem said, bending over a tiny canister and squeezing in clear liquid from a plastic packet. He attached a purple alligator mask to a large tube and gently slipped it over Tina's head. She moved a little, but stayed asleep. Jem flipped a switch, and the low hum of the machine filled the office and white steam filled the mask.

Lucy shifted in the chair, hoping the baby wouldn't wake while her mom was in the bathroom. The mask would be scary enough, but a stranger might be much worse.

Jem sat on the swivel stool and scooted toward the baby. He positioned his stethoscope in his ears and placed the flat piece against Tina's chest.

Lucy froze, surprised by how close he was. Their knees were almost touching, and Lucy was suddenly aware of every breath she took. She thought of how long ago she'd eaten lunch and hoped her stomach didn't growl. She glanced up, noting how he'd never really been able to tame that cowlick in the front and how his dark blond hair grew every which way. His hands were so sure, so gentle. He lifted the baby's shoulder and listened to her back. His head was bowed, just inches from Lucy's. She could see where he'd shaved and the tiny scar over his right eyebrow where he was snagged by his cousin's fishhook that last summer before college. He'd jokingly told everybody he'd been in a fight, but Lucy had known better. Jem wasn't the fighting type.

Lucy dropped her eyes to Tina's little face. Her eyelashes were long and curled up to touch her lids. Lucy wondered if the baby's father had long lashes, or if she'd inherited them from some other family member down the line. She touched the soft skin of the baby's arm, marveling at the milk-chocolate color, the impossible smoothness.

"Could you turn her a bit, so I can listen on the other side?" Jem asked. Lucy nodded and carefully maneuvered Tina to her other arm. Jem leaned close, listening.

Lucy's mama had said she was as dark as her daddy by the time she'd passed her first year. She wondered if her babies would be like her and her daddy, or like her mama and her sisters. Of course, it all depended on the father. Lucy's heart contracted a bit at the thought. In her mind, the only man she could see fathering her children was Jem. Maybe they would have his height, or that smile that went up on one side, or his love of science.

Jem scooted away to the desk to write down some notes, and Lucy wanted to kick herself. Jem wasn't marrying her and wasn't making babies with her. Some girls put a lot of thought into a future spouse, but Lucy had never been that girl. It was probably because Rebecca was getting married. Being in a wedding always made the women want to jump on the marriage train and start decorating a nursery. Lucy wanted to give her hormones a talk. She was young, not even thirty. There was plenty of time for marriage and babies.

It was a remainder of former sentiment;
it was an impulse of pure, though
unacknowledged friendship; it was a
proof of his own warm and amiable heart,
which she could not contemplate without
emotions so compounded of pleasure and
pain, that she knew not which prevailed.
—ANNE ELLIOT

CHAPTER EIGHTEEN

Stroking the soft skin of the baby's arm, Lucy admired the little ridge of baby fat above the wrist. A few lines started to run through her head, something she'd read that morning. She thought of Jem, his hands, how she'd gripped one of his at the presentation, how he'd held hers so gently a little while ago while he was singing a silly song about peanuts.

"What are you thinking?" he said without turning his head.

"I—nothing." She couldn't explain she was thinking of what color their babies would be and how she missed the touch of his hands.

He turned around, a half smile on his face. "You sighed."

"I did?"

"You won't get sick. If you wash your hands very well and turn your head when she coughs, you can keep most colds from spreading."

"Oh, no." Her face went hot. Did he think she was afraid of this baby's germs? She felt privileged to be here, holding her. "I was thinking of a George Eliot quote."

His eyebrows went up. "Which one?"

She opened her mouth and for a moment debated whether to tell the truth. She could say anything and he'd never know. But her mind had gone blank and she answered, "The one about friendship, about pouring out your heart."

He nodded and recited, *"A friend is one to whom one may pour out the contents of one's heart, chaff and grain together, knowing that gentle hands will take and sift it, keep what is worth keeping, and with a breath of kindness, blow the rest away."*

She nodded, reveling in the sound of his voice. Memories rushed back, of that summer when they would come out of the poetry slams unable to sleep, unable to stop talking to each other. And now a simple exchange felt too difficult.

"What made you think of it? The line about *chaff and grain together?*" His tone was causal. "She said it so well. We're all made up of chaff and grain."

Lucy stared down at Tina, at how her own dark

fingers looked against the baby's skin, how Jem's light hands had seemed to fit in the picture. She was afraid to tell him because even though the thoughts weren't hers, speaking the lines would make them hers.

She took a deep breath. *"Knowing that gentle hands will take and sift it."*

She stopped, the air in the room thick with her meaning. She looked up, holding on to her bravery, and said, "Gentle hands. That part, you made me think of that part when you were examining her."

His blue eyes went a bit wider, then he looked down at Tina and said softly, "Thank you."

His goodness made her realize how weak she truly was. He was always kind, nothing but kind. And she was afraid to be seen with someone her aunt felt wasn't good enough.

He cleared his throat. "I was going to have a Fourth of July party. I would like it if you'd come."

Lucy blinked. "Where?" she asked, then was embarrassed by her bad manners. "I mean, yes, that would be fun. I'd like to go."

A smile spread over his face. "Good. One of my friends, Lars LeRoux, runs swamp tours down where the Sampit and Pee Dee meet, but he's taking the weekend off to visit." Jem paused. "I'm not big on parties, but we're trying to get a friend of ours to be a little more social. Danny's had a rough few months and I thought a little fun might cheer him up."

"What can I bring?"

"I think he'll have ribs from Shorty's BBQ, but you can bring any kind of horrible vegetarian dish you can whip up out of the garden. We'll all just suffer through it."

She snorted. "You're on." Paulette had mentioned some party, but Lucy had tuned her out. She usually watched the fireworks from the back deck. Now Jem's invitation had sparked a bright flame of hope inside.

"I'd rather head down to Tombigbee and hang out at the lake for the weekend, but Lars thought this might be a good way to get Danny out of the house." Jem's smiled faded away. "I should tell you while I have the chance that Danny's wife passed away from cancer last summer."

"I'm so sorry," she said, wishing there were something better than that tired old phrase.

Jem nodded. "He hasn't been out, unless it's to head out to the pond and go frog giggin' late at night." He ran a hand through his hair, making it stand up in the front. "I would never force someone to be more social than they want to be, but Danny used to be the party man. He loves people and is a classic extrovert. Lars said that Danny wants to ease back into the world, but he feels as if he's lost touch with his friends."

"I think it's great that you two are hosting the

party for him, and I'd love to come." She paused. "Although, I'm not much of a wild party person myself. I don't know how much help I'll be in bringing him out of his cave."

Jem laughed, and she loved the little lines around his eyes. "I know you're not."

She opened her mouth to respond but couldn't think of a single thing to say. She wanted to freeze this moment, when he smiled at her as if they were friends, planning a happy moment together.

"Sorry about that," Kaniesha said, bustling back into the room. "I saw my cousin Jaylene's girls out there and I thought maybe they were sick."

She came close and Lucy transferred Tina's little form back into her mother's arms. Kaniesha settled into the chair and said, "And thanks."

"Anytime. You have a beautiful baby."

Her face softened. "She is. Takes after her daddy." She pressed a gentle kiss to Tina's forehead. "It makes me crazy when she's sick. I'm so glad Dr. Chevy could get us right in. We used to wait for hours because they only had Dr. Stroud."

"Now we've got more room, too," Jem said, head bent over the papers on his desk.

"Right." Kaniesha's brows were drawn together. "I didn't think it was such a good idea to move the clinic here. But it's worked out fine."

"Is it much farther from where you live?" Lucy asked.

"No." And her answer hung in the air like an unfinished sentence. Finally she shrugged. "I ran into a Crawford girl once. I wasn't much impressed."

Jem's head went up and he frowned. "I'm sure it was a misunderstanding."

"Probably not." Lucy sighed.

Kaniesha shook her head. "Nope, no misunderstandin'. I was working at June Bug Boutique, unpacking the boxes in the back. She came in there, looking for some big vase she needed. I brought it out and . . ." Kaniesha sighed. "There was an extension cord on the carpet. I didn't see it and lay myself flat out. I tumped that pretty vase right on the tile. Turned it into a hundred pieces."

Lucy grimaced. She could imagine what happened next. She didn't have to know whether it was Paulette or Janessa. Neither of them was overwhelmingly sympathetic.

"I figured that if she threw a fit, then they'd just order her another. But she needed it right then, and the only way she was gonna get some satisfaction was if Miss June fired me." Kaniesha shrugged. "I don't blame Miss June. She needed to keep her customers happy."

"I'm sorry that happened. Is there something I can do to help?"

"Nah, that was a long time ago, before I left school. I got a different job now at Kenny's

314

Cafeteria. I would rather be unpacking pretty glass things, for sure, but I don't mind it so much."

There was a tap at the door and Leticia poked her head inside. "Lucy, your aunt's looking for you."

Jem stood up, holding the door open. "Thanks for your help."

Lucy had the feeling of being shooed away but she just smiled. "Welcome."

A few seconds later she spotted Aunt Olympia's sullen face. She was standing in the far corner of the waiting room, clutching her little purse to her chest. "What are you doing in here?" she asked, loud enough to make everyone turn to look.

"Come on in the kitchen," Lucy said, pulling her toward the door.

"You better wash your hands. I can't eat anything you touch until you wash your hands. Those people probably have all sorts of diseases." Aunt Olympia let herself be led toward the hallway.

Sounds were coming from the kitchen and Lucy could smell something wonderful. "Hello, Mrs. Hardy," she called as they came in. "Just getting Auntie some sweet tea."

"How you doin', Miss Lucy?" Mrs. Hardy's dark face shone with sweat but she smiled. "Makin' your daddy's favorite dish for dinner."

"Chicken-fried steak?" Lucy washed her hands

at the sink, noting how much whiter it was when Mrs. Hardy cleaned it. She remembered how delicious chicken-fried steak was, especially with Mrs. Hardy's special white gravy, but her mama's early death had robbed Lucy's ever wanting to eat it again.

"Chicken casserole with green beans," Mrs. Hardy said, pointing to a row of condensed-soup cans and a large container of sour cream. "I think he like the way I fry the crackers in a pan after I mash them up."

Lucy went to the fridge and pulled out the pitcher of tea, pouring it into two tall glasses. She argued back the part of her that wanted to remind Mrs. Hardy they were trying to eat healthy. Sour cream and fried crackers wasn't the greatest base for a casserole.

"I can see what you're thinking," Aunt Olympia said.

"Oh?" Lucy had never learned how to keep her emotions wrapped up tight and they leaked out into her expressions.

"You think we're not feeding Willy right." Aunt Olympia's face was triumphant. "Tell her, Mrs. Hardy. Tell her what we had for lunch yesterday when she was at work."

"I made baked potatoes for Mr. Crawford and he enjoyed them real well." Mrs. Hardy stirred the crackers in the pan and nodded. "Fresh-baked potatoes."

"With a little butter?" Lucy was going to have to eat crow if her daddy ate something like that and didn't complain.

"Not even any butter. I just hollowed out the potato mash, filled it with pulled pork and topped it with chow chow."

"See?" Aunt Olympia took a sip of her tea. "That has all the food groups. The bun was real soft for soppin' up the sauce, too."

Lucy dropped into her chair. "Chow chow doesn't really qualify as a vegetable. It's a condiment."

"Of course it does. Cabbage, green tomatoes and peppers are all vegetables. We usually put potato chips on there, but this had a nice crunch to it, too."

"There ain't nothin' like a big, juicy pork butt rubbed with sugar and spices. Mmmm-hmmmm," Mrs. Hardy added.

"Look at that." Aunt Olympia pointed a bright-red fingernail at the glass door that led to the deck.

Lucy turned in time to see a group of kids circling Hattie, each reaching out to pet her fur.

"Zeke fed her chitlins and I don't think we can convince her to leave." Lucy had to smile at the way the kids all wanted to pet her at the same time.

"What? No, not the cat. I was lookin' at that woman. Can you imagine? Who in their right mind has all those kids? No wonder she's at the free clinic." Aunt Olympia clucked her tongue. "And I hate that we can see them running up and down our steps."

"We could cover this door, I suppose."

"Then we wouldn't have any view at all! Lucy, sometimes I don't think you have a lick of sense."

She'd heard those words before but had shrugged them off. For the first time those words didn't settle in as they should have. Lucy felt them drop one by one into her heart, and they didn't fit.

"I think I have more than a lick, Auntie." She stood up. "I've got to get back to the clinic. I'm volunteering there on Thursday afternoons."

Aunt Olympia's mouth dropped open, but Lucy didn't wait to hear what would come out next. She had somewhere to be.

"You look the very opposite of relaxed," Lars said. He had his feet propped up on the deck railing, a beer in his hand and a hat shading his face. "This is supposed to be fun."

"It is. I am." Jem checked the BBQ ribs one more time. "Maybe I should have got some chili-slaw dogs from Shorty's. Everybody loves those."

"Buddy," Lars said, dropping his shoes to the deck with a thump, "sit yourself down and stop fussing. You're reminding me of my aunt Glynna with all this temperature takin' and foil tuckin'.

This food is fine. As soon as the wife gets all her dishes out here, we'll start eating."

Jem settled into one of the deck chairs and looked out onto the acre of land that Lars had reclaimed from the kudzu. Guests were wandering in and out of the kitchen area, introducing each other, greeting old friends. A few had walked to the end of the yard to look at the goats. Jem blew out a breath. He wanted everything to go right. It was just a barbecue party but he felt as if maybe it could be something more. If she came at all.

"So, who's got you all tied up in knots?"

"Nobody."

Lars stared at him, eyes hidden behind his dark glasses.

Jem let a few more seconds pass. "I invited a girl."

"No kidding." Lars took a sip of beer and motioned with his other hand. "Angie was asking me where your girlfriend was."

"I don't have one," Jem said. Lars's wife was plugged into the gossip. She probably had heard something about Regan and her habit of running her hands up his ribs when he couldn't defend himself.

"Sho-o-ore." Lars made the word last several syllables longer than it needed to be. "And you wear nice shirts to every barbecue."

Jem smoothed the front of his shirt. "Nothing wrong with looking good. You should try it. I'm sure Angie would love it if you didn't look like a river rat all the time."

"A drowned river rat, at that." Lars shrugged and picked at the frayed hem of his khaki shorts. "This is my river-guide costume. If I change my look, I'll lose my mystique."

Jem snorted.

"Seriously, my friend"—Lars leaned closer—"who's the girl?"

Out of the corner of his eye, Jem saw Lucy walk through the arbor. She was wearing a peach-colored dress and her hair was down in soft curls that reached past her shoulders. She held a casserole dish in her hands and her eyes scanned the yard.

Jem stood up, his heart in his throat. As if he'd called her name, she looked over at him and smiled. Jem thought she'd never looked more beautiful, not even at the Strouds' party. She'd been quiet and sad then, but now she glowed with life.

"Is that who I think it is?" Lars said, pulling down his shades to get a better look.

"Lucy Crawford. I don't think you ever met her but—"

"Nope, never did, but I sure heard about how she dumped your sorry self." Lars let out a low whistle. "Boy, you are a glutton for punishment. But somehow I can't blame you."

Jem was already headed down the steps, a smile

spreading over his face. He should try to not care so much, but he couldn't help the way his heart beat faster just at the sight of her. As he got closer, he realized her dress had sequins across the chest. She looked as if she'd just walked out of a high school prom.

"You look beautiful." As soon as he said the words, he wanted to take them back. Not even a "Hey, how are you?" before he launched right into the compliments. Way to play it cool.

She beamed. "Thanks. I found this in the attic and I knew it would be just the wrong thing."

"Just the . . . what?"

She nodded toward a group of girls crossing the grass. They all wore little sundresses that barely reached halfway down their thighs, simple strings of pearls, strappy sandals. Peals of laughter floated on the air.

"I brought you something." He reached out for the dish, but she didn't let go. "I want you to know it took me a long time to choose a recipe."

"You shouldn't have worried. We've got lots of food."

"I know, it's not that. Just open it."

He cocked an eyebrow and peeled back a corner of the foil. "Cracklin' cornbread. My favorite." He leaned closer. "Wait a minute. This is plain."

Lucy nodded. "There's only so far I can go with this. And cracklins are my limit."

So far I can go with this. He realized why she was wearing a peach prom dress from the nineties at a twenty-first-century Fourth of July party. He felt his mouth go dry.

"Cracklins are tasty, so I don't know whether your limit is high or low." He tried to sound as if he were making a joke, but he couldn't stop staring into her eyes. She was telling him something about herself, and him, and that horrible party ten years ago.

"It's real high," she whispered. She took a deep breath. "I'm hoping one of your friends comes over to make fun of me, maybe tell me to get back in the kitchen with the catering staff."

He nodded. That had been the very worst moment. Aunt Olympia had shooed him toward the kitchen, thinking he was part of the cooking crew. "And I'll just stand in the corner like I don't know you."

Her face crumpled and he felt her pain as if it were his own. He wanted to take it back, but just like that memory, it was always going to be there.

She worked to get control and then said, "I'm sorry I didn't defend you. I'm sorry I didn't tell them you were my guest."

Jem hadn't thought he cared anymore, not really, but her words were tugging loose the hard, painful knot in his chest. "It's okay."

She shook her head. "It's not. It wasn't."

He reached out and cupped her cheek in his hand. He didn't know what else to say, and all he wanted was to touch her skin, let her know that he wasn't that boy anymore and that she wasn't that girl.

"Hi, honey!" The chirpy voice behind him made him jump. He turned and saw Regan trotting across the lawn. "I looked all over the house for you."

He dropped his hand. "I'm out here."

"Well, obviously, silly pants." She threw her arms around him and squeezed. Jem patted her awkwardly on the shoulder. Her strapless sundress was skintight until the little skirt flared out, but he was still afraid it was going to fall off.

"I'll take this inside," Lucy said, starting past them.

"I can do—"

"No, you stay here." Lucy's gaze flicked to Regan, clinging to his waist and giggling up at him. "Otherwise you might get lost again."

Jem watched Lucy walk toward the deck. It wasn't his fault that Regan was the Southern-belle version of an octopus.

"Let's go look at the goats." Regan let go just enough to turn him toward the back of the lawn. "I heard that goat milk can cure a hangover. I think I'll test it out."

"You're drunk?"

"No, but I can get there." She giggled and ran a hand along the back of his belt.

Jem detached her hand. "I'm not sure if goat milk will save you, but it does contain the amino acid cysteine . . ."

"And?"

"When alcohol works its way through your system, it releases acetaldehyde, which can be deadly in a large enough amount, and cysteine can neutralize that."

"Oooh, honey, I love it when you talk like that." Regan slipped her hand up his arm. "Nerds are so sexy. I had this biology professor who was so hot. I loved when he would come to class in his sweater vest. I could hardly concentrate."

Jem wanted to roll his eyes but managed to keep a straight face.

"He had the worst fashion sense, but it was kind of cute, ya know? Not like Lucy. That girl needs a real makeover." Regan glanced behind her. "Vintage can work, but it has to be the right era. She's got it all wrong with that nineties-prom thing. Even the shoes are those dyed-to-match kind."

"I thought she looked fine." Jem clenched his jaw.

"Of course you did, because you're a man." Regan giggled. "And that hair. I know Black hair is hard to work with. Paulette has to be at the salon practically every week. But Lucy is just letting it go wild. It's huge!"

Jem didn't know what to say. He'd seen Lucy wearing a silk sheath dress, with her hair smoothed down in a sort of forties-movie-star style. He'd seen her with no makeup, wearing jeans and a T-shirt. He'd seen her in a ponytail and office clothes. Now, he'd seen her with curly hair and a bad prom dress. Every single time, she'd taken his breath away.

It didn't matter what she wore, or how she did her hair, or what she put on her face. She was beautiful and his heart responded to the sight of her without his permission.

A small smile touched his lips. When he had put his hand to her cheek, her eyes had gone soft. He could have sworn that Lucy, just for a moment, wanted to kiss him. He had hoped that if he invited her to the party, they would get to know each other away from her family and her friends. He hadn't planned on Regan showing up, but it was still a major step forward that Lucy was here, and they had cleared the air.

That foil-covered pan of cornbread meant more to him than anything he'd been given since he'd left Tupelo, and Jem wasn't going to let her peace offering languish. He was determined to do his best to carve out some space, somewhere, for him and Lucy. Maybe, if God willed it, in time they could find their way back together.

"All the privilege I claim for my own sex
(it is not a very enviable one: you need
not covet it), is that of loving longest . . .
when hope is gone!"
—ANNE ELLIOT

CHAPTER NINETEEN

"Hello, I brought a side dish," Lucy said, setting it on the counter. She almost laughed at herself. It was the sort of awkward greeting that matched her costume.

A red-haired woman looked up from where she was washing her hands at the sink. Her pink-flowered shirt matched her pink shorts, and her gaze took in Lucy's outfit several times before she spoke. "Thanks. I cooked up a few dishes because I was afraid if we left it to the guys, our two dinner options were going to be barbecue ribs and beer." She wiped her hands on a towel. "I'm Angie, Lars's wife."

"I'm Lucy. Jem invited me," she answered, and hoped that was enough information.

"So, I'm thinking"—Angie frowned at Lucy's dress—" 'ninety-six? No, wait. 'Ninety-four?"

Lucy grinned. "I don't really know. I found it

in the attic. The mystery might never be solved."

"And should I ask why? Or is that classified, too?"

Lucy took an immediate liking to Angie. She was clever, but in a gentle way. "I was hoping to make a point to someone."

An eyebrow went up. "And do you think this someone got the point?" Angie hitched up one shoulder. "Because if that someone was a man, I'm thinking a text might be a better choice."

"I think so." Lucy had wanted to tell him she was sorry for so long that, when the time came, she could hardly get the words out. But she'd done it, and he'd accepted her apology.

"Well, good." Angie looked around at the dishes. "We should start bringing these out to the deck. I'll see if I can find Danny. He's hiding around here somewhere."

"Not hiding," said a tired voice. A man was leaning against the doorjamb. His brown hair was a little too long and his face was pale, but the corner of his mouth twitched when he looked at Lucy. "Nice prom dress."

"Thanks. I thought somebody better wear one. All those little sundresses with spaghetti straps are so boring."

He smiled outright. "I'm not so worried about the sundresses. It's all the girls in them. The chatter, the giggles, the inanity."

"I saw goats. A party can't be all bad when you have goats."

"Yep, Angie is a regular Heidi. She milks them and makes cheese. Probably sings while she does it, too."

"You bet I do." Angie handed Danny a dish. "I don't want you to hide in here all evening."

"Already said, not hiding." He wasn't smiling now. "Seriously, I think this was a mistake. I went out for a few minutes earlier and . . ."

"It's just a party. You eat some food and drink a beer and pretend you don't want to be crawdad fishing," Angie said.

"No, it's an echo chamber of sycophants and I can't listen to some bimbo recite her newest purchases while pretending I don't want to throw myself from the roof."

A laugh bubbled up in Lucy's throat and she couldn't keep it from bursting out.

Danny turned to her. "You think I'm kidding."

"I know you're not." Lucy was still chuckling. "I've been to these parties before. Plus, I'm related to some of these bimbos."

Angie took a dish and headed for the deck. "Just take a drink every time you want to say something rude. You'll be fine."

Danny shook his head. Angie was already out the door when he said, "I'll be drunk."

"Stick to Coke, maybe it will still work." Lucy picked up her cornbread dish. "We can raise our glasses together."

He smiled. "Sounds like a plan."

A few minutes later all the food was laid out, and Lars let out a shrill whistle, getting the attention of the guests at the far end of the yard. "Grub's on," he hollered.

"I'm glad the heat isn't so bad tonight," Angie said, looking up at the sky. "But I don't like the looks of that thunderhead."

"Gonna be a storm, for sure," Lars said, staring at the enormous cloud building on the horizon.

"Kelsey loved thunderstorms," Danny said, as if to himself.

Lucy saw Angie and Lars exchange glances.

"What?" Danny said. "I can't mention her name?"

"Of course you can. But I thought you were going to enjoy the party, meet new people." Lars pointed to the group coming across the grass. The girls were young and pretty, their laughter floating ahead. Lucy saw Regan's arm around Jem's waist and her stomach clenched.

"I won't be able to enjoy the party if I have to pretend she didn't exist." There was a hard note of anger in Danny's voice.

"Nobody's asking you to pretend that, but mentioning her name every five minutes sort of stops the conversation." Lars took a long pull on his beer.

Danny turned to Lucy. "Did it stop our conversation?"

"Not at all." She wanted to like Lars, but the guy seemed to not have the faintest idea of how it felt to be in love with someone who wasn't coming back. "When you love someone, it's hard not to see them everywhere."

"Ah, a romantic." Danny leaned back, threading his fingers behind his head. "I used to be one, until my wife died. And then I was just pathetic."

Angie made a noise and got up to rearrange the dishes.

Danny whispered, "I'm not supposed to say that I was suicidal and didn't shower for three months. I'm supposed to say I bore it like a man."

Lucy didn't know if Danny expected her to laugh, but her heart was heavy. "I've been where you are. Or were. You can't talk yourself out of that place."

His eyebrows went up. "You lost your husband?"

"No, I've never been married." Lucy saw Jem and Regan walk up to the deck. The words stuck in her throat, but she forced them out. "But I did love someone once." She felt as if she had to clarify. "And we broke up."

"That's nice," he said, and took a sip of his Coke.

Lucy narrowed her eyes. "You just used Angie's party advice. You took a sip of your drink and pretended you didn't want to be crawdad fishing."

Danny laughed, and it was a surprisingly warm sound. "You got me." He sobered. "You have to admit that breaking up with someone and losing a spouse are different."

"I know." She looked down at her hands, remembering Jem's touch from just a few days ago. "But that love is the same, and the loss is deep. I know how it is to look around you and see them everywhere. Everything they loved is still here, and it hurts to see it."

He nodded, closing his eyes for a moment. "True." He looked over the group of girls; most of them huddled around Jem. "But I think when a woman loses someone she loves, she can run to her friends for support. They take her out shopping or to the movies; they distract her with craft projects or get her hooked on *Downton Abbey*. Men have nothing to fall back on but whiskey and fishing."

"Do you really think a woman can be distracted from a broken heart by a knitting project?"

He shrugged. "Sure seems like it. Every TV show I see, the girl is drowning her woes in chocolate and throwing herself into some new hobby."

"Huh. And you take that as truth because TV is the last word on the female heart."

"People wouldn't watch it if it didn't make sense to them."

Lucy could see Jem watching them from a few feet away. He was probably wishing she would stop arguing with Danny and ask him about something normal, such as fishing. "I'm not sure about chocolate or hobbies, but I do know one thing. When women have their heart broken, they don't run out and find another man. Not usually. But men, it's the first thing you hear. They've got a new girlfriend and call her a rebound relationship."

"I've known guys who did that," he conceded. "And although I didn't, it may have been less about not wanting to than that I hadn't showered recently enough to attract any sane woman."

"Right." She sighed. "I wish it was different, really. But women will wait for a man long after a man has given up waiting for a woman."

Danny stared out at the thundercloud building in the distance. "When I think of how long I have to wait before I see her again, I wish I could skip to the end of my life."

Lucy reached out and touched his hand. "I know. Looking too far ahead is the worst kind of torture. One day at a time, as they say."

The corner of his mouth turned up. "Or one party at a time."

She smiled and turned her head just in time to see Jem's expression—of concern, anxiety and something else. Regan was chattering away in his ear and rubbing her hand up his arm, but he didn't seem to be listening.

"Time to eat, everybody," Danny called as the last of the guests straggled onto the deck.

Lucy stood up, feeling tired and spent, as if she'd run for miles instead of sitting at a picnic table and discussing broken hearts. She hoped, for Danny's sake, that Jem's plan would succeed. Maybe Danny would decide life held some happiness after all, but she didn't think a barbecue would make the man forget the love of his life. She was almost certain it wouldn't because she knew just how he felt.

"Dare not say that man forgets sooner than woman, that his love has an earlier death. I have loved none but you. Unjust I may have been, weak and resentful I have been, but never inconstant."

—CAPTAIN WENTWORTH

CHAPTER TWENTY

Lucy carefully outlined her eyes with a brown pencil and stared at her reflection. If she could change her color at a whim, she would be the spitting image of a Regency girl from Theresa's movie. Her pale-pink dress fell in silky folds from the bodice, and the velvet-ribbon piping around the scooped neckline was a shade darker than the fabric. A lace overlay created an elegance that was timeless.

"Almost ready?" Rebecca's friend Shelby popped into the room. She was wearing a matching gown in pale-green, but hers covered an obviously pregnant front. "We've got about fifteen minutes before the ceremony starts, and the priest wants us near the front doors so we can process in as soon as it's time." Her red hair was piled up in a small shower of curls.

"I'm done here. I just need to get my gloves." Lucy started to pull on the elbow-length gloves.

"These remind me of my cotillion. Except I wasn't pregnant, of course."

Lucy snorted. "My dress was such a giant poofball I had trouble getting in and out of the car."

"Who knew we'd put all that fancy training to work in an Austen wedding." Shelby shook her head. "I've always told her she's obsessed, but she never listened."

Caroline Ashley popped in, glancing around the room. Her blond updo was elegant and her blue-green eyes shone. The pale-blue of her dress made her seem like an ethereal ice princess, except her skin glowed with health. Lucy had known Caroline since high school, and they had more in common than most people would think. Their friendship was cemented after college, when they met over long lunches to bemoan the pressures of caring for their widowed parents while simultaneously being expected to marry as soon as possible. Caroline had married her own true love last summer, and Lucy had felt one more friendship subtly change as others moved onto the next stage in life. She didn't want to be jealous and fought hard against it, but being in Caroline's wedding had been bittersweet. They had been comrades-in-arms and now Lucy felt as if she'd been left on the battlefield alone.

"Lucy, you say pink isn't your color, but you look gorgeous in anything," Caroline said. She reached over and gave Lucy a tight squeeze.

"Thank you. But I think anyone can pull off a Regency gown." Lucy adjusted a curl at Caroline's temple.

"We only have about five more minutes," Shelby said, checking her watch.

"Everyone looks perfect." Caroline sighed, smiling. "Oh, Shelby, you are just beautiful. That baby bump is precious."

"It's not a bump. It's a dorm-room-sized beanbag." She caressed her front. "If I was nice and tall like you, I would probably have a perfect little basketball."

"Don't count on it. My cousin Debbie Mae is only five months along and she looks like she's ready to pop," Caroline said.

Lucy watched this exchange and felt a sharp pain near her ribs. It was just hormones, just the biological clock ticking away, just being surrounded by married and pregnant women. But even as she told herself this, Lucy knew there was more to it. The more time she'd spent around Jem, the more she'd yearned for more. Now that they were almost friends, her dreams were about weddings and babies and little cottages with bright-green grass. Lucy forced herself back into the moment. It would be a shame to mope around Rebecca's wedding because she was being a jealous cow.

"Thank you for filling in, Caroline. I know Rebecca appreciates it," Lucy said.

"Not a problem. I'm glad I was in town and just the right size for the dress. I just feel terrible for her cousin. To get appendicitis and miss the wedding must be really awful."

"Hmm. I don't want to get appendicitis or miss the wedding, but I would have liked a more flattering style," said Shelby. "I feel like I'm wearing a tent."

"You're perfect. Plus, it's Rebecca's day to shine. If she wants us all to wear tents in a rainbow of pastel colors, we will, just to make sure she has everything her little Austen-loving heart desires, right?" Caroline linked arms with the other two and walked them toward the foyer.

"Right," they both responded.

Lucy stayed quiet as the girls whispered on the way down the hallway. They had dressed in a small group of rooms built on to the old church, and as they walked, Lucy noted the carved saints in every alcove they passed. She didn't know who any of them were, but it gave her a sense of peace to think of so many who had come before, trying to live as honestly as possible, even unto death. She could see how Jem treasured this place, this history. She wondered for a moment what it would be like to attend services here.

Would she be homesick for the community she'd grown up with? Or would it seem natural to be part of something so old?

Lucy remembered Jem's mama asking her where she went to church, and at the time it hadn't meant much, but she understood now. If she had married Jem, they would have had to choose which church to attend. And when they had children, they would have had to bring them up in one tradition.

She glanced at the stained-glass window that stretched the length of the hallway and wondered what all the symbols meant: keys and lions and quills and even a wagon wheel. She would have to learn it all. Maybe some people who attended services here didn't know or didn't care, but she would. She couldn't ignore all the history around her.

Lucy shook the thought from her head. Whether she would ever attend this church was a ridiculous thing to wonder about. All she was doing was walking down the aisle as bridesmaid, not taking her own vows. A second later, they turned the corner and saw the groomsmen lined up. Lucy's gaze went straight to Jem. He was watching them walk down the long hallway and a smile grew on his lips. His gaze never left her face.

She took in his blue morning coat, white vest, breeches and riding boots. He seemed at ease. The white cravat at his neck was tied in a simple knot, and his skin looked tan against it. When they were only a few feet apart, he stepped forward, blue eyes locked on hers. "You look beautiful."

"Why, thank you, Jem."

Shelby pretended to snag his elbow and lead him away. Lucy let out a soft snort. She had to agree that Jem was incredibly handsome, although Shelby's husband, Ransom, was just as attractive. He stood in the corner, a bit of a frown on his face. He seemed just like the Darcy Lucy imagined when she thought of Jane Austen. His face softened as he looked at Shelby. She let go of Jem and stepped to his side, looking up with an expression of complete happiness. He gently wrapped an arm around her and rested his hand on her hip. "Feeling okay? Should I get you a chair?"

"Just fine." She stretched up on tiptoe and gave him a kiss.

Lucy couldn't help smiling, even though it was painful to see a couple so in love. They'd been married three years and acted as if their own wedding were yesterday.

Caroline's husband, Brooks, stepped into the foyer and grinned. "I've never seen a nicer-looking group of Austen characters, but I'm glad I get to play a civilian this time."

"But you're so handsome in breeches." Caroline pretended to pout.

"You'll have to do with plain old regular me." He gave Caroline a kiss on the cheek. "I'm going to go sit down." She waved him away and rolled her eyes at Lucy. "I wish I'd taken more pictures the one time we'd gotten him in costume. I'm afraid that was a once-in-a-lifetime party."

Lucy opened her mouth to respond, but stopped as someone handed her a small, ribbon-wrapped bouquet of wildflowers and pleasant-smelling greenery. She glanced up at Jem and felt her cheeks go hot. He gave her a slight smile, but didn't speak. She hadn't had a chance to talk with him alone since the Fourth of July party. The way he'd touched her cheek, the tender look on his face, it all spoke of a man who felt more for her than bitterness and regret. Lucy dropped her gaze to the flowers, feeling her heart beat in her chest. They were going to walk down the aisle and witness the exchange of wedding vows. She wished she knew where they stood, if their friendship was growing, or if she should be content with simply not being at war with him. She felt as if the air were pulsing with questions and she didn't know where to start. He stayed silent beside her.

The organist started to play and Lucy turned to see Rebecca behind them. Her eyes were already misting with tears but her smile was joyous. The Regency wedding gown was a hundred times more beautiful than the picture Lucy had seen and she put a hand to her chest. She drew in a shuddery breath.

As if sensing her emotion, Jem took her hand, tucking it in his elbow and drew her close to his side. Lucy turned and focused ahead, straightening her shoulders. A lot of people cried at weddings, but Lucy had never been one of them. This was different. She felt tears pressing against her eyes and she gripped Jem's arm, willing herself to hold it together.

He looked down at her and winked. "Our turn," he said, and they began the slow march up the aisle.

Lucy glimpsed the delighted expressions of the guests and knew the two of them looked like something out of an Austen movie. Well, at least Jem did. She giggled a little and cleared her throat.

"Something funny?" he murmured out of the corner of his mouth.

"Just thinking how you're just like Captain Wentworth and I'm just like Tina Turner."

He let out a bark of laughter and quickly covered it with a cough. "Not sure who Wentworth is, but I can assure you that you're not Tina Turner."

"Shoot. She has really nice legs." Lucy couldn't help smiling as they neared the front.

"You have that in common." They started to separate and he whispered, "See you on the flip side."

Lucy took her place in the line of bridesmaids and turned to see Rebecca coming down the aisle. Lucy's heart swelled to see how happy Rebecca was, how the whole church had stood to welcome her. Lucy glanced at Tom, standing by the altar. His red hair was neatly combed and his face shone with happiness. She would never have believed the man in the Regency outfit was a computer programmer, but that was the beauty of Jane Austen. The most normal, run-of-the-mill person turned into someone noble and romantic. Her gaze slid to the right. Jem wasn't watching Rebecca, he was watching her. His eyes were soft and his lips were touched by the slightest smile. She stared into his eyes, wishing she could ask the questions that were beating against her ribs, but was then so thankful that she couldn't. For this moment, as they stood in the church to witness their friends pledging love and fidelity to death did them part, they were united. She was afraid that if they spoke at all, the spell would be broken and they would go back to being . . . whatever they were.

Rebecca crossed Lucy's vision and she turned away, still feeling Jem's gaze on her. *Lord, I never could have imagined anything about this moment. Your ways are mysterious and more than a little confusing. But thank you, for their love and for their joy.* She glanced back and Jem had turned his attention to the priest. Whatever happened after this moment, she would be thankful. She'd been able to make amends to someone she'd hurt very much, and even if she never got her heart's desire, that burden was lifted. She couldn't ask for more.

"Time will explain."
—LADY RUSSELL

CHAPTER TWENTY-ONE

Lucy gazed around at the freshly mown lawn at Rowan Oak, dotted with white tents and tiny lamps hung from the cedar trees. It was incredibly romantic and she thought she'd never seen a more beautiful setting for a reception. She caught Paulette's eye and raised a hand in greeting. Her sister changed course and greeted her with the usual sort of criticism. "That was a real nice wedding, but I think those dresses are a bit much."

Lucy frowned at the gown, wondering how anybody could find fault with such an elegant creation. "You don't think the men look silly? Just the women?"

"Oh, the men look wonderful. Those breeches fit just perfectly." Paulette gave her a sly grin. "But when I get married, Daddy says I can have it anywhere I want. I know he loves the—"

"Paulette," Lucy interrupted, grasping her hand. "Can I ask you something?"

"Well, I suppose."

Lucy looked down at their fingers, intertwined.

They were so similar. Lucy thought of their mama every day. Every time she cooked or picked out a dress or tried to keep their family from imploding, she hoped she was making her mama proud. Was Paulette so different just because she yearned for the approval of the parent who was still living?

"Do you really want to get married or are you just doing what Daddy says?"

For a moment, Paulette looked as if she were going to spit. But then her face slowly lost its fierceness and she seemed to crumple from the inside. She took several deep breaths and whispered, "He said he wants me to marry a successful man, someone he could do business with, but I don't think he really cares what I do, not really."

Lucy gripped her sister's hand tightly. Lucy knew how that felt. He never paid attention to her until she had the courage to step out of bounds, then he made it clear that good girls didn't disagree with their father.

"I think . . . I think he hasn't cared about anything since Mama died," Lucy said.

Paulette's eyes filled with tears. "I think we lost both of them that day."

Lucy reached out and hugged her sister tight. Paulette's marrying someone wouldn't make their daddy happy with her, and always being the perfect daughter wouldn't make him happy with

Lucy. She leaned back and looked her sister in the eyes. "I think we need to stop living for his approval."

"I don't think I know how to live without it." Paulette sounded small and lost.

"I bet you do. I bet you're stronger than you think you are."

Paulette shrugged. "And you? Are you finally going to tell him about Jem?"

It took Lucy a moment to catch her breath. "What about Jem?"

"Oh, Lucy, everybody can tell he's in love with you."

She stepped back, putting a hand to her chest.

Paulette gave her a little smile. "They say weddings always bring people together. Maybe you two can talk things through." Then Paulette turned and walked toward the crowded refreshment table.

Lucy stood stock-still, thoughts and feelings running over one another. She'd been so worried about Paulette's making decisions just for their daddy's approval, but maybe Lucy was just as guilty. She felt her heart pound in her chest. If it was right, if it was supposed to be, then she should be brave enough to be honest with Jem.

It was time to tell him the truth.

Jem stood in the corner and tried not to feel ridiculous. Rebecca had asked them to stay in their Regency costumes, but he was beginning to hate the pants tucked into the tops of his boots and the cravat that never seemed to stay straight. He would have paid big money to change into jeans and running shoes at that moment.

"You look lonely." Tom handed him a glass and cocked an eyebrow.

"Not lonely," Jem grunted.

"Grumpy, then. I misinterpreted the scowl on your face."

Jem couldn't help laughing a little. Tom always told it like it was, no honey-coating the reality. Sort of like Lucy. She didn't gloss over the truth, either. If you asked her what she thought, she'd tell you. The only reason he was still in the dark on her feelings for him was that he was too afraid to ask.

"And now it's back," Tom said.

"What is?"

"The scowl." Tom pulled a long face.

Jem rolled his eyes. "Stop harassing me and go back to your wife."

Tom jerked his chin toward a group of women near the refreshment table. "She's busy lecturing the guests on flummery. I'm not needed. And plus, I'd rather stay here and bug you."

"Lucky me."

Tom moved to stand beside him and looked out over the guests. "Lucy looks particularly beautiful tonight."

Jem shot him a look. Lucy was talking to Paulette, and they seemed to be having a serious conversation. "She always does."

"When she dumped you in high school, I thought she was sort of a snob. She doesn't seem anything like that now."

Jem sighed. "Sometimes I hate that we've known each other so long."

Tom looked surprised. "Old friends are the best, right?"

"Not when they continually remind you of how things went wrong in the past and you're trying to focus on the future."

"Oh, really?" A smile spread over Tom's face. "You're going to give it another try? Well, I wish you all the luck in the world. I know Rebecca thinks a lot of her."

"That's not quite what I meant." It was true; Jem had been making a general statement. But watching Lucy, and seeing the emotions cross her face as she talked to Paulette, he knew that everything in him wanted to take that step, to see if they could start over. He swallowed hard. But he would have to find just the right moment to tell her.

"Oh, my goodness, this is an Austen fan's paradise." A voice spoke from just behind her. Lucy turned and grinned as she saw Theresa Stroud.

She stood back to look at Lucy's dress. "You look beautiful, just beautiful."

"Thank you. I'm so glad you could make it to the reception. Have you had a chance to meet Rebecca?"

"Just now she came right up to me and gave me a great big hug. She said she really appreciated my coming in costume, but I told her it was really my pleasure. It's not every day we get to celebrate such a beautiful wedding, Austen style."

Lucy nodded. "It's certainly not the normal Tupelo affair." She glanced toward the open bar and saw Paulette putting in an order. Lucy repressed a sigh. She'd like to go to just one party without having to watch out for her younger sister. Turning her attention back to Theresa, she said, "You're not wearing the same dress as before."

"No, I have quite a few." Theresa blushed. "Okay, more than a few. But a woman must have a hobby, and if Jacob can have four Confederate uniforms, then I can have a few Regency gowns."

Lucy had to smile. The older couple seemed to get along so well, generously allowing space in their marriage for separate passions and hobbies. Her thoughts went to Jem, and his river-rafting friends. Would she mind if he went away for a week at a time? Would he invite her along? And the next moment she reminded herself that she and Jem were not Theresa and Dr. Stroud. But maybe someday they could be. She had the feeling of perching on the edge of a cliff, not sure which way was the safest and not sure whether she wanted to be safe at all.

She searched for something to say, trying to regain her train of thought, but Theresa spoke first. "I saw Jem on the way over here."

Lucy forced herself not to peer around the garden. He'd said something to her about having dibs on the first dance since they'd walked down the aisle together, but she hadn't seen him since. "I don't think he was thrilled to be wearing breeches, but it's funny what we'll do for our friends."

"That's the sign of a good man."

"Dressing up in a Regency costume?" Lucy asked, laughing.

"That, too, but I was referring to the way he treats his friends." Theresa looked out across the grass, watching the guests. "You can tell a lot about a man by how loyal he is to his friends."

Loyal. Lucy felt the word reverberate in her head. Jem had always stood by his friends, through moves and marriages and deaths and children. Lucy was the one who broke promises.

"You two are very similar that way," Theresa said.

Lucy looked up in surprise. She and Theresa had only just met. The woman didn't know much about Lucy's life, or her history.

Theresa went on, "I see how you take care of your sisters and watch out for your father. Loyalty is a rare thing these days. It seems as if we can make friends more easily than ever before since distance isn't an issue when everybody lives online most of their waking hours."

Lucy nodded, thinking of Marcus's hostess present for Paulette. The poster-sized selfie was the sign of a warped sort of world, where friendships started with a profile picture and hinged on gifts that fed the illusion.

"And we can lose friends just as easily. The click of a button and you can hide them forever, as if they'd never existed," Theresa said.

"Maybe I'm not more loyal than the rest of the people. Maybe I'm just not able to hide the people that irritate me. It's hard to block out a living person."

Theresa reached out, putting a hand on Lucy's arm. "But you could. The fact that you think you can't tells me a lot about you, Lucy Crawford. You've stepped into your mama's shoes, and nobody thanked you for it. It's a lot easier to walk away from responsibility, especially when it's not really ours to carry. Not everyone would stick around to fight for their family and their home." Theresa paused. "And not everyone would try to be friends with an ex-boyfriend."

Lucy dropped her gaze. The faint sounds of the band tuning their instruments sounded from the stage. "I think you might have misunderstood. We didn't just break up—I . . ." She was suddenly aware of how much she enjoyed Theresa's friendship and how she didn't want to explain what she'd done so long ago. Lucy didn't want Theresa to think any less of her. "It was my fault. I made the wrong choice. I know that now." Her voice was just a whisper.

"Then it means even more. You're humble enough to face him and want to be friends. Maybe there is a second chance for you two."

Lucy watched couples drift toward the dance floor, laughing and talking. Without obstacles, staying in love was easy. But Lucy had failed Jem so many times that he couldn't possibly trust her now. At dinner, when her father didn't welcome him properly, she hadn't said anything. In the clinic, he'd held her in his arms for one shining moment, and then she'd jumped away when she'd thought her aunt had walked through the door.

"I think I've used up all my second chances." Lucy lifted her chin. "He's the most wonderful man I know. He deserves better."

Theresa blinked, shocked. "Better? Than you? Girl, I know how it is to look at a man through the lens of a deep and passionate love, but Jem is still a human being. He has his own faults, his own failings."

Lucy nodded, but wasn't convinced. Jem

needed a woman who would never let him down.

"You should really watch the rest of *Persuasion*."

"I'm sorry I haven't made it back to finish the movie."

"Oh, dear, not a problem. We have all the time in the world." Theresa paused. "I know you think we Austen fans are crazier than all get-out, but there's a lot of truth in those books."

Lucy's lips twisted. She knew Theresa would love to give them a happy ending, but life wasn't as simple as fiction.

"You haven't seen the end, but Captain Wentworth realizes he loves Anne. He wants to ask for her hand, but he thinks she might be engaged to her cousin—"

"But if Jem felt that way about me"—Lucy hated the hope in her voice—"he wouldn't have any reason not to say something. He could say anything he wanted, at any time."

"What I was going to say was that it can go both ways."

"You mean, I should tell him how I feel?" The very idea made her stomach roll up into a ball.

Theresa glanced toward the band and smiled. "I'm tellin' you to take what opportunities present themselves."

The dance floor was filling with couples, and the fading summer light bathed everything in a warm glow. Lucy thought of how afraid she'd been to show up at his party, of how her hands had shook when she slipped on that ugly prom dress, of how her heart had pounded when she carried the pan of cornbread through the little garden gate. But she had done it because she knew that if she didn't take the opportunity to apologize, she would regret it forever.

Could telling Jem that she loved him be any worse than asking his forgiveness?

Caroline appeared beside them. She introduced herself to Theresa and said, "Are you two ready for the dancing? They brought a band in that is going to teach us some of the reels. My husband says he's not dancing, but I bet Jennie, the caller, can convince him." She grinned and waved toward the stage.

"I think they're the same ones who played at the Wrigley barn that night for the party I told you about." Theresa nodded to a tiny African American woman and four men who stood at the ready.

Someone brought her a microphone and she tapped it with her finger. "Hey, y'all."

The crowd started to quiet down. People drifted away from the punch table and toward the long dance floor in the middle of the grass.

"My name is Jennie, and this is my band." She introduced them one by one, and they stepped forward to take a bow. "I'm right tickled to be callin' the dances at this wedding." She waved a couple up to the front. "Brooks, come up here. Bring your pretty wife."

Lucy let out a laugh as Brooks turned and gave Caroline a knowing look. She hurried to him and they went to the front, hand in hand.

"We're going to show you a few moves. Real simple. I want you to practice with each other, and then we're going to have a real good time."

Jennie started calling moves, and everyone stood on tiptoe to see Brooks and Caroline. Lucy thought they looked like something out of a book, both blond and so clearly in love.

"Grab a partner and give it a whirl," Jennie called out.

"I better grab Jacob before some other woman asks him. Doesn't he look handsome tonight?" Theresa didn't wait for an answer but crossed the grass to Dr. Stroud. He was standing near the punch table, deep in conversation with several older gentlemen. As Theresa took his arm, Lucy smiled at the sight of the pair. He was wearing his seersucker suit and a bright red bow tie, and they seemed as if someone had gotten the eras confused when they'd hit the time-travel button.

"Would you care to dance?" Lucy knew who it was before she turned, but she still blinked in shock.

"I . . . yes. I do. Want to dance." She rolled her eyes. "Sorry. I haven't even been drinking. All of that was natural."

He was smiling, tiny lines radiating from the corners of his eyes. He held out a hand and she placed hers in it. Her heart was pounding so hard she was afraid he could hear it. Theresa's words had planted a seed of doubt. She knew Jem didn't hate her. He might even feel something for her. Would she ruin everything they had worked for? Would their tentative friendship be cut off with one awkward move?

They stood on the dance floor side by side. She tried to listen to Jennie's calls and watch the couples move from one place to another, but seconds later, she was lost.

"I have a bad feeling about this," she said.

"We'll fake it. And if push comes to shove, we can just sing 'Goober Peas' and waltz around."

She giggled. "Rebecca might not find that very funny."

"Rebecca is a Yankee. You can tell because there aren't any cheese straws on the snack table."

Again, they lined up facing each other. The fiddler started first, and the tune was slow and mournful. After a few bars the other instruments jumped in, and the rhythm picked up. Jem bowed to her and Lucy curtsied.

She realized she hadn't really been paying enough attention because when Jennie started to call out the turns, they made no sense. "Men allemande half to the left. Left one-half and half a hey," Jennie called to the beat, singing out steps.

"Ladies chain and circle right. Do-si-do and make it right, back to your man and face each other."

Lucy was being passed from hand to hand, unsure of where to turn or what to do.

Jem appeared and he was laughing at her expression, and then he was gone again. Theresa appeared and she gripped Lucy's right hand, swinging her in a circle and giving her back to Jem.

"There you are," he said, and saw a moment later than he was in the wrong spot. He shuffled forward, a sheepish look on his face.

Jennie called out, "Gypsy turn," and the couples put their palms together and turned in a circle. Lucy searched for Jem and found him alone, looking as lost as she was. She waved, and he rolled his eyes.

Jennie called out another gypsy turn and everyone moved in the opposite direction. Jem grabbed Lucy's hand and tugged her from the group.

She gasped, "But we're supposed to dance."

"I have no idea what I'm doing and neither do you." He steered her toward the refreshment table. She couldn't really argue with that and was relieved to leave the dance floor.

They stood in front of the dessert table. "What do you think this is?" Jem asked, wiggling the metal tray under a large gelatinous mound.

"I'm not really sure, but I think I see baby

asparagus and . . ." She leaned down, squinting into the molded dessert. "Green olives."

"Yikes." Jem chuckled. "So the food is weird, but the setting is nice."

"You can't do much better than the William Faulkner House." She looked out at the evening sky. The sun was still bright but the heat of the day was gone. She thought of what Theresa had said about taking the opportunity if it presented itself, and of how Paulette had known that Lucy was in love with Jem. Everything and everyone seemed to be leading her to this moment. She prayed that she wasn't making a huge mistake. "Have you ever seen the path that runs to the little footbridge?"

He frowned. "I don't think so. I've only been here once on a school trip."

"Come on, I'll show you." She took one last glance at the quivering food and headed for the edge of the grass. "It's not very far."

"At least I'm dressed for riding, in case I encounter a horse."

She snorted. "I'm sure you guys weren't real happy about the clothes, but you look very handsome."

He said nothing for a moment and they walked farther along the path, until the trees grew thick and close together.

"Are you sure you're not planning to lead me out here and then lose me in the forest?"

"Did you fill your pockets with bread crumbs? Or was it stones in the fairy tale?"

"I think bread crumbs get eaten," he said. "But I'm a little wary of filling my pockets with rocks right near a river, either."

"Very Virginia Woolf." Lucy looked at him, trying to not trip on the edge of her gown. "But why would I be trying to lose you in the woods anyway?"

He shrugged. "It would be easier on you."

She stopped. "If you weren't around?"

"Right."

Lucy shook her head. "I don't understand."

"I know it's hard for you to have me in your house." His face was half in shadow but she could see the set of his mouth.

"Only because . . ." And then she stopped, knowing that if she was really truthful, she would tell Jem exactly why it was hard to have him near.

"The patients? Your aunt?" He ran a hand through his hair. "I wish it didn't have to be this way."

She tried to speak, but all she could think of was the day when Jem would leave again. She hadn't realized it, but even though it was painful to know he was near, she couldn't bear the thought of his leaving. Looking down at the edge of her dress, she felt the burn of tears and tried to force them back.

"What is it? Did I say something wrong?" He let

out an exasperated noise. "Just ignore me. I've never been really good at words."

"Not good at words? But that's all we had, really. We lived and breathed words, that's when we fell in love, how we learned to listen to each other."

His blue eyes turned dark. "No, it wasn't then. It was all those times we weren't even talking." He stepped closer. "Those hours we spent under the trees near the trailer park. That afternoon under the willow. Even your back porch."

Lucy's face went hot. She remembered every single one of those times. "So, how do we learn to understand each other now? We're not teenagers anymore. We've grown up and have to have conversations like adults."

The corner of his mouth slid up. "Maybe not all the time."

She realized what he meant the moment before he reached out for her. She walked into his embrace, her heart pounding so loudly she couldn't hear what he whispered against her lips. All she knew was the press of his hands against her back, the crush of his arms around her, and she had never felt so happy. One kiss slid into another, and another. He kissed a trail down her neck and she thought she was going to slip to the ground. Her knees felt weak and she couldn't quite grasp a full thought, but only knew that she had waited for this moment for ten long years.

"Lucy," he groaned against her mouth, and almost lifted her off her feet.

She had never yearned for a man who was rough or anything less than absolutely respectful, but when his hands threaded into her hair, releasing it from the Regency style, she shuddered.

"Oops," someone said, laughing.

Jem lifted his head.

A blond girl giggled, stumbling against her friend, a tall man with a crew cut. "Oh, I know you. You're that new boyfriend of Regan's. She's gonna have a duck fit," the girl said. "She can't stand a cheater."

"Nobody's cheating on anybody," Jem said, and didn't let go of Lucy.

"Kaycee?" Regan's voice called out. "Kaycee, you've got my keys in your purse." The next moment, Regan appeared, looking irritated and sweaty.

Regan's gaze traveled from her friend to Jem to Lucy. Regan's eyes widened as she took in Lucy's hair falling loose around her shoulders and Jem's arms around her waist. Regan stalked forward, face furious. "I . . . You . . ." She reached out and slapped him hard across the face. Lucy felt the shock travel through his body and into her arms. Regan turned on her heel and stomped back down the path. The sound of her sobs carried back to them long after they couldn't see her anymore.

"Told ya so," Kaycee said. "All you cheaters think you can get away with it, but the girl always finds out."

Lucy looked at Jem and started to move away.

"No, I don't know what she's talking about." He gripped her arms, holding her in place.

"Not at all? Not even a little?" Lucy could feel doubt push against her heart, like a wave of icy-cold water. She'd seen him flirt with Regan, and he'd let her touch him in a way that Lucy would never have dared. Maybe it wasn't just that he was too embarrassed to move her hands away. Maybe there had been more to it after all.

"Not even a little." His mouth was a tight line. "I mean, I knew that she thought we were dating, but I figured she would get over it."

Lucy shook her head. "I don't even know what that means."

"It means just what I said." He sounded frustrated and his tone was sharp. "I thought she would just move on after a while."

Lucy looked up and saw Kaycee and the blond guy with the crew cut, smirking. A numbness filled Lucy's chest and traveled down to her feet. She couldn't have this conversation here, not now, in front of these people.

"Let me go," she whispered, and tugged against him.

He released her, his eyes dark with pain. "Lucy—"

"I'm going back to the reception. I shouldn't have led you here in the first place." She paused. "Maybe I'm like Regan, throwing myself at you when you're really not interested, and you just go along with it, hoping eventually I'll move on."

"No, it wasn't like—"

She'd already moved past him and was hurrying up the path. Tears burned behind her eyes, but she bit her cheek, forcing herself not to cry. It was so juvenile to wander into the woods and make out with a guy at someone else's wedding. More than Jem, she was disappointed in herself. She was a grown woman, not a teenager. All it took was a pretty dress and some Regency costumes, and she had let herself act like someone much younger, someone who had never had her heart broken.

"I can listen no longer in silence.
I must speak to you by such means
as are within my reach."
—CAPTAIN WENTWORTH

CHAPTER TWENTY-TWO

Jem wandered up the flagstone path and watched Zeke pouring chicken feed in metal containers. Jem felt exhausted and hollow, as if someone had scooped out all his working parts and left him full of dust.

Zeke looked up and called, "Morning."

Jem trudged closer, not able to muster a response. He couldn't imagine making his way through a workday.

"You look like a hound dog." Zeke pulled an exaggerated face.

"Tired," Jem mumbled.

"Lucy's that kind of tired, too."

"What?"

Zeke threw him a sly look. "She's mopin' around the house like someone took her shoes and gave her lead feet. Can't hardly get her to say a word to me. And you can't convince me that it's a coincidence."

Jem sighed and plopped himself on the old bench. Hattie trotted out from the tomato plants and wound around his ankles. He stared at his feet, chin in his hands.

"Well, now I know you got it bad. Nobody can resist Miss Hattie's charms unless he's sick at heart."

"I'm fine." Jem shrugged. "When I came here, I wanted to serve this community, really help out the people who got overlooked. And I feel like all I've done is pour energy into my own problems."

Zeke sat down next to him and tilted his hat back on his head. "I didn't think nobody cared about these people until Dr. Stroud started his clinic. And now you're here, too." Zeke jerked his chin toward the back door. "You make a difference just showing up."

"I wish it was that easy." Jem stared out at the garden, thinking of how they had come so far and now were right back at the beginning. "As for Lucy, I've really made a mess of things."

"Glad it's your turn. I was worried Miss Lucy had done it again."

"Again?"

"When Miss Olympia persuaded her that it would never work between the two of you." Zeke shook his head. "She cried for weeks."

Jem straightened up. "She told me she wanted to date other people. I was sure her aunt had something to do with it."

"She never dated nobody." Zeke looked out past the garden. "Lots of nice young men come callin' and she was real polite, but never took to any of them. Not like you."

Hattie jumped onto Jem's lap and he rubbed her fur, his mind churning with this information. He'd always assumed she'd found someone else and had been trying to let him down easy by being vague.

"Jem, I don't give much advice." Zeke rubbed the white whiskers at the side of his jaw. "But you need to get this all straightened out. I don't want to see Miss Lucy nursing a broken heart for another ten years."

Jem's eyes went wide. Had she loved him all this time? Had he spent the last decade being bitter and resentful for nothing?

"She's not home. She's up at the center, gettin' ready for the reenactment tomorrow." Zeke answered Jem's unspoken question.

Jem stood up, and Hattie slid onto the ground with a mewling protest. "Sorry, girl." He reached down. "Wasn't thinking." He grinned at Zeke. "I'm got some work to do. Tomorrow is a big day."

A slow smile spread over Zeke's face. His dark eyes shone with moisture. "It's about time, son."

Jem jogged up the path to the clinic entrance. His heart was pounding in his chest and he felt as if he couldn't catch his breath. Something had gone wrong ten years ago, and maybe they'd been given a second chance to make it right.

He was going to tell Lucy exactly how he felt, and he was going to do it in a way she couldn't possibly misunderstand.

Lucy tugged on the blue wool jacket and checked her reflection in the mirror. Her hair was tucked up into her hat, but she still looked like a woman. She smoothed down the front of the jacket and frowned. She wasn't sure how flat-chested Hattie Winter was, but she must have been smaller than Lucy. With no makeup, the rough outfit and the hobnail boots, Lucy certainly felt less like a woman, but she was clearly a woman in a man's uniform. She slipped the leather strap over her head and positioned it across her chest. Now it was even more obvious. She frowned at the mirror. Well, she was going to do her best, and if people laughed, then so be it.

For a moment, she looked into her own eyes. Ten years ago, she'd been weak and cowardly. One hundred and fifty years ago, Hattie Winter had walked into a war to find the man she loved. Lucy couldn't change the past, but a small part of that broken heart felt satisfaction at playing Hattie today.

Her throat tightened at the thought of the battle reenactment. She'd been through dozens before, but this would be different. Jem would be here, somewhere, fighting on the Confederate side. At least she wouldn't see him, if she was lucky. She'd be with the artillery unit on the rise, while he would probably be near Dr. Stroud somewhere.

She hadn't seen him since the reception, but she'd heard from Paulette that Regan was now dating Danny, Jem's old friend. She almost smiled, wondering again how it was even possible that a man such as Danny could stand being around such a flake, but maybe she was just what he needed. He would never be able to replace Kelsey, and it was easier to go in the opposite direction, falling in love with a girl who never stopped talking long enough to look at the clouds.

Lucy took a deep breath and headed out of the bathroom. The center was already full of tourists, and she kept her eyes straight ahead. Once a soldier was in uniform, you didn't break character. If you ran into your own mother on the way to the battlefield, you didn't stop to chat. She could hear the whispers and a few clicks of a camera, but she didn't pause.

The sun was bright and hot, but thankfully the humidity wasn't so bad. Lucy grabbed a rifle from the regiment pile and saluted her commander. Parker McNabb saluted smartly, then let his hand fall slowly to his side. "Miss Crawford, is that you?"

"No, sir. Leroy Carver, sir."

Parker's face smoothed back into a neutral expression, but he looked as if he wanted to laugh. "To your station, son."

Another salute and she was on her way, down the path toward where the 1841 howitzers were lined up. She had no intention of standing anywhere near the cannons when the reenactors set them off, but that's where she'd been assigned, and Hattie always did her duty. As soon as she came into sight, the group stopped their preparations and gawked.

She saluted. "Leroy Carver, Bouton's Brigade of United States Colored Troops."

A potbellied, middle-aged man stepped forward. "Lieutenant James Gillison." He leaned near her and whispered, "Sorry, Miss Lucy, you ain't foolin' any of us. You're too pretty to be a soldier."

She frowned. "Maybe a little dirt?"

"Maybe so." He nodded.

She bent down and wiped her fingers in the clay, then scrubbed them on her skin. Looking up, she asked, "Better?"

"Hmmm." He turned to the group and barked a few orders. Lucy took that to mean that she was accepted into the group.

The sun rose in the sky and she could see groups gathering at either end of the battlefield. Tourists set up chairs and umbrellas, carrying little coolers of drinks and snacks.

"Five minutes," called the lieutenant.

Lucy felt her stomach tighten. It wasn't real, none of it was real, but she still felt as if she were heading straight into battle.

Faster than she could say, the first shots sounded and horses emerged onto the field, carrying riders who bellowed directions with their sabers drawn. Her regiment worked furiously to load and fire the cannon, never setting it off, but heaving the metal balls from place to place.

A soldier ran up and saluted. "Message for Miss Hattie Winter," he shouted over the noise.

The men froze, looking from her to the messenger.

"There's no Hattie Winter here," she said, but a suspicion was growing in her mind, and as he started to turn away, she called out. "Stop! I can deliver it to her."

He shrugged and handed over a folded piece of paper, sealed with a blob of bloodred wax. It was clearly something written by a reenactor, maybe even someone on the field that very minute.

Lucy opened it, sucking in a sharp breath at the sight of the familiar handwriting, which not even a quill pen could disguise. She scanned the words. At first it didn't make sense, nothing made any sense at all. Her knees went weak and she stumbled to the grass. The paper shook in her hand.

Dear Lucy,

Thoreau said that it's only when we become completely lost or turned around that we begin to find ourselves. I can't waste one more day hoping but not knowing whether you feel the same. There will never be a perfect moment to tell you how I feel and I can't wonder any longer if you love me. I have to know.

There was never anyone but you, Lucy. Even when I was angry and bitter, my heart was faithful to you. I thought of you when I woke up in the morning and thought of you when I lay down to sleep. I tried to forget you and even convinced myself that moving back home to Tupelo wouldn't be a problem. One look at your face told me that I was wrong.

I've tried to show you what I feel, and I thought, maybe, you understood me. When I danced with you in the clinic, I never wanted to let you go. When you brought your cornbread apology to the party, I wanted to tell you then. When we kissed at the reception, I thought we'd finally understood each other. My hands are shaking as I write this, but not knowing is a worse agony.

I am yours, heart and soul. I always have been, and always will be.

Jem

I'll be near Dr. Stroud's amputation tent (probably getting something removed). If you love me, come to me after the battle is over. I'll look for you.

Her breath came in gasps and she read and reread the lines, unable to believe that his letter was real. She stumbled to her feet.

"Soldier, where are you going?"

She ignored the lieutenant's call and began to run down the grass slope past the Union medical tent. In a minute, she'd overtaken her own troops, and soldiers in blue were on all sides, horses trotting at the edges of the group. She pushed on past them, threading her way between lines of men, dodging rifle barrels and sheathed swords. Her side began to ache but she didn't slow down. The hobnail boots were several sizes too big and her feet slid around the insides, but she focused on the dots of gray in the distance and kept running.

"Hey, soldier! You're headed into enemy territory," a man called out as she ran past.

She waved a hand, noticing for the first time she still held Jem's letter, smudges of red clay from her fingers marking the paper like blood.

The path cleared and the empty green field stretched out before her. She could hear gunfire and cannons in the distance. Suddenly, a line of soldiers in gray approached from the side, confusion on their faces.

"Deserter from the enemy camp," someone shouted.

They converged on her and she fought her way through, using her elbows and knees. She connected with someone's middle and heard the whoosh of air as it left his lungs. Then she was through, panting and exhausted. The battle raged on behind her, the sound of gunfire and the screams of wounded men fading into the distance.

Tourists were pointing and laughing; some grabbed their cameras while others flipped through the pamphlet, wondering which Civil War soldier had broken ranks and run to the other side in the middle of the battle. She slowed to a limping walk, scanning the area for Jem.

"Lucy," she heard him call, and she turned to see him standing by the battlefield emergency tent. His gray Confederate uniform was stained in several places, and the rifle at his side was missing its bayonet. He took off his cap, and his expression was a bright flame of hope.

She walked toward him, her ankle throbbing with every step, her breath coming in gasps and her heart nearly pounding out of her rib cage.

"I feel like I just watched Night Train Lane go coast-to-coast for a touchdown," he said, the corners of his mouth turning up.

"Very . . . funny." She tried to laugh, but it came out a sigh. "Hattie . . ." She stopped, working hard to get her breath under control. "Hattie Winter loved a man so . . . so deeply that she went to war to find him."

He nodded, gaze never wavering.

"I wanted to be like her. I wanted to be strong

372

like that." She looked down at the letter in her hand, and the smears of red clay reminded her that she was standing in front of him with dirt on her face. This wasn't the way she had dreamed of this moment and she wished it could be different, but she wouldn't walk away from him. She *couldn't* walk away from him. She had waited too long to tell him the truth.

She looked him in the eye. "I made a mistake ten years ago, and if you'll give me the chance, I want to show you that I'm different now. I'm not afraid anymore. Nobody can tell me how to be happy, or who I need." She swallowed. "I need you."

"Come here," he said.

"Where?"

"Here."

She limped toward him, ignoring the tourists just feet away. They were creeping forward to get a good picture. They must look like a perfect photo opportunity, a Confederate soldier and a Union artilleryman.

"Closer."

She stepped closer. She could smell him, see his chest rising and falling, and hear his breathing. She couldn't look above the collar of his rough cotton shirt, the soft skin of his throat. Once upon a time she'd known that skin as well as her own. She'd known how his chin felt under her lips, how his stubble looked in the sunlight, as if someone had thrown sand across his face. She knew how his breath felt, so warm against her neck, and there was that spot under his jaw she once loved. She finally dragged her gaze up, up to meet his eyes. He was looking at her as if he'd been waiting his whole life for her.

"I'm here," she whispered.

"Thank God," he said, and his eyes filled with tears. He reached out and wrapped her close, whispering into her ear, "You're here. And you've had my heart all this time."

Her lips found his and she barely noticed the clicking of cameras and laughter from the other reenactors. After a few minutes, Jem lifted his head and looked around. "Hmm. This will be a mighty confusing picture."

She didn't want to let him go, didn't want him to ever stop kissing her, but Lucy couldn't help laughing. "Rebel soldier, I don't think my friends will approve of you."

"Union deserter, I'm fairly sure my commander will demand you be taken to the prison camp." He brushed a kiss across her temple. "The next time we decide to kiss in public, I have a request."

She frowned. "You do?"

"Let's just wear normal clothes."

Laying her head on his chest, she let the laughter take her for a moment. "Jane Austen, Civil War, it's all the same."

He reached out and tugged off her cap. Her hair

fell around her shoulders, dark curls startling against his white shirt. "Does this mean you want an Austen wedding, too?"

She looked up at him, surprise stealing the words from her mouth.

"Or we could have a Civil War theme, but that could get complicated," he said. "Seeing as how you're a deserter now and all."

She reached up and tugged him down to her, pressing a kiss to his mouth, his jaw, his cheek. "I love you, Jem Chevy. And I always have."

He pulled her close and murmured something she didn't quite catch over the beating of her heart, but his words echoed what she knew to be true. Beyond color, beyond history, beyond hurts and meddling relatives and poverty and anger and bitterness . . . beyond all of those things was a grace so powerful it could turn an enemy into an ally, and two lonely people into a family. It was a grace so miraculous it could mend broken promises and hand out second chances.

Lucy looked up into Jem's eyes and felt, for the first time in a long time, absolute happiness.

Dear Reader,

I hope you enjoyed reading *Persuasion, Captain Wentworth and Cracklin' Cornbread* as much as I enjoyed writing it! I fell in love with Jane Austen's story all over again and grew to appreciate her talent in a whole new way. Jane is famous for her wit, but there's not much humor in *Persuasion*. It's a sad story, and the only action to break up the monotony of heartache is a child falling out of a tree, Anne falling off a log, and Louisa throwing herself off the Cobb. But with nary a Miss Bates in sight for comic relief, Miss Austen gave us a gripping tale of love lost and second chances.

On the outside, Lucy Crawford and Jem Chevy have nothing in common. They have vastly different family histories, are in different economic classes and are different races in one of the few places where race can still be an obstacle. But if you look closely, they both love history, poetry and literature, care about poverty and live their faith. If you look a little deeper, you can see these two are fighting the same battles in a world that would rather they sit down and hush up.

Jem and Lucy are quiet but they're also tough,

courageous people. Together, I don't think anyone will be able to stop them!

I wish you courage, grace and the wisdom to know when to stand up for your beliefs . . . and a little bit of blackberry cobbler to sweeten the journey.

Sincerely,
Mary Jane Hathaway

RECIPES

Cracklin' Cornbread

Before we get started, let me say I know all about the great war over cornbread. Sweet or not? Bacon grease or butter? Hot skillet or cold? If you've got the perfect cornbread recipe, just guard that baby with your life and ignore this one. But if you love cornbread and are willing to try something new (or are up to tweaking this one to fit your mama's recipe), then come on over!

Ingredients
3 tablespoons bacon grease (or vegetable oil
    or real butter)
1½ cups cornmeal
½ cup all-purpose flour
1 teaspoon baking powder
1 teaspoon salt
2 cups milk (My sister uses buttermilk, but
    I've never liked buttermilk cornbread . . .
    and now she knows!)
2 eggs
¼ cup vegetable oil
1 cup cracklins or chitlins

Directions

Preheat the oven to 425°F and put the skillet inside so it gets nice and hot. Add the bacon grease or the butter and rotate it a bit (carefully: those skillets are heavy) to coat the bottom and the sides. Put it back in the oven. Getting the skillet to the right temperature is what makes that crispy bottom edge that everyone fights over.

Combine the cornmeal, flour, baking powder, salt and baking powder.

In another bowl, combine all the wet ingredients. Mix wet and dry together, and add the cracklins. Don't bother trying to get all the lumps out.

Remove the skillet from the oven and pour the mix into the skillet. Bake at 450° for about fifteen minutes and then test it. Heat longer if needed.

You can also substitute bacon for the cracklins, or turkey bacon for the bacon, or just pull a Lucy and leave it all out. But then it wouldn't be cracklin' cornbread, would it?

Let it sit for another fifteen minutes on the stove top, slice, and enjoy!

Chow Chow

The first time I heard someone mention chow chow, I thought it was a Chinese dish. No one can tell me where it came from, or how it got its name. But, boy, is it delicious! Think peperoncini, but with more flavor, and you can make it right out of your own garden. Plus, it only takes about thirty minutes to prepare (instead of jarring and pickling, which can take a whole day), and it lasts up to a week in the fridge.

Ingredients
2 cups apple cider vinegar
1 cup sugar
1 tablespoon celery seed
1 tablespoon dry mustard
1 tablespoon turmeric
1 tablespoon mustard seeds
1 teaspoon cayenne pepper (I make a little
    batch for my husband that has a few
    chopped chiles de árbol and 2 teaspoons
    of cayenne, but for myself, I don't like it
    burn-your-face-off spicy)
1-inch piece fresh ginger, peeled and grated
2 pounds firm green heirloom tomatoes, cut
    into quarters
2 medium onions, diced

Directions

Combine vinegar, sugar, celery seed, dry mustard, turmeric, mustard seeds, cayenne pepper (or not) and ginger in a stockpot and bring to a rolling boil. Reduce and let it simmer ten minutes. Your house is going to smell delicious! Now, add the tomatoes and onion. Stir gently but don't mash. It's more of a chutney than a sauce. Reduce heat and simmer for twenty minutes. Remove from the heat and let it cool slowly to room temperature. Place it in a piece of pretty vintage Pyrex and put it on the picnic table between the sweet corn and the roasted baby potatoes. (Well, that last part isn't essential, but it always works for me.)

Although I love the flavor of Black Zebra, Black Krim and Cavern heirloom varieties, they don't look nice in this sort of dish. It looks like chunky, fragrant mud. I usually use a combination of Candy's Old Yellow, Siletz and German Red Strawberry, if they're all available at the same time. You can usually find heirloom tomatoes at your local farmers' market if you don't have a little plot of your own.

I always use Walla Walla sweet onions (which are like Vidalias for Northwesterners), but you can use normal yellow onions, too. I have a friend who makes this with purple onions and adds red cabbage and it's beautiful! I'm not a cabbage fan, so I'll stick with onions.

This recipe makes quite a lot of chow chow, but we go through it pretty quickly in the summer with all the barbecues and picnics.

Enjoy!

Easiest Blackberry Cobbler Ever

Preheat the oven to 350°F and grease a nine-by-thirteen-inch pan. I've always used a large, round Fiesta baking dish that holds about three quarts. The cobbler doesn't rise much, so don't be afraid to fill the dish.

Ingredients
1¼ cups sugar
1 cup flour
1¼ teaspoon baking powder
1 teaspoon salt
1 cup milk
stick butter, melted
1 teaspoon real vanilla
2 cups fresh (or frozen) blackberries

Directions
Mix 1 cup of the sugar and 1 cup of flour, along with the baking powder and salt together. (I usually forget to limit the sugar to 1 cup, putting in all the sugar at once. It won't ruin the recipe, but the ¼ cup that is meant to be sprinkled over the top gives it a special something. So, if you remember, just add 1 cup at this point.)

Whisk in the milk, then the melted butter and the vanilla. Pour the batter into the baking dish.

Add the berries on top. They'll sink down a bit, and if the tops of the batter are showing, it will be okay. The cobbler rises a little and the berries cook down. Now sprinkle the remaining ¼ cup sugar over the top.

Cook for about an hour until the cobbler begins to turn brown around the edges and the middle is firm. Test with a wooden skewer, and if it comes out clean, remove the cobbler from the oven and let cool for fifteen minutes before serving. My friends like this with vanilla frozen yogurt, but it's perfect as is, too.

During peach season, this is a great recipe with peaches as a substitute. Instead of vanilla, you can add a bit of cinnamon.

A perfect recipe for a Sunday-morning brunch with family or when you need an easy dessert for company.

ACKNOWLEDGMENTS

Many people provided assistance and support during this project, mainly through gifts of chocolate or caffeinated beverages or pretending to listen to me while I plotted out loud. Mindy Postlewait, your enthusiasm for trying out new recipes in a tiny kitchen filled with small children is a gift in itself. Here's to hot lattes, homemade salted caramel ice cream and 1877 cookbooks that list carbolic acid as an ingredient. Christalee Scott May, I appreciate your Southern input on food, manners and dialect. Thank you for the perfectly timed shipments of chai (chia!) tea, fingerless gloves and never-ending pep talks. Our 2:00 a.m. conversations kept me awake and inspired. Cindy Ferreira Whitney, thank you for your generous assistance with marketing and advertisement design. Stacey Brower, for your willingness to Skype with me when I haven't showered in four days; you deserve an award. Thank you for all those times we held books up to the tiny laptop cameras and described our latest reads. Not many people would make the effort to continue a long-distance relationship that was begun in a toy kitchen at the local Children's

Museum. (To Mr. Brower, Jimmy and Mindy . . . because I can't leave you out.) To Sandra Bell Calhoune, for giving me advice on Lucy's hairstyles and how to accomplish them. To Stella Hale-Wheat, for keeping me company on the other side of the world while I write in the middle of the night. Thanks to my football-loving friend Jason Postlewait, for what I think is the funniest line in the entire book. To Barbara and Larry Nafziger, for being the best neighbors a thirteen-year-old girl could have, and the best friends a forty-year-old mom could have.

Many thanks to my editor, Beth Adams of Howard Books. Your insight, humor and keen editorial eye have made this series so much more than it was when we started. As hard as I have worked, you have always worked harder. I hope you know how rare that is and how much I appreciated it. A big thank-you to administrative coordinator Katie Sandell for her gracious and capable handling of any concerns I had. No matter how many e-mails I sent in a row (or how many times I forgot to send the attachment) she replied with speed, precision, grace and perception, even on a Monday.

A huge thanks to Mandy Rivers over at the *South Your Mouth* blog for posting such delicious recipes that kept my family happy while making me laugh at the same time. Thank you to the many regional Jane Austen Society of North America coordinators who agreed to review this book. To the vibrant Facebook communities who keep the rest of us entertained with all things Jane, including Austen in Boston, My Jane Austen Book Club and All Things Jane Austen.

Last but never least, a heartfelt thank-you to all the readers who have enthusiastically embraced this quirky series. I've enjoyed your letters, input, forwarded links and family histories. You were always willing to weigh in on whether chow chow is better than muscadine jelly, whether a Confederate soldier was better off using a Lorenz or a Whitworth rifle, and whether Mr. Tilney deserved to marry Catherine Morland. (The jury is still out on that last one.)

About the Author

Mary Jane Hathaway is the pen name of an award-nominated writer who spends the majority of her literary energy on subjects unrelated to Jane Austen. A homeschooling mother of six young children who rarely wears shoes, she's madly in love with a man who has never read a Jane Austen novel. She holds degrees in religious studies and theoretical linguistics and has a Jane Austen quote on the back of her van. She can be reached on Facebook at Pride, Prejudice, and Cheese Grits.

Center Point Large Print
600 Brooks Road / PO Box 1
Thorndike, ME 04986-0001 USA

(207) 568-3717

US & Canada:
1 800 929-9108
www.centerpointlargeprint.com